# THE NIGHT BEFORE CHRISTMAS

## NICOLA KNIGHT

To Jenn,

Thank you for everything

with lots of love
always,

Nicola K

x x x

**BLOODHOUND**
— BOOKS —

*For D & R. My darling ones.*

*(Can we get another cat yet?)*

# CHAPTER ONE

It was Christmas Eve, and Felicity Brooks was ready for whatever the night could throw at her.

She was all alone at the rescue centre, which was just how she liked it. Her man-eating boss, Andrea, was on a festive date with a mysterious Spanish man she'd met online, so she would be MIA for at least twenty-four hours while he tried his level best to get her wellies off, and in the meantime, Felicity was in charge.

On her way over, she had ducked into the little M&S at the petrol station and picked up armfuls of snacks, which were now strewn all over Andrea's office. Nothing festive mind, nothing too Christmassy. But, grinch-like as she was, even Felicity couldn't turn down a packet of Santa-hatted Percy Pigs on Christmas Eve. Or any night for that matter. Armed with a couple of ready meals, her PJs and sleeping bag, a well-thumbed copy of *The Hobbit* and a pristine copy of *Ulysses* – she knew she wasn't ever going to read that one, but quite enjoyed carrying it around – she hunkered down for a familiar anti-Christmas Christmas with her beloved animals, who she knew wouldn't ask her any awkward questions.

Now, if she could just stop her mind from whirring and clanking away like an old-fashioned slot machine, she would be feeling quite peaceful. In a pathetic attempt to block out her own thoughts, Felicity put on the cranky old TV in the corner, leaned back in the office chair, and flicked through the channels. *Die Hard* was on at 10pm. Sorted. The only seasonal movie she could tolerate. Well, that and *The Grinch* of course.

*Wow, what a cliché I am*, Felicity thought dismally, sticking her hand deep into a bag of salt and vinegar twists.

Every half an hour or so she would get up and wander between the cages to check on the centre's tiny residents. It had been a relatively uneventful few months, rescue wise, but Andrea and Felicity knew all too well that as soon as the festivities were over, their phone would be ringing off the hook as all those kittens and puppies mistakenly given as presents ended up unwanted or abandoned. Once, they had found a carrier bag with the body of a kitten in it just dumped by the side of the road. It made her heart hurt so badly, Felicity cried herself to sleep that night.

A high-pitched mewling drew her back to the present. Bobby Charlton, a little black kitten with four white socks and a big personality, was hanging off the bars of his cage in the cat nursery in an effort to get her attention.

'Come on, Bobs,' she said, opening the door and carefully scooping him onto her chest. Not for the first time since working here she wished she had a more ample bosom like Andrea's, a 'kitten shelf' if you will, but he seemed content enough with her offering and snuggled into her gratefully. As she began to stroke his soft fur, he mewled a little more softly, and nuzzled her chin.

Bobby had been abandoned shortly after he was born and had somehow survived for three days or so before Andrea and Felicity found him in the alley behind the centre. It had been touch and go for a while as he was absolutely tiny, very skinny, and very quiet, and neither of them really thought he would pull through. Felicity's heart gave a lurch at the memory and she held him a little closer, breathing in his familiar baby-powder-like smell. Bobby was not the first kitten who had arrived on their doorstep, of course, but he was probably the one who had made the biggest impression on Felicity. She knew she wasn't meant to have favourites, but he was such a fighter, and he was becoming so bold and friendly that you couldn't help but fall in love.

The puppy room, with its sunny yellow walls, was also miraculously quiet. There were only a couple of dogs in over the holidays this year, and Felicity had insisted to Andrea she would be able to cope. Secretly, though, she was a little worried about one of them. Felix and Freddy were two tiny dachshunds – one black and tan, one a lovely mahogany brown – who had been brought in by the RSPCA a few weeks ago. Both of them were extremely cute, and usually very friendly, but for some reason when Felicity went anywhere near the brown one, Freddy, he would bare his teeth or bark the place down. Even now, as Felicity crept past Freddy's cage, he gave a low growl from his basket. Andrea insisted he would come round but that was easy for her to say, the animals always adored her instantly. Felicity wondered, not for the first time, what had happened to him to make him so wary of strangers.

It was nearly time for *Die Hard*. An old friend. Felicity hit the record button on the remote, just in case. She'd completed her final rounds and in theory all her furry charges were tucked up for the night but one could never be too careful where animals were concerned. Of course, there would be some fidgeting and whining, and she'd have to give little Bobby his night feed in a couple of hours, but for now, there was a brief moment of peace. Idly, she spun on the chair to stare out of the window behind her. As she wiped the condensation away with her sleeve, her reflection appeared in the glass. Felicity stared dispassionately at the tired eyes looking back at her, the too-pale face without even a hint of a freckle to make it interesting, the ever so slightly sticking out ears only partially hidden under her red hair. She tutted and tried to get out of her own way to examine the world beyond but there was nothing to see. Just the same old pitch-black darkness that seemed to go on and on, and the occasional tap-tap-tap of rain against the filthy windowpane.

Just then, a strange scuffling noise came from down the corridor.

There was a brief pause, and then frantic banging on the front door, loud and shocking in the quiet of the night. Felicity's heart clanged in her chest. Freddy's too, from the sounds of it, as the little dog began barking furiously.

Who would be knocking on the door at this hour on Christmas Eve? Not Santa, surely?

*If it's Father Christmas*, she thought, trying to calm her nerves, *he's a bit early. Still, I can probably find some sherry knocking about the place, knowing Andrea.*

She crept up behind the door. Freddy's frantic barking was at fever pitch now and Felix, not wanting to be left out, was making a high-pitched whining sound that really added to the atmosphere.

No way was she opening it.

No way, no way, no way.

Instead, she shouted in the general direction of the scuffling. 'Who is it? Can I help you?'

'Oh, thank God, yes, yes please, I really need your help,' came a deep male voice.

*That's what a murderer would say*, thought Felicity. *Do murderers work on Christmas Eve?*

'Do you want me to call someone for you?' *Like the police, for example.*

'It's not for me,' came the voice. 'It's... well, I really need to show you. I found something and I didn't know what to do and then my feet fell off and it's really wet out here. Can you let me in?'

*Okay, it's probably not a murderer, but it may be a mad person. Is that better? What to do, what to do?*

'Just stay there a moment,' yelled Felicity over the noise of the dogs, and stood on her tiptoes to peer through the glass porthole in the door. But even with the side of her nose pressed right up to the filthy glass, all she could make out was a glimpse of a dark shape with flashes of white. What *was* that? Not Father Christmas, that's for sure.

'Please hurry, I think it's dying,' came the voice again and this time Felicity's heart started thumping so hard she could feel it in her ears.

*He's got an animal. It needs help. I must open the door. Even if I get murdered.*

She took a deep breath and unlatched the rickety wooden door.

There, standing in front of her, was a giant, rather dishevelled penguin with bare human feet and a human face. It was very wet and muddy, and it was clutching something in its hands that resembled a ridiculously small wet ball of dirty fluff. This was not good.

'Come in,' she said, backing away to let this strange spectacle into the centre. She closed the door behind it, said a quick prayer of protection from murderous festive penguins, and turned around.

# CHAPTER TWO

THE PENGUIN, as it turned out, was a very tall man in a costume. Which was something of a relief. Felicity held out her hands and he gratefully handed over the tiny bundle, which she drew in close to her chest. After a few anxious seconds, she could feel its little body moving under her fingers.

'It's alive,' she said, swallowing the lump in her throat as she turned and headed towards the cat nursery in search of towels and blankets. The dogs were quietening down, thankfully, and she chatted to them soothingly as she went past the door to their room, reassuring them all was well.

Penguin Man followed her wetly, explaining as he went that he had been walking home from a fancy dress party when he heard a cry coming from a brambly ditch beside the road. When he peered into the darkness with his phone torch, he had found a small damp creature, eyes shut, mouth open, yelling its tiny head off. By instinct, he had scooped it up and climbed out of the ditch, losing one of his penguin flippers along the way. The other one had to be sacrificed as he clambered and then fell over the low gate outside the rescue centre, his 'bloody costume' proving rather a hindrance. And so here he was, barefoot and wet. Cradling a small ball of fluff. A ball of fluff that had gone worryingly quiet.

'Never mind about your feet,' said Felicity. 'Pass me that heat lamp, can you?' She indicated a high wooden shelf above the row of cat cages behind him.

'It's blowing a hooley out there,' said Penguin Man, handing her the lamp and then wiping his soggy face on one equally soggy wing. 'I thought I was going to end up in the ditch with it. Poor thing. Is it going to be okay?'

'I don't know. I hope so,' she said, grabbing the softest blanket she could find and gently wrapping the tiny kitten up in it. As she did so she looked it over carefully, feeling for any cuts or breaks, but it seemed to be in one piece. Best guess in the circumstances, it was a female kitten but perilously young, perhaps not more than a couple of days old. She was very cold, and her filthy coat was matted and soaking wet. She smelled like damp leaves. Felicity gently placed her into a bed under the heat lamp and stroked the top of her tiny head with one finger.

'Now, Penguin Man,' she said, looking at him properly for the first time. He was even taller and broader up close, and he was looking at her anxiously with big grey-blue eyes, the intensity of the moment being slightly dampened by the large drops of water from his costume, which were making their steady way down his nose.

'Now, Penguin Man,' she said again. 'This is important. When you were out there, did you see or hear any sign of another cat anywhere around?'

'No, none,' he said, slight panic crossing his face, 'but I wasn't really thinking straight, to be honest.' His eyes widened as realisation dawned. 'You think there could be more.' It wasn't a question.

Felicity nodded quickly. 'The mum might still be about, and this kitten stands a much better chance if we can find her. There could be other babies too.'

Penguin Man's eyes never moved from her face as this sank in. It was a little unnerving and she felt her face flush. He was surprisingly handsome. For a soggy penguin.

'What do you need me to do?' he said.

After making the little scrap of fur as comfortable as they could, they headed back out into the darkness, cat trap, towel, and torch in hand.

There wasn't even time to discard the penguin costume although Felicity had managed to find some wellies to save his bare feet. Penguin Man's suit was still soaking wet though, and he was shivering as they trudged across the road and headed towards the ditch. Freezing rain pattered steadily onto the pavement, and they made their way with some difficulty thanks to a rather strong headwind that made walking challenging and talking virtually impossible.

Nevertheless, they located the section of the ditch where he'd found the kitten within minutes. There was a large entanglement of brambles stretching several metres along the side of the road and reaching across to a cluster of trees on the other side of the deep trough, which had water at the bottom of it. Felicity gingerly lifted a large bramble bush that was hanging over the edge and waved her torch about into the depths below. Nothing.

She took a deep breath and started making a mewling sound the way Andrea had taught her. Kitten sounds in the first few days are surprisingly loud and she hoped it might encourage the baby's mum to come forward. She glanced across to her neighbour as she did so and could swear Penguin Man's eyebrows lifted for just a moment but, to his credit, he managed not to laugh.

And within a few moments there – miraculously – was a distant but clear answering cry. Somewhere deep in the ditch was at least one other cat.

'Hold this,' she told her new assistant, who was looking suitably impressed, and handed him the torch. Then she crept forward slowly, managing to put one foot in a large puddle right up to the ankle. Felicity pulled her now dripping-wet shoe from the murk, swore under her breath, then crept forward again, crying out and listening for the answering calls, which were still coming but seemed to be growing fainter. The sides of the ditch were very slippery in the icy rain, and the wind was whipping her face and threatening to knock her off balance but eventually, perhaps through sheer force of will, she managed to find a safe position to perch, and steadied herself.

'Do you see anything?' said Penguin Man, from somewhere above her.

'Not yet...' she said, eyes following the torch beam as he moved it round slowly. 'Wait! There!'

Piercing the darkness, a little further along the bank, were two bright wary eyes staring back at her.

'I bet that's Mum,' said Felicity under her breath. 'Be really quiet. We mustn't frighten her.'

She began to clamber along the side of the ditch towards the cat, only to find the cat reversing away from her at precisely the same speed so that, after a few minutes, neither of them had made any progress at all, except that Felicity's other foot was now also covered in mud.

'This isn't working,' muttered Felicity.

'You think?' said Penguin Man from somewhere overhead.

'Now I'm getting sass from an overgrown penguin. That's all I need.'

Despite the situation, there was a hint of a grin as she climbed out of the ditch, grabbing his hand to help her negotiate the steep last section. When she arrived in front of him there was a momentary and somewhat intense pause. She quickly let his hand drop.

'Thanks for resisting the urge to push me in,' said Felicity, turning away and wiping her soaking hair away from her face, suddenly aware of how close they were in the darkness.

'No problem,' said Penguin Man with a nod.

She could feel his eyes still on her as she set up the cat trap with some tuna fish as bait, and she found her hands were shaking, but whether it was with the cold or his presence, it was hard to tell. They retreated a safe distance. Felicity crouched down and Penguin Man attempted to follow suit but his costume was not built for such strenuous activity, as it turned out, and there was a distinct ripping sound.

'Was that you?' whispered Felicity, giggling.

'Um, I'd prefer not to answer that, if you don't mind,' came the reply.

'Fair enough.'

'So, what happens now?'

'Now, we wait,' said Felicity.

And wait they did. In fact, they managed approximately ten minutes before the teeth chattering and shivering really set in.

'We'll come back in a while,' said Felicity. 'We need to check the little dot back at the ranch. And you should probably get changed before you catch pneumonia,' she added, throwing him a sidewards glance as they headed back towards the shelter.

Gamely, he flapped his soggy wings at her.

'I'm kind of attached to this thing now,' he muttered, shrugging his shoulders.

# CHAPTER THREE

BACK AT THE SHELTER, Felicity found Penguin Man – 'It's James, call me James' – some dry clothes and he dripped off down the corridor to change while Felicity tended to the tiny kitten in the nursery, padding around in a pair of Andrea's threadbare welly socks while her own dried on the radiator. Their tiny patient had recovered a little body temperature under the heat lamp but was still disturbingly quiet. Felicity mixed up some milk powder, then gathered her up to her chest and began to feed her some droplets from a tiny syringe while she contemplated the strangeness of the night so far. It was only then that she realised something. It was five past midnight.

'I guess we should say Happy Christmas,' she said, looking up at Penguin Man – 'Honestly, call me James' – as he approached. He was now dressed in a pair of her black tapered-leg running trousers and a white T-shirt that was several sizes too small and certainly enhanced the, well, sheer *broadness* of the man. He ran his fingers through his short, blond still-damp hair and made a face.

'Do we have to?' he said.

*Hmmm, that's interesting. I wasn't expecting blond,* thought Felicity.

'Don't tell me you were all dressed up with nowhere to go?' she said, gesturing to the carrier bags that now contained the sodden remnants of his alter ego.

'Ugh. Not exactly.'

'Care to expand on that?'

Penguin Man let out a long sigh. 'Well, let's just say that when your niece has her birthday on Christmas Eve it becomes very difficult to refuse the invitation. It's become a 'Thing' in our family. If a kid's birthday party wasn't bad enough, this year she decided she wanted fancy dress. Only... guess who forgot to tell Uncle James?'

He paused and Felicity found she was listening a little too intently and tried to hide it by focusing on the kitten in her hands. As she did so, it shifted position, clearly wanting some more milk. A good sign.

'It was so late that this was the only bloody costume they had left in my size. Okay, that's not quite true, it was Penguin Man or Wonder Woman,' he said, with a lopsided grin, 'but I just couldn't pull off those tiny pants.'

She smiled a little too broadly at this, as a vividly detailed image of pulling off his tiny pants appeared in her mind without so much as a by your leave.

'I just realised I don't know your name,' he went on, studying her face with a faint expression of amusement, as if he had guessed her thoughts.

'Oh. Ugh, it's Felicity. I know. It's awful. People always think I must have grown up in the Pony Club or something. My brother got it worse. He's Tristan. I think our parents had ideas above their station.' She was babbling now. *Take a breath.*

'I like Felicity,' said James, still looking at her steadily.

'Er... thanks, I think. At least someone does. So, um, why all the festive grumpiness?' she asked, scratching around for a distraction.

'Because I hate fancy dress. And I bloody hate Christmas. That's why,' he said quietly, dropping his eyes to the kitten in Felicity's hands.

'I hate Christmas too!' she exclaimed before she could stop herself. It wasn't the sort of information she normally divulged to any old person, but to find a fellow Scrooge on Christmas Eve of all nights was just too perfect.

He stared back at her. Eyes wide.

'I *bloody* hate it,' she said, on a roll now. 'That's why I'm working here tonight, in fact.'

'Seriously?' said James.

She nodded vigorously. 'I work in here every year. Keeps me busy. I hate everything about it. Every bloody thing. I hate the food and the presents and the stupid tree and the Christmas jumpers that say things like, "Touch my baubles" and "Champion Sprout Hater", and I hate the rubbish television and the music and the shopping and everything.'

'Everything?' said James, taking an involuntary step back.

Felicity realised she may have come on a tad strongly. 'Okay, well not *everything* everything. I quite like mince pies. And those big tins of Quality Street. Oh, and the fact they always show *Die Hard* on Christmas Eve. That's really the only saving grace.'

James looked at her earnestly, his eyes looking more blue than grey now against the white of his T-shirt. She stared across at him and they held each other's gaze.

'I bloody love *Die Hard*,' he said, quite sincerely.

For a second something like lightning crackled between them. It was Felicity who was the first to look away, her heart pounding hard against her ribs. She looked down at the kitten again.

'Then there's only one thing for it. She shall be called Holly. Holly McClane,' she announced, holding the kitten aloft.

'Perfect,' said James, smiling from ear to ear. She liked his smile.

# CHAPTER FOUR

'So, here's one for you, Penguin Man. Did you know that the costume department for this film made a whole series of vests for Bruce Willis? They were carefully developed so each one looked slightly dirtier and more bloodied and ripped than the last.'

James chuckled, and it sent a pleasant tingle down her spine.

'Well, that's ruined the magic. Thanks very much. What vest do you think he's on now?'

'Ooh, I'd say maybe five or six, wouldn't you?'

They were huddled in the office together watching the movie with the heater blasting. Felicity was curled up on the chair under a musty old blanket she'd managed to locate in a cupboard. James had insisted he was happy on the floor beside her, despite her polite protestations that he was the 'guest', if that was even an adequate way to describe it. She had found him a cushion at least, and he was leaning on the chair arm for support, meaning there was only a few short inches between them. Felicity had been studiously trying not to notice.

Despite the late hour, neither one of them felt tired. The

excitement of the kitten rescue, combined with their mutual hatred of the festive season, seemed to have given them a burst of adrenaline. So, when evil Hans Gruber met his gruesome end and the credits began to roll, Felicity suggested going back out to check the cat trap and the pair of them virtually skipped out of the door. It had stopped raining, but without the cloud cover the night had cooled considerably and the wind had a sharp, icy edge. Felicity could see her breath as they splashed through the puddles and mud towards the ditch.

As they approached, they could hear a high-pitched crying. Crying and what sounded like a rattling of bars. An escaped convict, perhaps?

'It's her,' said James, this time taking the lead, barging straight through the undergrowth ahead of her.

*What the hell is he planning on doing when he gets there...?* Felicity wondered idly as she followed him. But, to his credit, he was right. It was her. Or it was a cat at least. She was well and truly caught – and was extremely not-happy about it. Felicity bent over the trap and surveyed her, trying not to shine the torch right in her eyes.

The little cat was only young herself, not more than two or three years old, with big wide eyes, matted fur, and a painfully thin body. She had an astonishing-looking face, half bright ginger, half black, as if she was wearing some kind of mask, and her green eyes flashed with fear as she huddled in the corner of the cage. She was making the most mournful wailing sound, and every so often she would hurl herself against the bars in what seemed to be more a gesture of desperation than a serious escape attempt.

'I know just how you feel,' murmured Felicity, making soothing noises to try and calm her. She could sense James' gaze turn towards her as she said this, but she ignored his silent question. Now was not the time. They spent a few moments searching the area to make sure no more kittens were about but there was no sign of any other life in the damp hollow.

'Let's get you home,' she said, turning back to the little cat with the big eyes, trying to swallow the nervous feeling rising in her throat. She carefully placed the towel over the trap and, almost immediately, the crying began to ease. 'This should help keep her calm,' she said, sending silent thanks to Andrea for that tip.

As she picked up the trap and turned to go, she caught James' eye at last.

'We got her,' she said, and felt a sudden urge to cry which she only partially managed to stifle. James nodded but kept his lips tightly shut and Felicity realised she wasn't the only one feeling a bit overcome. She nodded back at him in true British style and, without another word, they headed back to the centre, their quarry moving round and round the trap impatiently as they did so, occasionally rebounding off the sides like a furry bouncy ball. A bouncy ball with claws.

In her time at the rescue, Felicity had never had the opportunity to reunite a baby animal with its mother and she wasn't sure what to expect. She could feel the nerves threatening to take over as they got closer to the centre and briefly considered calling Andrea for advice but then dismissed the idea. She could do this.

As they headed towards the cat nursery, it was clear she needn't have worried. The mother seemed to know her baby was near, from the moment they opened the front door, in fact, and had immediately set about wailing at the top of her voice from the cat trap. And as they entered the nursery carrying their precious cargo, they could hear an even more astonishing noise, which turned out to be coming from the ball of fluff under the heat lamp. Soon the two cats were calling to each other and responding as if they were having a conversation.

By this point, Felicity had tears rolling down her cheeks and made no effort to hide them. She placed the cat trap very gently down on the table and indicated to James to close the door so Mum couldn't escape. A move that was entirely unnecessary, it turned out, as she was so desperate for her baby that as soon as they opened the trap, she trotted straight over to her and began licking her all over. The kitten seemed to revive her strength a little as she did so, and James and Felicity looked on in awe.

'Look what you did,' whispered Felicity.

Again he nodded, transfixed.

It was only then that Felicity looked at the clock for the second time. 3.37am. As the relief kicked in, tiredness washed over her, too, and her eyes began to droop. What a night this had been! But still, she couldn't relax. This baby urgently needed to feed if it was to have any chance of survival.

Keeping her movements slow and gentle so as not to frighten the cats, she reached down into the cupboard by the door and grabbed a pouch of food. This she rumpled deftly before tipping its contents carefully into a dish for the mother, along with some fresh water. The mother cat pressed herself against the bars until Felicity's hand had moved well away from the cage, then took a couple of tentative steps forward and, finally, began eating furiously, as if she had never had a proper meal before. They stood and watched, holding their collective breath.

Finally, when the mother had eaten her fill, she sniffed her kitten all over, as if to double check it was hers and not an imposter, and when she was satisfied that all checks were complete, she lay down with her body wrapped protectively around the kitten's, like a cocoon. Felicity held her breath as the baby slowly responded to her warmth and her nearness, nudging and edging her way into the right position against her mother's belly, whimpering softly, eyes still closed. Then, joy of joys, she began suckling contentedly.

James finally came out of his trance.

'She's feeding,' he said. His voice was hushed but Felicity could practically see the huge lump in his throat.

'Got something in your eye there, have you, Penguin Man?'

He smiled but his eyes were glistening. 'No comment.'

'This is very good progress,' said Felicity. 'Baby may not be able to see yet, but she could obviously smell the milk. And I think this little cat is going to be a great mummy.' Felicity put a hand on James' arm. 'They probably need a bit of peace and quiet now. I'll check on them in a while.'

They crept out of the room, shut the door quietly, then stood in the corridor.

'That was amazing,' said James, turning to her with his suddenly very blue eyes wide. 'I can't get over how they responded to each other like that. I've never seen anything like it.'

He shook his head as if in disbelief.

'It's such a rush to see them safe, isn't it?'

'And you...' He turned a 1000-volt smile her way. 'You knew just what to do. I can't thank you enough.'

Felicity blushed from the top of her head to the soles of her feet.

'It was nothing, really. I guess you just go into autopilot or something,' she mumbled, suddenly unable to look at him.

'It was the opposite of nothing. It was genuinely incredible. I mean that.'

She forced herself to look up at him, and was immediately and acutely aware that they were alone together in the middle of the night. Parts of her she had thought were long mothballed began firing off in all directions. Metaphorically speaking.

'You realise it's nearly four in the morning? I can honestly say this has been rather an unforgettable Christmas Eve, but don't you, you know, have a home to go to?'

Her brain and mouth seemed to be out of sync. Of course, she didn't want him to go anywhere. But it was too late. Her words had broken whatever kind of magic had been woven between them.

'I... should,' he said, backing away from her. 'You're right, it's Christmas and it's so late and I've outstayed my welcome I'm sure... besides, well, look at me in these clothes.'

She unconsciously looked him up and down as he said this, and it was perhaps rather more suggestive a look than she intended. He immediately stopped reversing and raised an eyebrow.

'It's been... I mean... I could stay of course. If you wanted some company. Assuming you're staying that is?'

Felicity flushed and nodded, indicating the break room behind her.

'There's a camp bed of sorts. It's not exactly the Ritz. I'm on duty until Boxing Day so I just stay. It's easier. Anyhow, I couldn't leave our two little ragamuffins now, could I?'

She grinned but found she couldn't meet his eye.

'Well, how about I come over tomorrow and check on you... all?' he said.

'Don't you have plans?' she asked, and then instantly cursed herself again.

He shrugged. 'Probably about as exciting as yours. I was planning on sitting about in my pants, getting slowly drunk and eating snacks. I could do that just as easily here. Fully dressed of course. Providing you have more snacks.'

Felicity tried – and failed – to avoid thinking about him in his pants. Again.

'Not just any snacks. I have M&S snacks.'

'I think I love you,' he grinned, blue eyes flashing.

# CHAPTER FIVE

TRUE TO HIS WORD, James the Penguin Man did return the next day.

He was respectfully late, presumably to allow Felicity a well-earned Christmas lie-in, but of course she'd already been up three times in the night checking the cats, and had managed to get zero sleep in between on the tiny camp bed the size of a matchstick. So, by the time James knocked on the door at 11am, she felt like a complete wreck. Her hair was beyond unruly, and her mascara was smeared attractively under each eye. *Like a sexy panda*, thought Felicity with a grimace, as she caught her reflection in the internal window of the puppy room. Despite this, there was an unmistakeable and unexpected bubble of anticipation in her stomach as she opened the door.

This time, he wasn't dressed as a soggy penguin but a respectable human being with dry hair and everything. He was wearing a navy shirt and smart jeans, and something about his blue eyes made her think instantly of McDreamy from *Grey's Anatomy*. Only blonder, of course. She felt even more of a wreck by comparison in her scruffy 'Animal Saviours' T-shirt and old work trousers, but if he thought the same, he didn't let it show.

If anything, Penguin Man looked rather pleased to see her.

'Well, good morning,' he said, a big grin on his face.

She tucked her hair behind her ear as he handed over a familiar-shaped present that was rather shonkily wrapped in cheap foil paper.

'I thought you hated Christmas?' she said, feeling slightly betrayed.

'I do,' he said, quickly. 'But you'll forgive me when you see what it is.'

She ripped the wrapping off to reveal a tin of Quality Street.

'Bloody fantastic,' she said, touched that he had remembered. 'I don't have anything for you, I'm afraid.'

'Oh, don't worry about that,' he said, pulling another parcel from the enormous bag for life at his feet.

The cheap paper this time revealed a box of cat food.

'It's all I could get from the dodgy newsagents on Bell Street. It's some sort of bank holiday today, apparently.'

She smiled. 'No, don't worry, that's super thoughtful. Thank you.' She paused. 'Do you want to see them?'

James grinned and strode past her towards the nursery. 'Why else do you think I came?'

They peered down at the two balls of fluff, who were snoozing contentedly in their basket in the middle of the room. Even little Bobby Charlton was asleep, tucked up in his favourite blanket in the corner of the cage, snoring gently.

'Typical,' hissed Felicity. 'They've been up mucking about all night and waking me up with their noisiness every five minutes and now when you get here, they're flipping asleep. But don't you dare wake them!' she added quickly, as James went to poke the mother with a finger.

'It's so tempting, though,' he said, hastily retracting his finger. 'Just look at that.'

They gazed at the sleeping pile of cat in companionable silence. Now that the baby had been thoroughly cleaned by mum, she looked less like a dirty cotton ball and more like a kitten, and there were even tiny glimpses of what looked like ginger fur emerging. The mother, meanwhile, had patches of black and ginger all over her body, except for one white leg and a tiny white bib under her chin that just made you want to reach out and touch.

When Felicity spoke again it was in a whisper, afraid to break the moment.

'What shall we name the mother then? She's stunning. Tortoiseshell, I think.'

'Is that what you call that colour? She's beautiful. I have no idea about a name though,' said James, thinking very deeply. After a beat he continued, 'Wait. It's coming to me...'

Felicity shrugged. 'I hope so. I'm out of ideas. I can only think of one woman in the whole of *Die Hard*.'

James looked triumphant, as if she'd read his mind. 'Gennaro. That's it. As in, Holly Gennaro. Or is that a bit geeky? She could be Gennie for short.'

'I love it,' she said, a bit too intensely.

They stared at each other for a moment. Felicity pushed a strand of hair behind her ear, suddenly feeling awkward.

'Right,' he said. 'I think it's time for Christmas lunch. M&S style.'

The dingy office managed to look a tiny bit cosy once they'd laid a blanket on the floor and nicked the bedding from the stowaway bed from hell. Felicity – face washed and hair hastily finger-brushed – laid out the M&S banquet, which seemed rather meagre now it was stretched to feed two, but James proudly produced his contribution, consisting of a crate of beer, a family sized box of (genuine) Maltesers and an enormous bag of (imitation) Doritos, and they tucked in happily.

'Thanks for not mentioning the C word,' she said after a while, mouth full of crisps.

'You're most welcome,' said James, raising an eyebrow. 'But I didn't think you were that kind of girl, to be honest.'

Felicity laughed a little too loudly at that, only just managing to stifle a snort.

'Not that C word, you numpty,' she said, throwing a Malteser at his head. 'The other one.'

'Oh, that,' he said. 'To be honest this is the best C word I've had for quite a long time. Maybe for years, in fact.'

She stopped munching and looked at him intently.

'Actually, me too,' she said. And meant it.

*In fact, this is the best day I've had for quite a long time, full stop.*

'So, why do you hate it so much?' he asked, returning her stare as he screwed the cap off his bottle of beer in one smooth move.

She shifted position on the slightly (extremely) uncomfortable pile of cushions she had constructed on the dingy orange carpet tiles.

'Do we have to do this now?' she said, tilting her head to one side.

He smiled. 'No, you're right, let's not do that today. Tell me something good instead. A really fat juicy secret. Or something you're proud of.'

Felicity reached for a veggie sausage roll, and pondered.

'That's a good question. I once got my ten-metre swimming badge. Does that count?'

'It really depends. Do you mean "once" when you were ten years old or "once" as in, you know, last week?'

'Hey, ten metres is ten metres!'

'True, true. Okay, fine, that counts.'

'But I was ten. Well, maybe eleven. Just for the record. Your turn.'

'Okay. Erm. I rescued a kitten from dying last night.'

'No, no, no.' She shook her head. 'That doesn't count because I know that about you already. I mean, it's awesome and everything, don't get me wrong. But... I want to know something about you I don't know.' She realised even as she said it that she knew hardly anything about him at all.

'Okay, okay. Erm... I can identify every British plane from the Second World War. I used to go to air shows every year with my dad. I just love them. There you are. I nearly went on *You Bet* with that one.' He grinned. 'You're probably too young to remember *You Bet*.'

'Sadly not,' said Felicity, with a chuckle. 'You're a plane geek. I love that.'

'Your turn again,' he said, waving a fake Dorito at her.

Felicity's left leg was slowly going to sleep where it was crossed beneath her, and she began an ambitious attempt to pull it out from underneath her without toppling off her cushion pile.

'Hmmm, how can I top that one?' She wobbled, sticking her arms out for balance. 'Okay, I see your plane geekdom and I raise you one East Midlands chess champion – under fourteens.'

James smiled. 'This went dark quickly. I wasn't expecting that at all. I think we need a tournament. It's not just planes that make me go all geeky, you know.'

'You're on,' said Felicity, 'but bear in mind I'm seriously sleep-deprived and, also, I'm not fourteen anymore.'

'I'm very glad to hear it,' said James in a low voice and Felicity felt the blood rush to her ears.

'Quickly, tell me another.'

'Fine, well I can't think of any juicy secrets as such, but I do have a confession, does that count?'

Felicity nodded.

'I'll warn you, it's a biggie.'

'Go on...? And also, for the record, you're scaring me.'

'I think it's me that should be scared.'

'Is that so?'

'Yes. You see, the thing is... I've never owned a cat. Or a dog. Or even a hamster. Don't hate me.'

He put his hands protectively over his head as he spoke, and Felicity laughed again.

'Whether or not I hate you depends almost entirely on whether you are about to tell me you can't stand animals or whether it's simply because you had a deprived childhood?'

James laughed but didn't remove his hands from his head. 'I obviously hate all animals, what can I say?'

Felicity threw another Malteser at him. This was promising to descend into a full-on food fight.

'Just kidding. It's definitely the second one,' he said. 'I deeply regret it. My parents were clearly inhuman freaks.'

'You could always... rectify the situation,' she said, waving an arm vaguely around the centre. 'We have one or two...'

'Ah, as it happens, I'm holding out for a particular one or two,' he said, nodding his head towards the cat nursery.

Felicity felt her heart turn to liquid. 'Aw, Penguin Man,' she said. 'You're smitten!'

He smiled a broad smile. 'I think I might be.'

They gazed at each other, and this time it wasn't just

Felicity's ears that went hot. She yanked at the collar of her polo shirt to try and cover the spreading blush on her neck. What was it about this man?

'I think it's time for me to thrash you,' she said, trying her best to keep a straight face.

And that is how they ended up spending a sleepy and rather drunken Christmas afternoon sitting on the office floor, surrounded by carpet picnic detritus, and playing round after round of chess improvised with Andrea's desk ornaments and empty beer bottles. Every so often they would amble around the centre checking on the animals, who all seemed to be behaving, even Freddy the dachshund who of course had taken an instant liking to James. Typical.

Let the records state, it was very, very bad chess.

And a very, very good Christmas.

## CHAPTER SIX

Two DAYS LATER, Felicity's friends arrived at her flat for an enforced Christmas party. Which makes it sound like they were invited, but it was rather more complicated than that.

Rebecca ('Bex') and Sophie had known Felicity since school and although they knew she had rather strong feelings about Christmas, they were the tiny but resilient remnant who would still try and encourage her into a bit of festivity. Most years, she managed to avoid them during the critical period with excuses about work, but for some reason this year she had finally relented and agreed to a 'small affair' at her place providing they didn't 'go too mad'.

And tonight was the night. It had come round far too quickly for Felicity's liking, and she was still knackered from her completely sleep-deprived Christmas at the centre. But, she sighed, with the briefest of glances in the mirror as she quickly ran a brush through her hair and changed her top for one that was slightly less crumpled, there was no going back now.

Bex and Sophie arrived half an hour late as per usual, absolutely laden with huge bags full of fizz and chocolates and leftovers from their own rather more traditional

Christmases. Both had donned the most ridiculous festive jumpers and hats they could find, and Felicity could only stand aside as they bustled in like two little Christmas elves and swept up any mess they discovered on the way, fluffing cushions, clearing dirty crockery, and even making her dishevelled bed.

Then they set about making Felicity's tiny flat a little bit cheerier. They were careful not to call it 'Christmassy' as such, but Bex had brought streamers and blown up pink and purple balloons and Sophie had even made a sort of tree for Felicity out of some branches sprayed with white paint and covered in glitter. Sophie was that sort of person. Good At Crafts. Equipped With Glitter.

It was all a bit much, but for some reason Felicity didn't feel as cross about it as she thought she might. The 'sort of tree' was actually quite pretty, once it had pink and purple baubles hanging from its shimmery branches. And the food, she had to admit, was delicious. No roast dinner here, Felicity avoided those whenever she could, but Bex's home-made turkey curry and rice served with crispy poppadoms went down a treat. Sophie had brought the desserts – chocolate yule log and a very boozy 1970s style trifle, with glacé cherries on top and everything. They had even brought crackers, although both women knew better than to try and make her wear the paper hat.

*I suppose*, thought Felicity grudgingly, as she finished her second helping of sherry trifle, *it's quite nice to have some company*. That was before Bex pulled out her phone and attempted to put Christmas songs on the Bluetooth speaker, anyway, at which point Felicity felt she must intervene.

'Nope.'

'What do you mean, nope?'

'I mean it. Nope. Absolutely not. No Mariah, no Cliff, no

Shakin' Stevens, no bloody Mr Blobby or East 17. None of it. I am playing *my* playlist, or the party's over.'

'Yikes, darling, you seriously need to relax. Have some more bubbles.'

Bex was already pouring more cheap Prosecco into her glass, but she obediently put down her phone and allowed Felicity to put on her favourite anti-Christmas tunes instead. It was Sophie's turn to roll her eyes as The Eels' classic 'Christmas is Going to the Dogs' began to play but Felicity instantly felt that all was well with the world again.

*One festive step at a time.*

Later, as Bex and Sophie curled up like bookends on the sofa and Felicity relaxed back into her battered old armchair with the stuffing hanging out, she contemplated telling them about Penguin Man. She had just decided against it on the grounds that a) it wasn't anything yet, and b) some part of her didn't want to jinx anything, when good old Bex piped up.

'So, Felicity darling, what did you get up to for Christmas then, dare I ask? If you even had one in the end?' She was slurring her words slightly, a half empty glass precariously balanced between her elegant forefingers on the sofa arm, her other hand glued to her iPhone as always.

Felicity took a deep breath, mainly to buy some time.

'I was working. Andrea was – well, busy, let's say – so I worked the whole time. I say busy, but what I mean is, she had another date with that guy she met online.'

There was a pause.

'It was quite eventful this year, though.'

Bex looked up from her phone.

'Eventful how?'

'We had to carry out a rescue on Christmas Eve. It was really exciting, actually. There was a tiny little kitten stuck in a ditch near the centre. She was so cold and wet, the poor little thing. I thought she'd died at first.'

Both of her friends were listening intently now. At this, they gasped in unison.

'She was still alive though, and that meant we had to go back and try and find her mum in the pitch black. That took a while. It was all very dramatic.'

It came out all in a rush.

'Oh no, that's awful,' said Sophie.

'I know. I thought they'd been abandoned, but I think the mum was just a bit feral, bless her. She must have had the baby in that horrible muddy ditch. God knows how we managed to catch her, she was so scared... but we did, and in the end, we brought her back and reunited them, which was really cute.'

There was another pause.

'I thought Andrea was off banging that Spaniard?' This was Bex. Ever tactful.

'She was,' said Felicity.

'But you said "we". "We had to carry out a rescue", you said.'

'It's just an expression.'

'You said it a lot of times.'

'I know, but–'

'So, you rescued these cats by yourself?'

'Not exactly.'

'Someone helped you?'

Felicity shifted in her seat. 'Er. Yes.'

'Hold that thought, I'm out of fizz.'

Bex swung her long legs out from underneath her and strolled casually to the kitchen while Felicity desperately tried to think of how she could backtrack. She could tell them another time. It didn't need to be now. It was no big deal.

Sophie, meanwhile, was studying Felicity's face from the other end of the sofa.

'It was a man,' she said, calmly. Felicity didn't reply but she could do nothing about the huge smile that arrived on her face without warning.

'What?' said Bex, rather too loudly given she was only on the other side of the room.

'It was a man!' yelled Sophie.

'I bloody knew it!' said Bex, slamming her fist on the melamine kitchen counter in triumph.

Felicity ducked behind a cushion.

'I don't know anything about him, really,' she said, when they had exhausted playing their new favourite game, *Twenty Questions about Penguin Man*, in record time.

'You really don't, do you?' said Sophie, narrowing her eyes.

'He's not a psycho or anything. At least, I don't think he is. Fair enough, I thought he might be a murderer when he turned up on Christmas Eve banging on the door and I was on my own and everything.'

Sophie's eyes were nearly closed, they were so narrow now.

'But obviously he wasn't. A murderer, that is. He's nice. At least, I think he is. He seemed like a decent human.'

'It's a good job he wasn't though,' said Bex, through a mouthful of toffee penny. 'A murderer, I mean.'

'You think?' Sophie shot her a look.

'He saved a kitten,' said Felicity, and she could feel her voice rising a little. 'A tiny little kitten. You should have seen him, he was dressed as a penguin, for a start, and he was all soaking wet and he had no shoes on and yet he didn't seem to mind coming with me to rescue the mother and... what are you both grinning at?'

'Wow,' said Bex.

'Yup,' said Sophie.

'What?' said Felicity.

'Your face,' said Sophie. 'It's bright pink.'

'That's just the alcohol. Honestly, you two.'

'Honestly nothing. I can't remember the last time I saw you gooey over a man.'

Felicity stood up suddenly from her chair. 'I am NOT gooey,' she said, one finger in the air, all the alcohol rushing to her head at once.

'Woah.'

She paused as the room swung around her head once or twice, then seemed to behave.

'I am NOT gooey,' she announced for the second time. 'And I'm going to the toilet. So there.'

Her dramatic exit was hampered somewhat by the fact her armchair had been pulled too close to the coffee table and she had to sort of shuffle along the edge of the chair for a bit before she was free and clear. Sophie and Bex watched her go and as she manoeuvred her way out of the room, she knew they'd be exchanging one of their 'looks'. Eyebrows raised to the heavens.

'Well, this is a turn up for the books,' said Sophie.

'I heard that,' said Felicity from the bathroom.

'If you can hear us, we can hear you,' replied Sophie.

Felicity couldn't think of an adequate response to that.

Much later that night, when Sophie had fallen asleep on the sofa, Bex and Felicity chatted quietly – or semi-quietly – across the room.

'You should ask him out,' slurred Bex in her best stage whisper.

'What? No... I can't!' whispered Felicity.

'What have you got to lose? You like him, don't you?'

'Of course I do. He's completely gorgeous.'

'Well then.'

'Well then, nothing. He might not even be available. I'm betting he lives in an immaculate mansion in Chelsea Downs or somewhere like that. With a jumbo fridge and one of those barista coffee machines. And a girlfriend called something like Precious or Chanel who only eats egg whites and kale and gets her eyebrows tattooed on.'

Bex giggled and slopped Prosecco over the arm of the chair. She mopped at it feebly with her sleeve.

'Unlikely.'

'Look, I'm not in a position to date anyone right now. I never thought I'd meet anyone, working at Saviours, if I'm honest, and that suited me just fine. And it's not like I have a great history when it comes to relationships.'

'You can't hide out here forever,' said Bex, waving an arm around the tiny flat.

'I'm not hiding.' Felicity felt weirdly offended. But also, seen.

'Sure, whatever you say.'

'Anyway, he's bound to turn out to be a psycho in the end, isn't he? It's only a matter of time with me.'

'Anyone ever tell you that you have trust issues?' said Bex.

'You do. Regularly.'

'Well, there we are then.'

'You don't count. You know too much. At any rate, we're both forgetting something crucial. I may well never see him again. This is a big town. I'm a rather small person. I never go out. And I don't have his number.'

Bex's mouth formed an O shape which made Tipsy-Felicity giggle.

'You didn't get his number? What were you thinking?'

'I wasn't thinking. I was flustered. He was so handsome. And tall. Did I mention tall?'

'But the cats. Won't he want to visit the cats? He's bound to want to see how they're getting on.'

'He won't just turn up out of the blue, surely. Who does that? He's probably forgotten all about us. Or he's told all his mates about his crazy cat lady Christmas. Had a good laugh.'

'Oh no. He won't have done that.'

'How do you know?'

'Because then he'd have to tell them about the penguin suit.'

'Fair point.'

Felicity rubbed her eyes. 'So, what about you? Are you seeing anyone, Miss Know-it-all?'

Bex took a long time to reply. Into the silence, Sophie suddenly let out a Miss-Piggy-style snore and Felicity stifled a giggle. Sophie had never struck her as the snoring type.

'You know me,' said Bex, eventually, playing with a strand of her long dark hair. 'There's always someone.'

'That's no kind of answer.'

'I know, but there's not much else I can say right now. It's complicated for me, too.'

She seemed sad but Felicity put it down to the booze. Bex had drunk an awful lot of Prosecco, even by her standards. She always got maudlin after Prosecco.

'What about Sophie, then?' whispered Felicity. 'They're doing okay, aren't they?'

'Boringly so, yes.'

'Come now. You're not jealous surely?'

'Of Sophie and Marcus? No way. Urgh. It's a bit too perfect for my liking. All that couples yoga and crafting with the kids.

They even make their own Easter eggs, for God's sake. Who does that?'

'Ha! There's no such thing as too perfect. Admit it. If you had their life, you'd be happy as a clam.'

'I'd be bored senseless. I'd probably have ten men on the go, because, you know, why not?'

Felicity laughed. 'You'd have ten men on the go now, if you had the time.'

Bex shrugged.

'At least,' she said, with a grin.

# CHAPTER SEVEN

Penguin Man did, in fact, turn up out of the blue.

It was the day after the day after the day after Boxing Day – whatever it's called – when the rest of the world was lost in a fog of cheese and wine and *Morecambe and Wise* repeats and Felicity and Andrea's universe had shrunk down to being almost entirely focused on nursing Gennie and Holly back to health.

'There's someone here to see you,' Andrea had said, slyly, when she spotted Felicity walking past her office door.

'What? Who? Where?'

Andrea just smiled and waved her pen in the general direction of the cat nursery. Felicity's mouth went dry. She ran her fingers through her hair and wondered if she smelled of dog food and whether she could quickly duck past the doorway and make it to the toilets to check.

But as she approached the room all thoughts of her own appearance went straight out of her head. James was standing by the central table, peering down at the two new arrivals with a look of absolute reverence on his face. He was wearing a soft-looking vintage brown leather jacket over a striped shirt and jeans, and his blond hair was just the right amount of tousled.

Her memory had definitely underplayed the level of handsome.

Felicity leaned on the door frame and tried to look cool and effortless and not at all embarrassed about being covered in cat hair from head to toe.

'Well now. If it isn't Mr Penguin Man himself.'

*Smooth.*

James lifted his head and a slow easy grin spread across his face. His eyes seemed to her in that moment to be the bluest blue that anyone's eyes had ever been.

'Well good morning. How are you?' He was speaking in low tones, not wanting to wake the sleeping pile of floof in front of him, and her heart gave a little appreciative twinge.

'Good, I'm good, thanks,' she replied, attempting to lower her voice to match his, even though it seemed to have gone all squeaky for some reason. 'How's you?'

'Yeah. Good thanks. I brought snacks.' He nodded towards the side counter which was covered with paper bags overflowing with fresh doughnuts and cookies alongside several boxes of food for the cats.

'No wonder it smells like a bakery in here, wow. Are those Yum Yums? Andrea is dead partial to a Yum Yum.'

James shrugged and turned his attention back to the cats, but she could see he was suppressing a smile.

'Just a little something to keep you all going.'

'And more cat food. That's amazing. Thank you. Can I get you a coffee or something? It's about that time.'

'Sure. Coffee would be great.'

'Okay. But first you have to meet my boss. Don't say I didn't warn you.'

James raised a curious eyebrow but there was no time to explain further. The mention of coffee was like a homing beacon to Andrea and within mere seconds, James, Andrea and

Felicity were huddled together in the tiny break room, munching their way through baked goods, licking sugar off their fingers and sharing what felt like a reasonably companionable silence as long as Felicity didn't catch Andrea's eye.

That's all she had to do.

*Whatever you do... Don't. Look. At. Andrea. And stop letting your leg linger against James' thigh like that even though it's right there next to you and his jeans are stretched over it, all tight and everything.*

'So,' said Andrea eventually, her mouth full of doughnut.

'So,' said James.

'Here we all are then.'

'Looks like it.'

'How did it feel to see Holly and Gennie again then? Thanks so much for the treats.'

'Oh, you're welcome. Great, actually, it's great to see them again. Holly is so tiny I was sure she wouldn't make it.'

'We're not out of the woods yet, but she's a little fighter. I hope she's going to pull through.'

'Oh God yes, me too. And Gennie of course.'

'She's very nervous, the mum, but I think she'll come right. You two did well.'

Felicity had completely lost the power of speech but Andrea, to her credit, was doing a great job of making small talk, not something she was normally fond of. Felicity was doubly grateful for this as it meant that as the two of them chatted, she could take a break from trying not to squirt jam down her front and could legitimately go back to pretending to listen/staring at his lovely face, in side profile now but no less appealing as a result. He'd taken his jacket off to reveal his extremely solid-looking forearms, which were so distracting that she almost missed Andrea's crowning moment.

'Why don't you stay and help us with the cats this

afternoon, James?' said Andrea, brightly, as they reached a slightly awkward lull in the conversation. 'If you don't have anywhere you need to be, that is.'

'Love to,' said James, standing up and brushing down his jeans. 'But sadly, I have a lunch thing I really can't miss. Maybe another time though.'

'Sure, of course, anytime.' It was Andrea's turn to raise questioning eyebrows at Felicity, who studiously ignored her and led James out of the tiny room towards the back door. He hovered there a moment, then turned back towards her.

'So.'

'So.'

'Thanks for coming to see us. Them, I mean. Thanks for coming to see them.'

'My pleasure.'

'And for the doughnuts of course.'

'No problem. I'm so glad Holly is doing okay.'

'All thanks to you.'

'Oh no, that was all you. I was basically just the entertainment.'

Felicity giggled. The sound tailed off into a long silence.

'You seem rather quiet today. Everything okay?' James was looking at her intently.

'Am I?' She glanced up at him then found she had to look away. 'Just tired, I guess. And... I had a party the other night. Why is it that when you're eighteen you can survive on two hours' sleep and drink yourself into oblivion with no ill effects whatsoever, but when you're in your thirties it takes three days to get over a teeny tiny bit of Prosecco?'

'That is both one of life's greatest mysteries and its biggest cruelties.'

'You're not kidding.'

A pause.

'Surely you of all people didn't go to an actual *Christmas* party?'

*Don't say it was just your mates, don't say it was just your mates.*

'Oh, no, it was just a couple of mates.'

*Damn.*

'And a tiny bit of Prosecco, you say?'

'Well... maybe a couple of glasses.'

'Sure. And the rest. Well, I hope you behaved yourself anyway.'

'I can neither confirm nor deny.'

'You forget I've already seen what you're like to party with.'

'So you have. Great fun. The life and soul, that's me.'

'Of course. Like a tiny Christmas elf.'

Felicity snort-laughed before she could stop herself and her hands flew to her face in horror.

'Oh God. Pretend you didn't just hear that, please.'

'Hear what?' He gave her a flash of that grin and her insides did a little flip. Felicity smiled up at him gratefully. 'I'd like to come back sometime. See how they're doing. Is that okay?'

*Be cool.*

'Of course.'

'Great. I'm heading to a party on New Year's Eve but I was thinking I could drop in for a bit on the way over. Are you working? It'd be sometime in the afternoon, most likely.'

*Another party?*

'Oh right. Yeah, I'll be here... Quite the socialite, aren't you? Which poor animal's likeness will you be ripping off this time, pray tell?'

His blue eyes crinkled. 'I don't think it's that kind of party. Mind you, if I remember rightly it's black tie, so I might end up looking like a penguin anyway. Probably should find the invite, now you mention it.' James' brow wrinkled ever so slightly as he began patting down his coat.

She waited a moment, trying to picture him in black tie and then deciding that was a dangerous train of thought. As the silence extended between them, she found herself wondering if he might even invite her. Attempted to project the words into his mind through telepathy. Tried to summon the courage to ask if he was going alone.

But it was James who spoke in the end, breaking the tension abruptly. 'Must have left it at home. Dammit. Anyway, see you on New Year's.'

'See you.'

And with that he turned and headed out of the door.

*Dammit indeed.*

She watched him go, taking long decisive strides. *He was just so... broad.*

He didn't turn or wave. As he disappeared from view, she felt a pang of disappointment.

'He came back.' Andrea had sidled up behind her in the doorway.

'Yup.'

'Interesting.'

'Is it?'

'Isn't it?'

'I'm not sure yet,' said Felicity. Her face was burning suddenly and she didn't dare turn around. Hopefully the back of her head still looked reasonably nonchalant.

'Is that a real leather jacket, do you think?'

Felicity shrugged. 'I don't know. I suspect so.'

'Hmm, I'm not sure how I feel about that.'

'I think if it's vintage that's okay, right? It's not like he's harmed any animals to make it?'

A long pause. She could practically hear the cogs in Andrea's brain rotating.

'I guess you're right.'

'Come on. It's better than that awful plastic stuff, isn't it? For the planet, I mean.'

Another pause.

'I like him. Let's assume it's vintage.'

'Good call.'

'He's got a great arse.'

'Andrea!'

'What? Well. He has.'

'And that makes the wearing of dead animals okay, does it?'

'No. Of course not. But it doesn't hurt.'

'You're impossible.'

'I'm charming and endearing. You like it.'

'Don't have much choice, do I? You're also my boss.'

'You make an excellent point. Now get back to work.'

'Gladly.'

# CHAPTER EIGHT

JAMES THE PENGUIN MAN hadn't even touched her yet, let alone kissed her, but despite what she'd said to Andrea, despite her conversation with Bex, despite the fact he was clearly going to a fancy dinner with his model tennis player Nobel Peace Prize-winning girlfriend or something equally irritating, deep down inside Felicity couldn't shake the slightly irrational hope that he'd come to the centre to see *her*, not just the cats, cute as they were.

And now here he was, coming back on New Year's Eve, apparently. Her heart leapt at the thought. Despite having been out of the dating game for longer than she cared to mention, she felt a tiny bit hopeful that they had some kind of an understanding, as Elizabeth Bennet would say.

So, she was beside herself with despondency when the day came and James didn't show up. Andrea tried to reassure her that it was only a matter of time, that he'd probably got held up, but she had a bad feeling right down in the depths of her stomach as if she'd forgotten to eat. She tried to focus her attention on the cats, and as Gennie had started to show signs of wanting to play and even purring a little when Felicity was near, it was easy to distract herself for a few minutes at a time. But then she would remember the time and the pit-of-the-stomach feeling was back.

When the door banged shut at 7.30pm that evening, she felt she should be mad in some way and she fully intended to make him suffer a bit, but somehow Felicity found she couldn't help the huge smile that instantly lit up her face. She turned from the sink in the cat nursery, arms covered in suds from the washing up, wiping her hair away from her face with the back of her hand, fully expecting to see James walking in with some kind of perfectly reasonable explanation for being late that she was entirely ready and prepared to accept.

Except it wasn't James at all.

'Hello, Felicity,' said a familiar voice, and instantly the blood started pumping wildly around her body as if it was getting her ready to run.

A tall, dark, and very slick-looking man was standing in the doorway, polished tan shoes and smart navy suit looking hugely out of place amongst the paraphernalia of the rescue centre. He wrinkled his nose slightly at the smell of cat food and other related aromas as he moved towards her, deliberately ignoring the cats, who had immediately begun clamouring for his attention from their cages on either side of the room.

She took a deep breath.

'Adam,' she said.

He smiled that familiar dazzling smile that showed all his bright white teeth at once and not for the first time the mannerism reminded her of Tom Cruise.

*Top Gun* Tom, not *Tropic Thunder* Tom, mind.

He kept moving until he was only a few feet away from her

and she had a sudden panic that he was going to try and kiss her in greeting. Surely even he wouldn't be that bold. But, no, to her relief he stopped just short, right in front of her – inches away, really – and, in a panic, she grabbed a tea towel to dry her hands and give her something to focus on other than the familiar scent-and-lotion smell of him.

'What are you doing here?' she said, neurons firing in all directions. *What the hell is he doing here?*

'Merry Christmas,' said Adam. His jaw muscle flexed, and she could feel his eyes roving all over her face in that familiar way he had, as if he were trying to memorise every detail. 'Or should I say, Happy New Year?'

Felicity stared up at him, barely able to speak.

She couldn't believe he was here.

And, after all this time, she couldn't believe that he still had the power to make her feel the way she always had when he looked at her. As if she was completely inadequate. As if he'd mistaken her for some other woman. Some fitter, blonder, more attractive woman probably. Under his intense gaze she knew she was blushing, and she cursed herself for not wearing more make-up that day even as she hated that failed-feminist part of herself.

*Being a woman is so complicated.*

'Surely you didn't come all this way to say that?' said Felicity, trying to keep her tone reserved even though she felt anything but. 'You know I hate Christmas.'

At that he laughed. He actually *laughed*.

'I know you do,' Adam said, his dark eyes boring into her. 'It's delightfully charming, just like you. I missed you.'

'It's been three years, Adam. *Three* years. And you walk in here as if you just popped out for a bit!'

'I know, I know. It's shameful really. I've been watching you though.'

She looked at him properly then, a bit shocked.

'I mean, not, like, in a stalker way, I mean I've been keeping track of you. No, that sounds worse.'

It was his turn to blush now, but in a very cool and collected way of course, the luminescent brown skin on his cheeks flushing slightly with pink.

'You mean you've been facestalking me.'

'Yes, yes that's it. I've just kept up with you on social media, on Instagram and stuff. I wanted to know you were doing okay. Nice profile pic, by the way.'

She had thrown him a lifeline and he had seized it gratefully, not realising that it was a trap. And now she had him.

'I'm not on Instagram,' she said quietly, raising an eyebrow.

An awkward pause ensued, in which a look of anguish passed briefly across his features, but he quickly regained his cool.

'Okay. *Fine.* If you must know the truth, I've been asking around about you for ages, and I had no joy, and then I bumped into a couple of your friends on a night out last week and they told me you worked here and, well, I had to see you.'

*Bex and Sophie. It had to be. But why didn't they tell me?*

He moved even closer then, or so it seemed, still looking her up and down slowly.

*He looks a bit pale. Tired, maybe, or just older. Still handsome though, the cheeky git.*

'I've worked here for a while. I can't believe it's taken you that long to hunt me down, Poirot.'

Adam shrugged; his face annoyingly passive.

'Anyway, why on earth would you need to see me?' she said, feeling the old familiar mix of anger and desire rise in her chest as he came ever closer. 'Don't you remember what I did to you? How I treated you?'

Adam made another dismissive gesture, a wave of the hand

as if he was batting away a fly, which Felicity found intensely irritating.

'It's all well under the bridge and gone now. That was a long time ago, after all. Don't worry about it.'

'How can you say that? You were there. I was *awful* to you. Really awful. I always swore to myself that I would never be like... well, you know. Like *him*. And then I did exactly the same thing.'

Adam looked blank for a second. 'Him?'

'My dad.'

'Oh yes, right. What did he do again?'

Felicity felt her jaw clench. Adam had known her since she was a teenager. How could he not remember this?

'My dad. What he did to my mum. I swore I'd never be like him. I *swore*.' Hot tears prickled behind her eyes and she swallowed.

Adam leaned forward, his brown eyes softening, and took her hand. 'I forgive you,' he said. 'It's time to forgive yourself.'

She nodded dumbly. His hand felt warm against hers and the contact had a strangely numbing effect on her senses.

'I got you something,' he said. Without breaking eye contact he reached into his jacket pocket, turned her hand over and carefully placed a small box wrapped in pale blue and cream paper into her palm.

Mechanically, and really just so she had something to do with her fingers, she unwrapped it, revealing a beautiful sky-blue box with 'Tiffany' written across the top.

Felicity stared at it for a long moment, then lifted her eyes to Adam's face in astonishment.

'It's from Selfridges,' he said, with a shrug. As if that was no big deal. As if they popped in all the time. He was so close now she could feel his breath on her face. Selfridges. Shop of Legends. Her very favourite, or, at least, it would be if she could afford to shop there. Her mind raced. She had no idea how to handle this situation.

'See. You're forgiven. Now, aren't you going to open it?' He smiled, indicating the box.

'Not yet,' was all she could manage. 'Not yet.'

Fortunately, or unfortunately depending on your point of view, she didn't have to. For, of course, that was the moment that James finally decided to make an appearance.

# CHAPTER NINE

'Sorry I'm la–' came the voice from the doorway, tailing off rapidly as he took in the scene before him.

Felicity thought she might faint.

James walked further into the room, and for the first time in their brief friendship he looked distinctly rattled. He barely glanced at Adam, instead turning questioning eyes on Felicity.

Adam stayed completely cool, of course. He turned casually towards the interloper at the doorway, fixing his Tom Cruise grin to his face, and making no attempt to move away from Felicity, who was trapped in the corner of the room between Adam and the sink. Short of giving him a shove, she knew she couldn't put any distance between them without it looking too obvious. In fact, she could swear he had moved even closer when James appeared.

James stopped short about ten feet away from them, frowning openly. He was wearing bashed up Levi's and an extremely well-fitting dark T-shirt under his leather jacket. *Strange get-up for a black-tie party*, thought Felicity vaguely, trying not to notice the way the shirt stretched even more tightly across his chest as he crossed his arms.

'All right, mate?' said Adam, apparently oblivious to such non-verbal cues and greeting him like an old friend. Felicity threw him a glance. Had he been expecting this somehow?

'All right?' said James, but he was still looking at Felicity, who was trying valiantly to edge round Adam and make some space between them. She could almost feel Adam's heart racing next to her, or was that her own? Despite the blood rushing around in her ears, Felicity attempted to take charge of the situation.

'James, hi, this is, I mean, this Adam was just, I mean this is Adam, he's an old friend and he was just on his way out,' she said, casting a meaningful glance in Adam's direction.

'I just got here,' said Adam – *another shrug* – but to Felicity's relief he did take a small step backwards.

'And I was just arriving,' said James coolly, never taking his eyes off Felicity. 'I'm sorry I'm late, but I did bring us dinner. It's New Year's Eve, after all.'

From somewhere behind him, James produced an enormous pizza box and a six-pack of beer, waving them in her direction. At this clear display of male dominance Adam retreated a few steps further, and Felicity took the opportunity to duck past him. She tried to look like she had some important purpose as she moved down the room towards the door.

'You're late,' she said, 'but you're just in time to help with rounds,' and she threw the damp tea towel playfully at James as she went past. Hopefully he couldn't see that her hands were shaking. *Don't look back, don't look back.* James seemed to relax a little at that and – just as she hoped he would – he followed her out of the door. After a moment, Adam sauntered along behind.

*What now?* Felicity felt a cold spark of panic. *I have to get him out of here.*

And there, as if by royal appointment, was Andrea, waiting

by her office door. 'We have lots to be getting on with. A potentially busy night as you can imagine. Shall I show you out?' she said to Adam in a tone that implied this was not up for debate.

Felicity kept her head down and kept moving, heading into the puppy room to start her rounds, James hard on her tail. She prayed Adam had finally learned to understand tone of voice. It had never been one of his strongest traits.

Just as they had a few days earlier, Andrea, James and Felicity sat around together in the break room after Adam had gone, but this time there was a heavy, weighted silence. They all stared at the pizza boxes but no one made any move towards them. When James finally excused himself and went to the bathroom, Andrea took her chance.

'Well... this is awkward. Who the hell was that guy?' she hissed.

'My ex,' Felicity hissed back. 'Adam. Thanks so much for getting rid of him. I could have kissed you for that.'

'Don't mention it. He's gorgeous by the way!' said Andrea. 'He looks like that actor, ooh, what's his name? Dev something.'

'Patel. Dev Patel. I know. A cross between Tom Cruise and Dev Patel, I always thought.'

'That's it exactly!' said Andrea and Felicity shot her a look. 'Sorry!' she added, lowering her voice.

Felicity rolled her eyes and pulled her chair closer so she could whisper properly.

'He's hot and he's trouble, that's what he is. I haven't seen him in years, and then in he walks out of bloody nowhere and tells me he misses me. God knows why. He must be drunk, I guess. Or high. Or something.'

'Talk about bad timing.'

'I've no idea what he's up to. He said he's been trying to find me for ages, fed me some story about how he "just happened" to meet some of my friends in town and they told him where I was. But who? And why? What does he want? And why hasn't he been before? It's all a bit weird.'

'And besides, you don't have any friends,' said Andrea, helpfully.

Felicity laughed. 'Yes, thanks for pointing that out.' It was a running joke. Her friend count was decidedly, deliberately low.

Felicity remembered the Tiffany box then, and her palms started to sweat. As far as she knew, it was still sitting there, on the counter near the sink, but she hadn't had an opportunity to retrieve it since Adam left. What the hell was in that box?

'What I don't get is, why today of all days?' she said, her brain starting to hurt.

Andrea shrugged as if this sort of thing happened to her all the time. 'It's New Year's Eve. The night when you regret all the terrible decisions you ever made and all the people you let go. It's obvious really. He can pick his moments though.'

'You're telling me.'

'How did you feel when you saw him again?'

How *did* she feel? It was a good question. Confused, mainly.

'Oh, nothing, I felt nothing, it's been too long, and I mean, I *properly* messed it up. Like, it was an absolute disaster. I'm amazed it's only taken him three years to forgive me, to be completely honest with you.'

At that point, James came wandering back into the room. 'What are we talking about?' he said, a little too loudly.

'Who's going to kiss who at midnight,' said Andrea, quickly.

James nodded as if she'd said something very profound and handed them both a beer, not looking directly at Felicity as he did so. Felicity gave a nervous smile and tried to wipe her sweating palms discreetly on her jeans.

'Shall we get started on this pizza then, folks?'

'Don't you have a party to be going to?' The words were out of her mouth before she could stop them.

James gave a short, almost nervous laugh and glanced at his watch. 'Oh yes. I suppose I do.'

'Leave the poor man alone, Fliss,' said Andrea hastily, throwing her a 'look'. 'For all you know, he'd rather be hanging out with us. I mean, the man's clearly got taste.'

'Well, this is true.' James nodded enthusiastically and dived in for a slice of pizza.

Felicity looked from one to the other in amusement. 'Okay, fine. Stay if you like. No one's about to kick you out or anything.'

'I'm very glad to hear it,' said James through a mouthful of pizza crust.

*Thank God for Andrea.*

## CHAPTER TEN

ANDREA AND FELICITY met when Felicity was at rock bottom.

Well, one of her many rock bottoms. A particularly rocky bottom, this one.

Felicity had left university with a reasonable degree in English and Art History and no clue at all what she was going to do with it. After her first of several cataclysmic break-ups with Adam, she had resolved once and for all to sort her life out, so on a whim she cut her hours at her not-actually-awful job in the café in town and embarked on trying to find some work that would give her a bit more of a sense of purpose.

She had contemplated teaching for about thirty seconds when she found out they paid a golden handshake just for signing on, but even then, the overly complicated process to get qualified and the prospect at the end of it of having to stand in front of a room full of people and decant some kind of useful information into their brains had paralysed her with fear.

She worked in an insurance call centre instead, which lasted approximately three weeks, before she got fed up with having to tell the manager when she was going to the toilet and how many minutes she intended to take. As if that sort of thing could be predicted.

When things got a bit dire financially she took some hours as a cleaner, but that went horribly wrong when she found something unmentionable under a wardrobe and instead of putting it back, she accidentally left it out for the husband to find. Turns out it was not something the wife had ever used... *with him*, but only when the man from number 43 popped round for a coffee. Needless to say, she wasn't welcome in that particular house any longer.

There was a brief highlight when she found a role as a library assistant, which seemed like her dream job for a couple of months because she quite enjoyed moving stacks of books from one place to another, until she was made redundant when the library closed with two days' notice.

Things got a bit desperate after that. Felicity signed up to various medical experiments but chickened out when she was asked to sign a 400-page waiver document and confirm she didn't have an allergy to fish in order to give what was supposedly just one vial of blood.

Her last venture was as a rep for a slimming club, but the pay was miserable and the weigh-in sessions each week were even more miserable.

'So, Karen, you've put on half a stone this week. Where do you think you might have gone wrong?'

'Well, Felicity, I ate two massive pizzas and ten Mars bars, and I enjoyed every second of it.'

'Um, good for you!'

Besides, because Felicity was naturally slim and petite, none of the members ever fully bought into her story about how she had once needed to lose ten pounds to get into a special dress. They always looked at her with narrowed eyes as she delivered her cringeworthy Tip of the Week from Head Office. ('If you fancy a chocolate digestive, why not replace it with an apple or a few frozen grapes?' 'Try cutting up a chocolate bar into small pieces to make it last longer.' And other such tripe.)

One particularly low day, she encountered Andrea in a supermarket. They were both alone and both clearly trying to rush to get the experience over as quickly as possible, and when they bumped trollies getting to the checkout, there had very nearly been pistols at dawn. Andrea would have looked quite scary except that she was dressed in an ancient bobbly old fleece with 'Animal Saviours' printed on the front, and she was covered head to toe in fur. She even smelled a little bit of cat hair, if Felicity was to be completely honest, like she could do with a good hoovering. But even in that get-up she was surprisingly attractive, with a long salt and pepper plait down her back and striking pale blue eyes.

After a bit of 'After you', 'No, after you', through gritted teeth, Andrea had let Felicity go first and as she was putting her meagre selections on the conveyor belt – Super Noodles, Pringles and red wine, dinner of champions – she decided to attempt a conversation to clear the air. She asked Andrea what Animal Saviours was, and they were like the magic words. Andrea's face shone as she told her how she'd set up the charity after finding an abandoned litter of puppies under a hedge and how she had never been without a puppy or a kitten to bottle feed in her house ever since, until one day she came into some money from a deceased aunt and decided to invest in a proper centre.

When it emerged that Andrea had lost her only helper two months before after an unfortunate incident with a hamster, and that she was desperate for someone 'nice and normal' to come and cuddle the rescued animals, that was it. By the time they were walking out of the supermarket door together, they had arranged for Felicity to visit. And by the time she visited, she was already planning a career in animal welfare and considering retraining as a vet.

A year and a half down the line, and although she was a way off being able to afford the vet thing, working at Animal Saviours had given Felicity a real sense of fulfilment at last. That, and her relationship with Andrea, who had become almost like a surrogate mum. Sure, on the surface Andrea was a bit of an animal rescue cliché: ruddy cheeks, long grey hair, partial to a 'wolf fleece', living in a tiny cottage in absolute chaos, no apparent form of income and yet complete and utter dedication to the cause. But Andrea was also completely authentic. No side to her, as they say. She was direct, occasionally even abrupt and didn't suffer fools, gladly or otherwise, but she was kind too, and completely selfless. She had given Felicity a job when she really needed it and supported her unconditionally ever since. She was, perhaps, the only stable thing in Felicity's life.

A rare treasure indeed.

# CHAPTER ELEVEN

It was a tense evening.

With Adam's unexpected arrival, the memories of how she had behaved towards him, the way she had treated him – all of it had been unlocked. Her head was full of questions and her stomach was churning.

And James didn't seem to want to leave. There had been no more mention of the mysterious party he was meant to be going to, and he'd even offered to help with the evening feeds. Felicity watched him carefully as he made his way among the cages, popping food in the bowls and giving each furry recipient a little head scratch or stroke on his way. Her heart felt like it was being squeezed in a vice. She longed to warn him, to tell him to run away from her at 100mph and never look back. What was he doing hanging around her anyway? Surely he had someone else – someone who wasn't a complete emotional wreck, perhaps even someone who'd won a Nobel Peace Prize – that he could be spending New Year's Eve with?

To his credit he had so far resisted the urge to ask her who Adam was, although she knew he must be dying to. As they sipped their (Irish) coffees in the break room after rounds and waited for midnight, neither one looking directly at the other, it seemed as though James may be on the verge of saying it... Of saying something, anyway. But just as he opened his mouth to speak, there was a loud shout. James and Felicity leapt up and raced instinctively to the cat nursery, where they found Andrea holding aloft a pale blue box.

'What on earth is this?' said Andrea. 'You haven't even known each other five minutes and already, a ring!'

James looked at Felicity and Felicity wondered if she could somehow make herself invisible. Was it Harry Potter who could do that? What were those words again? *Spellus invisibilianus*, or something?

'What *is* that?' said James, reaching forward to take it from Andrea, who went a deathly shade of pale.

'You mean it's not from you, James?' she said, glancing at Felicity in horror.

Felicity shook her head slowly.

*Oh God, oh God, oh God.*

She felt as though her insides might be folding in on themselves.

Swallowing her panic, Felicity thought fast. She decided to attempt nonchalance.

'It's from that bloke, Adam,' she said, in what she hoped sounded like a breezy version of her voice. 'The stupid idiot hasn't seen me for, like, years, so I have no idea what he thinks he's playing at.' She gave a forced kind of laugh which came out much louder than she had intended, but the others were looking down, mouths agape, at the open box in James' hand and didn't even seem to notice.

James stared at the ring, for that is what it was, for a long time. And all the while, Felicity and Andrea waited, exchanging nervous glances, Andrea trying to mouth an apology across the room, Felicity trying to hold back the tears, but also trying to keep her face neutral, as if it really did mean nothing.

'I should go,' said James, slowly, taking a few steps backwards. 'I'm late.'

Andrea had somehow managed to edge towards the door, looking contrite, and it was obvious she was trying to give them some alone time to make up for her monumental cock-up. But when she heard him say that, she stopped short.

'You'll do nothing of the sort,' she said.

James looked at her, a bit taken aback.

Andrea blustered on. 'It's New Year's Eve. It's 11.30, it's far too late to turn up to a party now. You'll miss the big moment. Anyway, you said it was black tie.'

James glanced down at himself as if he'd forgotten what he was wearing.

'Why don't you take Freddy and Felix out for a quick walk round the block? That would be a huge help, actually.'

James crossed his arms. 'It's nearly midnight. Why on earth would two tiny dogs like that need a walk at midnight on New Year's Eve?'

Andrea didn't miss a beat. 'It's part of their training for a new home. They need to get used to being taken out at all hours. It was scheduled anyway, and Felicity was due to do it... only, Freddy hates her.'

Felicity nodded. 'He does, it's true,' she said, with a feeble attempt at a smile.

James stared at Andrea for a long moment, as if trying to make her crack. To her credit, she stared back at him boldly, daring him to accuse her of lying. Then, in a devastating final blow, she crossed her arms back at him, and that was that. Defeated, James turned with a sigh, grabbed a couple of leads from the higgledy-piggledy pile on the hooks in the corner, and headed in the direction of the puppy room. He didn't even look at Felicity as he walked past, and she felt a bit woozy – like it wasn't just her insides that were giving up the ghost. Now the entire universe felt as though it was on the verge of caving in around her.

'I need a beer,' she announced in a feeble voice to no one in particular. But if she was honest, all she really wanted was to take a proper look at that ring.

The evening had really gone downhill from there. Midnight had come and gone with an awkward 'Happy New Year' and a pathetic attempt at a verse of 'Auld Lang Syne' and then, before they could make up another task for him to do, James was leaving, muttering some excuse about needing to be up early the next day for something vague he couldn't possibly miss even though they all knew it would be New Year's Day and who the hell ever had plans on New Year's Day?

He stared at Felicity for a long moment as they reached the door.

*Say something.*

'Look...' she said, wondering which words were going to come out of her mouth next.

'You don't have to explain anything to me,' he said. His jaw was tense.

'I do...'

'No, you don't. It's really none of my business.'

She flinched. 'Look, it really didn't mean anything, honestly. I've no idea what he was doing here... and maybe the ring's not even *for* me? He probably bought it for someone else. Maybe Andrea? She's a dark horse after all!'

A smile tugged at his lips then, just for a split second. 'And why would you think I care?'

He moved towards her in the shadows of the entranceway, and looked down at her upturned face so intensely her entire body began to tingle with anticipation. She resisted the urge to put her hands on him.

'Happy New Year, Felicity Brooks,' he said, a hint of regret in his voice, and with that he turned and stalked off into the night. She almost wanted to laugh out loud as she watched him strop off, the memory of him in his soggy penguin suit on the first night they met popping into her head. And then her knees gave way and she had to lean against the doorway for a moment.

Damn, but that was one very attractive man.

# CHAPTER TWELVE

Felicity didn't open the box for several hours.

Instead, it sat on her nightstand next to the precarious pile of books waiting to be read (which seemed to always be growing rather than shrinking), burning a proverbial hole in the painted wood. Every so often she touched its pale blue top (well, stroked it really) and tried to picture what might be inside. She hadn't been able to get a good look when James and Andrea were poring over it and although part of her was desperate to, now that she was finally alone, there were warning bells going off all over the show. In the darkness, lurid images of her time with Adam swirled around her head, interspersed with that memory of James leaning in to nearly kiss her and the feeling he generated whenever he was near her, as if her whole body might burst into flames at any second.

She couldn't believe it. Her past and her present had collided, and not for the first time.

When she was at university there had been a boy called Tom who she absolutely adored. He was everything she had ever dreamed of, in fact. Tall, dark-haired, chisel-jawed, charming as all hell. Practically every girl she knew had fancied him that first term. He had been Head of the Social Soc and was incredibly popular as well as funny and handsome, so she'd been beyond flattered when he'd asked her out. But, only a few days later, Adam had come to visit her in Halls and when Tom saw them together, he immediately ended it.

It didn't matter how much she had insisted nothing had happened, how much she insisted that Adam was just a friend. As soon as he saw the – *what was it, the chemistry?* – as soon as he saw whatever it was between her and Adam, Tom – tanned, sporty, clever, funny Tom – had backed away from the deal, as if he knew he was on to a loser, just like James had. And of course, he'd been right. Adam and Felicity got back together a year after she graduated and it had seemed like that was it for good. For a while.

*What was it about Adam, anyway?*

Felicity lay on her bed and stared at the ceiling in the dim light, trying to ignore the shadowy damp patch that was creeping across the surface. *Must get that seen to,* she thought idly.

Adam and Felicity met when Felicity was fifteen.

She'd been in a bad place at that time. Her family had fallen apart long before, her mum was basically a non-parent; and school, which had always been her safe place, had become more and more difficult as she'd got older. That was, until Adam arrived on the scene. He was a year older than her and had just started at the sixth form next door, and the first time she saw him he was waiting at the bus stop after school, looking for all the world like he'd just dropped out of a rock band on tour.

His hair was dark and dishevelled and he was chewing gum and kicking at the back of the bus shelter, while one of his mates tried to get his attention telling some story or other. As she walked past, Adam glanced sideways and caught her eye – accidentally, she had assumed at the time but, later, she realised it must have been deliberate. No words passed between them, and it was a fleeting moment, that's all, but in that single look, that one moment in time, a whole conversation had happened between them. Felicity knew with complete certainty she would be going out with that boy by the end of the month.

Her friends had all noticed him too, of course, had discussed his tight trousers and his lack of tie and his rule-breaking haircut at great length. And he was the only Asian boy in their school at the time, which just made him more exotic. Felicity was careful to keep quiet, to not give anything away, but one day, when they were all giggling together as they tried to work out his name, her friend Katherine had caught Felicity chewing her lip to hide a smile and guessed immediately that this new stranger was spoken for.

It took him two more weeks to approach her. Two weeks of sideways glances and eye contact and hot blushes. And then one day he stepped out in front of her as she walked behind the bus shelter, and she stopped immediately and bit her lip again.

'All right?' he said, standing just a bit closer than was really decent.

'Yes thanks,' she managed to squeak out, her voice failing her.

'What's your name then?' he said, his deep brown eyes catching hers for a moment and then flicking to his shoes.

'Felicity,' she said, trying to sound casual, finding herself trying to catch his eye again, bring his gaze back up to hers. 'What's yours?'

'I'm Adam,' he said, looking up for a split second. She hastily looked away. 'I like your red hair.'

Her hand had flown to her hair in embarrassment, and she felt herself blush hot and hard.

'What are you doing on Friday night?' he said with a grin.

And with that, it was done. He took her to the cinema and bought her popcorn and kissed her in (almost) the back row and then they were officially 'going out' and from then on it was 'AdamandFelicity' in one word as naturally as breathing. As if they'd known each other in another life and the universe had brought them back together. Felicity was the talk of the school of course, dating a sixth former and the most handsome boy in the school to boot, and it rocketed her to the top of the popularity ratings even though that was the last place she wanted to be. But where she did want to be, she was certain, was anywhere Adam was.

# CHAPTER THIRTEEN

In the early morning light, she sat up on the bed and opened the box.

Sitting there, on a perfect pillowy Tiffany's cushion, was the most beautiful ring Felicity had ever seen.

It had four diamonds shaped like petals interspersed with delicate little leaves crafted intricately out of what looked like rose gold, and an exquisite narrow band with 'Tiffany & Co' imprinted on the inside.

For a moment or two, Felicity had the strangest sensation that she was falling. What did this mean? What the hell was Adam playing at? As per usual she felt oddly annoyed with him, despite this kind gesture, and the anger was muddled into all the old love and desire and everything she had ever felt for him coming back in a rush.

She tried to think calmly. What was going on? It had been three years since she'd seen him. And the last time she had seen him... well, she'd been so awful to him, so cruel, she could hardly bear to think about it. Felicity had ruined everything. She had accused him of cheating and – even worse – she had kicked him out of their house on Christmas Day. Just told him to get out, no chance for him to explain, never even stopping to wonder whether she had jumped to conclusions. Just one of the many reasons that Christmas was not her favourite time of the year.

And now there was a ring.

Did this mean he forgave her? *Could* he forgive her for that? Adam had seemed pretty, um, forgiving when he came to the centre. She felt rather hot as she thought about how close he had been, how good he had smelled. He may be a little intense at times, but he had always known what he was doing in that department.

She got up to get a glass of water and try to stop that particular train of thought when she realised that at some point in her reminiscing, she had slipped the ring on. Onto her engagement finger, no less. She quickly pulled it off again and put it back in the box. Then she put it back on again, took a quick picture with her phone – man, oh man, it looked amazing on her finger – and then whipped it off again quickly. Who was going to see? She was alone after all, but for some reason she felt guilty. As if she was betraying James somehow. Which was a strange thought given they'd only just met.

As she ran the tap for her drink, something else occurred to her. Felicity put down the glass, grabbed her phone and googled *Tiffany flower ring*. And there it was, plain as day, on their website. A rose gold and diamond flower ring. It was called The Victoria. And it was priced at a very reasonable £2,800. Felicity laughed out loud at the absurdity of it all. What on *earth* was Adam playing at? Did he really think a ring – even one that beautiful – was going to make everything okay?

Felicity got no sleep that night. Or for several nights afterwards, truth be told. Bloody men.

❄

Returning to work a few days later, it was back to earth with a bump.

There were no handsome men dressed as penguins waiting on the doorstep when she arrived at the centre. There was no James turning up out of the blue with his broadness and his blue eyes and his, well, whatever it was that made her want to grab him and kiss him every time he walked past. There was no Adam getting down on bended knee while she was doing the washing up and befuddling her brain. Andrea wouldn't even let her play her anti-Christmas playlist anymore to cheer herself up.

'It's the New Year now, Felicity. No more Shaky or Cliff for a whole year. I would have thought you of all people would be delighted about that.'

Andrea was right. She normally *did* feel delighted to get Christmas out of the way. Most years, it was a huge relief, as if she had sidestepped a landmine. But this year, for the first time in many years in fact, she didn't feel delighted at all. For some reason she couldn't quite put her finger on she felt... bereft.

A couple of days later, Felicity was left to hold the fort while Andrea took Holly and her mum to the emergency vet. Holly was the most adorable little kitten, all ginger fluff and toe beans, heart-meltingly cute. But the reality was, she hadn't got any better since New Year. She seemed very weak and was not putting on much weight despite constantly suckling from Gennie and all the extra feeds from Andrea and Felicity. They were so worried that – even though they had absolutely zero money in the bank this month and they'd had a load of new arrivals – they made the call and told the vet to do whatever he needed to, to get her better.

And now Felicity was covered in scratches because although she understandably had not wanted to be separated from Holly again, Mummy Gennie also really *did not* want to go to the vets. For some strange reason that had absolutely nothing to do with recent events of course, Gennie was suddenly suspicious of all boxes and cages and other trap-like containers, and she had definitely got some of her fight back now she was feeling better.

Felicity sat on the office chair rubbing Germolene into her war wounds and waiting for Andrea to return, when a sneaky thought wormed its way into her mind.

James would definitely want to know about Holly.

Definitely.

He'd be worried.

Really worried.

He might even be upset that she hadn't told him.

Once the thought was in her head, she couldn't shake it. She waited as patiently as she could, kicking her legs under her and subconsciously counting the seconds as they ticked by, and then she caved and at 11.05am precisely she texted the number he'd left on their noticeboard ('for emergencies'), which had been burning a hole into her eye sockets ever since.

> James, hi, it's Felicity, Holly is really sick.
> Please come.

*Shameless*, she thought, and deleted it.

*Try again.*

> James, hi, it's Felicity. I hope you're okay. Holly
> is not doing so great; she's going to the vet's
> today. I thought you'd like to know.

That was better. Less needy. That was good.

She hit send and closed her eyes, hardly daring to hope. She had been half expecting never to hear from him again, so jumped in surprise when her phone beeped a rapid reply.

> What can I do?

She smiled. He was such a fixer.

> Scrap that, I'm on my way.

She felt weirdly triumphant for a second. He was coming.

And then there was a small moment of panic. She hadn't really thought this through. Felicity jumped up and ran to the toilets to check her face. Her ears were sticking out of course, as per bloody usual, and she looked quite drawn, paler than normal if that was even possible. Less usual still were the red raw scratches all the way up her arms, some crusting over with blood, others raised and furious-looking despite the pink smears of hospital-corridor-smelling Germolene. She rearranged her hair and nodded at her reflection. *It's not perfect*, she told herself, *but he's coming to see the kitten, remember. Not you.*

When Felicity opened the door, though, yet again it was not her own appearance that was on her mind. It was his. Not just the tousled left-the-house-in-a-hurry hair – although that was very distracting – but the fact that he appeared to be wearing a uniform. Her uniform. A green T-shirt with the Animal Saviours red heart logo.

'Erm, hi?' she said, as he nodded in greeting and walked past her down the corridor.

'Any news?' he said over his shoulder, striding purposefully towards the cat nursery.

'Not yet,' said Felicity, following him into the room as he approached Bobby Charlton's cage and took him out for a cuddle.

James didn't reply. There was an awkward pause, punctuated by Bobby Charlton mewling with delight as James brought him up to his face for a kiss. *It's like one of those old Athena posters in here*, thought Felicity, feeling a sudden need for some fresh air.

'I know you like wearing my clothes and all, but how come you're wearing my T-shirt?' she said out loud.

'It's not your T-shirt. It's mine,' he replied while kitten wrangling like a pro. Bobby was purring noisily in his hands.

'How...? What...?'

'I've been taken on as a volunteer. Andrea was looking for someone, said things would be busy after New Year. And I... had some annual leave left over from last year that I needed to take. I thought this would be a worthy way to use it up. I'll be here for a week or two from next Monday. Thought I'd run in the uniform today.'

Felicity was conscious that her mouth was moving open and closed, but no sound was coming out.

'Is there a problem?' James said, looking up at her for the first time.

*Be cool.*

'No, no problem. Great news in fact. The cats will be delighted.'

She felt the opposite of cool. Whatever that was. Flustered? Flummoxed?

'And you? Will you be delighted?'

'Me? Oh sure, it'll be great to have some extra help around here. We're pretty busy,' she said, trying to sound as casual as she could.

'Good. That's settled then.'

He looked at her for a second longer than was strictly appropriate, then turned his attention back to Bobby who was now casually lying along one of James' lightly tanned forearms like a furry fashion accessory.

'Cute,' said Felicity with a smile, and – face burning – she turned and left the room before he could respond.

*Make of that what you will, you sneaky handsome bastard.*

Felicity's heart pounded in her ears as she paced up and down in the break room.

James had properly thrown her off-guard. She had been expecting him to back away altogether to be honest, after Ringgate. He'd been so cross. So, what was this about, exactly? A genuine desire to volunteer? Bobby Charlton was a pretty compelling reason after all. Not to mention Holly and Gennie. Or... did he secretly want to see her again? Did she dare hope?

Her mind was working double time now. She was on the rota for the next five out of seven days. Whatever his reason, that was a lot of Penguin Man in prospect. A lot of Penguin Man plus cute baby animals. Not exactly unappealing, as workplaces go. Her phone buzzed in her pocket, interrupting that thought.

> Andrea: Holly not good. Needs to stay in overnight. Back later. Sorry. Can you stay longer?

She texted straight back:

> No problem x

Felicity felt a bit sick. She had been so busy focusing on the presence of Penguin Man she hadn't really registered how poorly Holly was. What if she died? That tiny little dot deserved a chance at life. If anything happened to her... well, that was an unbearably scary thought. She sent up a quick prayer. Her phone buzzed again. This time it wasn't Andrea.

> Adam: Please let me take you out for dinner. I'd love to explain a few things. It would be great to see you again properly. I think you owe me that much. Ads x

A shiver ran down her spine and she took a deep breath. Did she owe him? That phrase rankled even though she knew he probably had a point.

> I'm not sure that's a good idea, F xx

She stared at her phone for a long moment, then shook herself into action, making a mental note to think about it all later.

'You okay?' said a voice from the doorway.

James was watching her closely. Guilt leapt and flapped in her stomach, and she quickly slipped her phone into her pocket.

'Yes, all fine.' She nodded, although she wasn't sure, to be honest.

'Those look nasty...' he said, nodding at the scratches on her arms, which if anything were looking angrier than before.

*He had noticed, then.*

'Oh, I'll be fine, thanks. I should have gone with the towel method, but you live and learn.'

James nodded sagely, as if he talked about towel methods all the time.

Felicity smiled. 'It's where you use a towel to – well, grapple seems a strong word, but you know what I mean. It can help when they don't want to go in the carrier.'

'I knew that,' said James, mock-offended.

'Course you did. Want to help me with rounds then, Mr Expert Volunteer?'

He smiled, a proper warm, slightly cheeky smile, the first she'd seen from him for a while, and the cold guilt in her chest was replaced with a spreading warmth.

'You're the boss. Lead on.'

## CHAPTER FOURTEEN

HOLLY PULLED THROUGH. Andrea collected her a few days later and although she was woozy and still oh-so tiny, the vet had given her a clean bill of health and told them to persevere with everything they had been doing. Best of all, the vet was confident it wasn't fading kitten syndrome, which is the thing that Andrea and Felicity had both been petrified of even though neither of them had said the words out loud. It can take a kitten very quickly and the reason is not always obvious. They had lost kittens before, and lack of appetite and failure to gain weight were two huge red flags.

When Holly and Gennie were back and settled in their basket together, Andrea, Felicity and James – who'd turned up for his first shift that morning as promised – stood around the cage like proud parents.

'This is a weird little set up we've got going on,' said Andrea, after a few moments, and there was a hushed ripple of slightly awkward laughter. No one wanted to wake the sleepers.

'Oh, by the way, in case you hadn't worked it out, James is coming to help us for a couple of weeks, Felicity,' said Andrea in a low voice. 'He fancied some volunteering work and I know we could use the help.' This was all said with an arched eyebrow. So arched, in fact, it looked like it might disappear over the back of her head. Felicity resisted a sideways glance at James.

'Sure, makes sense,' she said, trying to keep a straight face.

'Good. I've put you both on shift tomorrow. It's my day off. Can you show him the ropes, please? It might be pretty busy. And Lisa from the RSPCA is bringing some pups in during the afternoon.'

'Sure, happy to.'

Andrea turned to look at her, both eyebrows practically on the ceiling now. 'Are you okay?'

'Sure, yes, why wouldn't I be?'

'Well, for one thing, you keep saying "Sure" in that weird voice.'

James cleared his throat and Felicity threw him a look.

'No, no, I mean, yes I'm fine, sorry, I was just listening, that's all.'

Andrea looked at Felicity, at James, then back to Felicity. She had a smirk on her face. Felicity shifted uncomfortably. Awesome as Andrea was, she could also be bloody embarrassing sometimes. She felt ready to kill her but also – and not for the first time – supremely grateful.

'Good. I'll see you both on Wednesday then. By the way, the vet said Holly would almost certainly have died if James hadn't found her that night. If you guys hadn't done everything you did for her. Well done, you two.'

James and Felicity exchanged a long look and Felicity felt her heart do a back flip. Then she looked down at little Holly, all snuggled up and sleeping next to her mum, and she said another silent prayer. *Please make it through this, little one.*

❄

The next morning, James and Felicity greeted each other solemnly, and Felicity felt so bewildered by his presence that she found herself giving him a mock – and rather proud – tour around the building before she remembered that he already knew it inside out. The centre had been converted from an old industrial building and was essentially laid out like a large barn with partitions between the rooms that didn't go all the way to the ceiling. That meant it wasn't very soundproof and sometimes the noise the dogs could generate when they were in full voice felt like it was reverberating off the ceiling and bouncing off the walls. Still, Felicity felt rather proud of the place as she showed it off.

James followed her about politely and let her talk, although he had an amused smile on his face, and occasionally a bemused one too. Felicity tended to talk rather fast when she was nervous, and could sometimes be virtually impossible to understand until she got her breathing and heart rate under control, but to his credit he nodded along and pretended to hear every word.

When she had calmed down a bit, they did the rounds, spending rather longer cuddling dogs and kittens than was strictly necessary. It had become clear very early on that James was a natural. He had a gentle, easy way with the animals – no sudden movements, no loud noises – and they seemed to take to him instantly. She even felt a pang of jealousy when 'her' Bobby Charlton mewled loudly at him, demanding to be picked up and cuddled. James handled him deftly and he settled into a purring position under James' chin as if he was born to be there.

*He doesn't even have a kitten shelf of any kind*, thought Felicity, crossly.

The morning flew by and when it was time for a break, James nipped out and grabbed them cappuccinos and fresh cheese and onion pasties from the bakery, guessing (correctly) that she had forgotten to bring anything to eat for her lunch, as per usual. As it was just the two of them, they ate in the office like naughty children, Felicity sitting on the desk, legs swinging, James spinning backwards and forwards on the ancient office chair, and munching happily. Felicity found herself thinking about their cosy Christmas spent on the floor of this very room, playing drunken chess and flirting shamelessly. She wondered if he was thinking about it too.

'So, you never told me why you hate Christmas,' he said, as if reading her mind.

'Do we have to do this now, Penguin Man?' she said.

'What else is there to do?' he replied, in a slightly suggestive voice (or was that her imagination?).

Felicity waved the remains of her pasty at him. 'Okay, fine, but you go first. I'm still eating.'

He paused, holding eye contact for a moment too long, his grey-blue eyes suddenly intense. Part of his blond hair was sticking up on one side and she resisted the urge to pat it back into place.

'If you insist. But it's not a pretty picture,' he said.

'What happened?'

'I got dumped on Boxing Day.'

Felicity's heart lurched in her chest. 'That's terrible,' she said, the sound of her own blood rushing and swirling in her ears.

He spoke slowly. Carefully. It was still painful, clearly. 'It wasn't much fun. I'd been with E... er, with my ex, for nine years. We were planning to get married. Then, I don't know what happened, she had a kind of midlife crisis at the grand age of thirty-six and decided she wanted to travel round the world. Without me.'

Felicity waited. As she had guessed, there was more to say.

A wrinkle-frown appeared between his eyes as he spoke, and she was overcome with sadness for him.

'I wouldn't have minded,' he went on, 'but I later found out she never went travelling at all. She just bloody moved to Coventry, got together with an accountant of all things, and carried on living her life. Same old life, just without me in it.'

'What a bitch!'

James winced.

'Er, sorry, I mean, that's awful! And this all happened on Boxing Day?'

He nodded slowly.

'That's really rough.'

'You could say that.'

'So, what happened? Do you mind me asking?'

'I think you already did.'

'That's true. I'll shut up.'

James gave a deep sigh and pushed his hand through his already tousled hair, making it even more sticky-uppy. Felicity attempted to avert her eyes, desperate as she was to touch it herself. It just looked so soft. *Inappropriate.*

'We'd spent Christmas with my folks. It had been nice, a bit sedate, nothing to write home about, you know, but also nothing she could object to, if you know what I mean?'

Felicity nodded obediently. *Don't look at his hair.*

'She'd been pretty quiet all day, but my mum is... well, let's say she can be quite domineering, she loves a party and causing havoc and being super loud, especially after a few sherries, and so Erika always tended to keep quiet around her anyway. So, I didn't think much of it until I found her bags in the hallway the next morning. As far as I was concerned, everything was fine. We were fine.'

Felicity noted the clear hitch in his voice as he said her name. Erika. Sounded rather exotic.

'She could have waited one more day, surely?' said Felicity.

'That's the kicker. To this day, that's the question I just don't have the answer to. Why Boxing Day? Why not an ordinary Tuesday in February? Why couldn't she have just waited even a couple more days? I tried asking her for an explanation later, but she couldn't even give me that much. She just said, "It was time" in that mysterious, mystical Japanese way of talking she had. What am I meant to do with that?'

Felicity tried to ignore the stereotypical images of beautiful and mysterious Japanese women that immediately entered her mind.

'Anyway, she basically ruined Christmas for me, and I was never a huge fan to start with.'

'I'm so sorry,' said Felicity.

*Why on earth did she ever let you go?*

James lifted his eyes to hers, his cool seemingly restored. 'Your turn.'

'Yikes, how long have you got?' said Felicity, meaning it. Then she had a crazy thought. *Damn you, Bex.*

'Take me out for dinner on Friday night and I'll tell you,' she said, looking him right in the eyes with what she hoped was a slightly flirtatious look. He stared back at her from beneath that blond fringe, his eyes suddenly twinkling in amusement.

'You are full of surprises, Crazy Cat Lady. But...'

'Don't worry, it's not a date,' said Felicity, quickly. 'It's just two friends sharing their tragic Christmas stories over dinner. Okay?'

'Fine. Okay. It's not a date. It's just two tragic friends. Gotcha.'

'Right then.'

'Right then.'

83

## CHAPTER FIFTEEN

WHOSE STUPID IDEA WAS THIS? thought Felicity, three days later, as she waited for Penguin Man to pick her up from her flat for what was seeming more and more like it might actually be a date.

Her phone had been pinging non-stop with messages from Bex and Sophie who had mystically discovered that she was finally going out with James (okay, she had told them) and had threatened to come and gatecrash if she didn't give them all the details immediately. Hell, even Andrea had dropped her a little good luck message. Bloody Andrea, who was twenty years older than her and had a much more exciting sex life. She smiled at the thought of the three of them: Bex, Sophie and – unlikely though it was – Andrea. They were her only true friends in the world. But man, they could be bloody annoying. And not just sometimes.

Bex: Time to get back on the horse, cowgirl.

*Ew. And also, dear God. The prospect of having sex with someone new after all this time is actually terrifying.*

> Sophie: Good luck, darling! Don't do anything I wouldn't do.

*Eye roll.*

> Andrea: About time you two had a bloody good shag and got it out of your system. Enjoy!

*Inappropriate. Wrong on so many levels, in fact.*

One small mercy was that little Holly was now well on the mend which meant at least Andrea wasn't quite so stressed. In fact, she had even seemed quite happy to let Felicity take the night off and go out for the evening with her number one volunteer.

'It's not like it's a date or anything,' she'd said, to which her boss had just raised her eyebrows. 'It's not. I mean it. We specifically discussed how it wasn't going to be a date. I have no idea if he's even single.'

'Single or not, it's definitely a date,' she said, waving away Felicity's protestations. 'The sexual tension between you two is off the charts. It's a date.'

Now, sitting in her flat, she felt as though Andrea might be right. God, she was unbearable when she was right. Felicity waited. Her palms were clammy. She wondered vaguely if she still smelled of Lady Swish shaving foam after mistaking it for her deodorant earlier and spraying it lavishly under one arm. That had not been an easy clean up. The clear gel had turned instantly to foam, seeping into her only acceptable bra and leaving a huge wet stain. Mortified, Felicity had dabbed at it desperately with a ratty old towel, but in the end she'd had to abandon the silk shirt and bra altogether and now her bedroom looked like a mini tornado had hit after she'd gone through the enormous pile of clothes on her chair-cum-wardrobe in double quick time to find something that would function as an acceptable alternative outfit.

It was the nerves. It had to be the nerves. She couldn't remember the last time she'd been on a date. Adam had been her childhood sweetheart. Had she ever actually been on one with anyone else? Did she go on one with Tom? She couldn't remember. Maybe? Although that's not really how things worked at university. You just sort of went to a bar and got a bit drunk and then you got a lot drunk and then you accidentally bumped faces or loins with someone and then you were going out with them and that was that. Simpler times.

Her stomach did another little flip flop. What did one do on a proper grown-up date? What happened if James tried to kiss her? What happened if he didn't? She had asked Bex and Sophie these questions on WhatsApp, but their replies had been less than satisfactory.

> Bex: If he kisses you, go for it. It's like riding a bike. You don't forget how to do it just because it's been a few hundred years and your fittings are a bit rusty. And by the way, if he doesn't, dump him immediately.

> Sophie: Ignore her. He'll kiss you. You'll see. If he doesn't then he's definitely married.

> Felicity: What kind of advice is that? Thanks for nothing you two.

> Bex: Don't be such a grump. You'll be fine. Just be yourself. But not too much. Channel the happiest version of yourself. Don't go on about Cliff Richard or anything.

> Sophie: Don't forget to shave your legs. And wear some decent pants.

At that, Felicity had muted the conversation. No bloody help at all.

Just as she was beginning to think she might pull out, make up some excuse, or perhaps emigrate to Australia, the doorbell rang. She opened it to Penguin Man dressed in a suit. An actual suit. No tie, fair enough, but a white shirt open at the top and a dark grey jacket and trousers, and proper shoes. He looked good. Really good. Very handsome and clean and not covered in cat hair or mud or a soggy wet penguin suit or anything.

'Good evening,' he said, in that deep voice of his.

He smelled amazing too. Like chocolate or coffee beans or something equally delicious. It sort of wafted into the hallway as he leaned casually on the door frame and gave her a flash of his blue-eyed smile. It was at this point that Felicity realised she hadn't yet spoken and quickly tried to think of an appropriate greeting.

'Good evening yourself,' she said in what she hoped was a light-hearted tone, smoothing down her soft navy-blue dress and wishing she'd been able to find some decent shoes herself rather than her scruffy trainers.

He didn't seem to mind. In fact, he stared for rather a long time.

'I hope this is okay, I wasn't sure what one wears to a non-date with a tragic friend.'

'You look amazing,' said James.

'Ah well, it'll be the lack of faded polo shirt that's made the difference there.' She grinned, heat prickling her neck. 'Or perhaps the absence of dog hair.'

'Shall we?' he said, holding out his arm.

'Oh yes, let's,' she said, taking it lightly and resisting the urge to squeeze.

❄

It sure felt like a date.

They'd talked about going to the pub, but unbeknownst to her, James had booked them into the poshest restaurant in town instead.

So, there was that.

The Victorian House was well known for its wonderful food but, as James explained rather proudly on the way over, it was almost impossible to get a table because spaces were so limited. There were only thirty diners each night for a single 8pm sitting, and the dishes were not served by menu in the usual way but...

'Well, you'll see,' he had said, mysteriously. Despite her badgering he refused to say any more, an enigmatic smile on his face. Felicity was already intrigued but her mouth dropped open when she walked in.

The restaurant was tiny. The size of a large living room, really, and it was intricately decorated like an authentic Victorian parlour, or at least, how you might imagine one to be. There was dusky pink patterned wallpaper in panelled sections on each wall, an elegant painted ceiling, fine bone china ornaments on every surface and glossy dark furniture. *This is all very Jane Austen*, thought Felicity, as she sat down at a table heaving with expensive-looking silverware and candles. She ventured a glance at James as they did so, and her tummy did a little boogie-woogie dance. He looked incredibly handsome in the candlelight. *Funny place to bring a non-date*, she thought, and a thrill of excitement prickled down her spine.

Excitement, tinged with anxiety.

The first course arrived, and they took it in turns to ladle onion soup from a large porcelain Victorian tureen, and then practised moving the spoon away from them daintily and slurping it off their spoons, little fingers raised, giggling like schoolchildren.

'This is way better than the pub,' said Felicity, mid-slurp.

'I'm glad you think so,' James replied with a grin.

As their plates were being cleared away there was a loud trumpeting sound from the hallway and Felicity jumped and banged her knee on the table, letting out a small yelp. The lady on the next table gave her a sharp look and she nervously looked up, fully expecting to see every single diner staring at her with the same wasp-munching expression. But – *thank you, God* – they were all far too busy. All around the room guests were murmuring and looking at the door expectantly. She followed their gaze just in time to see a troupe of waiters entering the room pushing wooden trolleys laden with enormous silver warming dishes.

Felicity let out another squeal – of delight this time – and there were audible gasps from the other diners. After a short pause, and with immaculate timing, the servers lifted the lids in perfect unison, revealing plates piled high with gleaming hand raised pies and steaming roasts, all semi-authentic to the period of course. Game pie, lamb cutlets, enormous hunks of roast beef, venison and pork, and vats of dauphinoise potatoes swimming in creamy, decadent sauce.

'Wow,' whispered Felicity.

'I know,' said James. 'Isn't it incredible? You can have as much as you want.' This last was said with eyes shining.

Felicity couldn't help but wonder how he knew all this. More importantly, who else he might have been here with, and whether that was an appropriate question if this was genuinely not a date. She was also wondering whether she was going to have to ask about a vegetarian option amongst all these piles of meat, when a very smart waiter arrived and presented her with her own individual hot water crust vegetable pie that was golden and glossy and looked like something out of a cartoon.

Felicity looked up at James, delighted.

'Did you tell them I was a vegetarian?'

*Because I think I love you.*

'I may have.'

'Thank you.'

'My pleasure.'

They stared at each other, faces flushed, eyes bright, until they were interrupted by the arrival of a waiter who began to serve James his choice of roast venison and potatoes from a silver dish.

'Please tell me you're also going to have some pie,' said Felicity.

He laughed. 'You're right. It's got to be done.' He turned to the waiter. 'A small piece of the steak pie too, please.'

'Very good, sir.'

When the waiter had gone, they looked at each other for another long moment, grinning like idiots, and then down at their plates, which were piled high with food.

'Shall we?' said James.

'Yes please,' said Felicity, diving in. And then, 'This is incredible,' through a mouthful of pastry.

'I know, right? I've always wanted to come here,' said James, sawing at an enormous slice of venison with a knife that was patently not up to the task.

*So... he hasn't been before.*

'Apparently the desserts are bloody fantastic too so make sure you save some room. If that's, you know, even possible.'

'It's okay, there's a different stomach for dessert.'

James laughed at that. 'I like a lady who can appreciate her food.'

Felicity wondered if that was a back-handed compliment but decided not to overanalyse.

There was a pause.

'Do you know something?' said James, after a few moments

of happy munching silence. 'I still can't get over how incredible you were with Holly and Gennie that night. I meant what I said. It was all you. You were amazing. You saved their lives.'

Felicity paused with her fork in mid-air. A chunk of carrot dropped back to her plate, flicking a bit of gravy at her face, which she chose to ignore.

'It was a team effort. You were the one who found her in the first place.'

'I know but still, seeing you whisk her away like that. Take charge. It was... just brilliant. Like watching a superhero at work.'

'Oh, stop it,' said Felicity, waving her fork at him, but feeling her cheeks burn. 'It most definitely was not. It's my job, anyway, isn't it? Although to be fair it feels more like a life obsession some days!'

'It was pretty damn sexy too. You taking charge and all that.'

Felicity nearly choked on her food. Which was definitely not sexy.

'I thought you said this wasn't a date, Mr Penguin Man,' she managed eventually, with a giggle.

'I know, I know, I'm sorry. I'm just telling it like it is.'

'Well, can you not do that while I'm trying to stuff my face with food, please? It's hard enough to maintain this sexy public image without accidentally choking in front of a room full of strangers.'

James threw his head back and laughed so loudly that a family at a neighbouring table looked over. He didn't seem to care.

He shook his head. 'You are a very funny girl, Felicity Brooks. Very funny indeed.'

Felicity grinned. 'And sexy. Don't forget sexy. Do I have broccoli in my teeth, by the way?'

'Ooh, broccoli, now you're just talking dirty,' he said, looking at her mouth, which she quickly hid behind a hand in case she actually did have broccoli in her teeth. 'And no. No, you don't. You're perfect, in fact.'

They looked at each other again. One Mississippi. Two Mississippi. Three Mississippi. It was just starting to get uncomfortably intense when the waiter came up to ask if everything was okay.

*Phew. For a non-date it certainly is getting hot in here.*

'So,' said James, later. 'We're on dessert and you still haven't told me your sad story. Go.'

'I'm not sure you really want to hear it,' said Felicity, scraping up the last of her crème brûlée (which the menu referred to as Trinity cream, of course, because Britain) and contemplating licking the bowl. She was almost painfully full, but it was so damn good.

'Besides, I want another one of these first.'

'Fair enough,' he said, clearly impressed. 'I get you another one of those and some coffee and you tell me why you hate Christmas. Deal?'

Felicity looked up at him. Looked him right in the eye. Resisted the urge to look away. There was a moment or two more of that heavy, loaded silence.

'Fine. Bring me more of this wondrous burnt custard and I'll tell you all.'

He smiled and looked over to try and grab the waiter's attention and Felicity took the opportunity to study the side of his face and tried to steady her nerves. Would he hate her when he heard her story? Surely he was going to think less of her. It was inevitable. Perhaps she should enjoy this last moment of bliss just in case? They'd had such a lovely evening so far and, apart from a bit of gravy, she had even managed not to drop anything down herself, which was quite an achievement.

When he had tried and failed to catch the waiter's eye for several moments, James stood. 'I'm going up there,' he announced, and before she could protest, he'd left the table to go over and order her an extra pudding. Felicity couldn't remember the last time someone had taken her out for a dinner like this, if ever, and she felt strangely proprietorial as she watched James chatting casually with their server. He returned to the table with a big grin on his face.

'Did he say I was a fat pig?' Felicity laughed as he sat down.

'What?! Oh no, nothing like that! There was no judgement at all, surprisingly,' he added, with a cheeky grin. Then, 'Ow!' as she gave him a swift kick under the table.

'So... what was he saying, then?' said Felicity, still giggling as a magical second bowl of Trinity cream appeared before her.

James gave a wide smile and for the first time she noticed he had a dimple in one cheek. It gave him a slightly lopsided smile which was far from unpleasant to look at.

'Never you mind...'

She glanced over at the waiter, who was now lurking in the corner of the room next to an ornate grandfather clock, watching them intently. He gave her a little discreet thumbs up and Felicity raised an eyebrow.

'This is very suspicious.'

'Oh, just eat your custard.'

They both laughed and the simmering tension dissipated a bit. Only a bit.

'Right then, enough distractions,' said James. 'I think it's time you told me your story.'

'Okay. But don't say I didn't warn you. You of all people

might decide you never want to speak to me again after you've heard it.'

'I seriously doubt that,' replied James in that low, slightly suggestive voice of his.

Felicity took a long, slow breath.

'Just you wait,' she said.

# CHAPTER SIXTEEN

'THE THING ABOUT ME IS...' began Felicity, trying not to look at James in case she lost her train of thought altogether. 'The thing is, I really don't let people in easily. Normally, anyway,' she added hastily, as she realised how short a time she'd known the man sitting opposite her. He smiled indulgently, waiting patiently for her to continue, his right hand flat on the table, his left thumb and forefinger around the base of his antique wine glass. Her mind began to drift.

*He has nice hands.*

*Right.*

*Focus, Felicity.*

*It's been a while since you told this story. And this time you need to keep it together.*

She took another slow breath and began.

'We grew up in a small community...'

*She knew better than to mention where, at this stage, or it would end up being a tourist's guide to The Island.*

'Quite a strange place, truth be told, where everyone knew your business and you had to keep up appearances, be the perfect family, if you know what I mean? That all went to pot when I was six, though, when my dad left us. He just walked out on my mum and my brother and me, and he did it...' she took a deep breath, 'on Boxing Day.'

James had been staring at the tablecloth as he listened, but he looked up sharply at this. A flash of something, empathy or pain perhaps, crossed his face but he stayed silent.

'So that's probably enough reason to hate Christmas right there,' she went on, the tears threatening behind her eyes. She hated telling this story. 'It was... rough... after that. My mum collapsed in a heap, and we had to fend for ourselves really. She just... imploded. I don't know how else to describe it. Because of how close the community was, it wasn't easy to hide but we got really, really good at pretending everything was okay at home.'

'That must have been tough.'

Tears loomed, and she nodded. She hadn't even realised she had been ripping a paper napkin apart with her fingers while she was talking. There were tiny pieces of shredded paper everywhere. Methodically, she began putting it all into a neat pile as she continued.

'We had to grow up super quick as there was a lot of cleaning and cooking and general caring to do, not just for ourselves but for... for her too, and we were both so young. We managed, somehow, with the help of some family members, our grandparents, some neighbours I suppose, but we always dreaded Christmas most of all. That's when we were always left alone with her for a few days, and we didn't have the refuge of school to escape to.'

James put his hand over hers. It was warm and comforting. She laced her fingers between his and stifled a sob.

'Don't get me wrong, she never beat us or anything. It was more like, well, basically she liked to relive the experience every year, torturing herself endlessly, wondering what she'd done wrong, what had made Dad leave like that, going over and over it in her mind, out loud, too, and all the while she'd be drinking herself into a stupor. It was painful to watch.'

'You were just kids,' said James.

'I know. I have no idea how you're meant to process something like that at that age. I'm not sure we ever did. The real irony was that it wasn't anything to do with her. He was just a total arsehole. By all accounts he walked out on us so he could start things up again with his childhood sweetheart and her three children. They got a new dad for Christmas, and we got... well, it was horrendous, frankly. We got a pure hatred for Christmas and each other. Thanks a lot, Santa.'

She took another breath, the tension lifting from her shoulders a little, the more she spoke.

'Christmas was at best a non-event. At worst, it was the single most miserable day of the year. We never even got any presents after that, as far as I can recall, even when we were still young. No decorations. No Christmas dinner. No different from any other day, really. Maybe we got one or two pity presents from those who remembered but nothing from... her. Nothing from our own mother. She didn't give a damn. It was like we'd left along with Dad. Like she'd... forgotten about us.'

James was watching her carefully. She liked that he wasn't immediately giving her his opinion. Felicity took a mouthful of her (second helping of) Trinity cream and steadied herself for what was to come.

'I always swore I would never be like him. I swore I would never ever treat anyone the way my mum was treated. It destroyed her completely. His cruelty ruined her life and ours... and so I decided I never wanted to be like him. But I am. It turns out I'm a carbon copy.'

'That's impossible,' said James.

'I'm serious. A few years back I was with... someone... for a long time. It was full-on, you know? We were talking about marriage, kids, the works, and then one day I found a couple of texts on his phone from a random girl, and I jumped to conclusions. My mind just went to the worst possibility it could think of.'

'He was cheating?' said James.

'That's just it,' she replied, her voice trembling a little, chest tightening with the shame. 'I never stopped to find out. I just told him to pack his bags and get out. I kicked him straight out of the house, and I never even bothered to find out the truth. He was heartbroken, and I've spent three years racked with guilt at how I behaved. I'm just like Dad.'

A hot tear rolled down Felicity's cheek and she wiped it away with the back of a trembling hand. For something to do she gathered a pile of the delicious custard onto her spoon, but her throat felt too constricted to eat. They both watched it wobbling for a long moment. Her hand was shaking. This was never going to work. She put the spoon down and sent up a silent prayer that he would be kind. That he would somehow understand.

Then, finally, he spoke. 'You are nothing like him.'

'How do you know that?' said Felicity. 'You never met my father.'

'No,' said James, his blue eyes lit with a new spark of intensity. 'But I have met you. That's enough for me.'

'Ah, but I didn't mention the kicker.'

'Oh?' he said, eyebrows raised.

'It was Christmas Day. I kicked him out in the cold on Christmas Day. He had to sleep in his car for two weeks. Couldn't have waited until – what was it you said? A "random Tuesday in February"? Oh no, I couldn't wait. I had to really make it count. Really make sure he suffered.' She bit her lip. 'So, let's face it, I am Erika, basically. I'm so sorry, James. I did tell you you'd hate me.'

James was looking down at the table again. He didn't say

anything for a long time. Felicity scratched at her arm with a fingernail and made it bleed. James silently handed her a napkin. If it was stinging, she couldn't feel it.

'I don't hate you,' he said at last. 'I'm really glad you told me.'

Felicity's heart was flapping around inside her like a baby bird. She put her hand up to her chest instinctively to try to calm it while she waited for him to say more. *Please say more,* she thought.

'No wonder you hate Christmas!' he said suddenly, looking up with a kind of nervous laugh. She could tell he was trying to find the right way to react and felt strangely touched.

'I really bloody hate it,' she said quietly, looking at him steadily.

He smiled at that, just as she hoped he would.

'Me too,' he said, his eyes meeting hers again. She inwardly relaxed and the baby bird grew still again.

'Tell me something,' he said.

'Anything,' said Felicity.

'This person, this guy who you walked out on.'

*Uh oh.*

'Yes?'

'Was it that guy. The ring guy? Did you forget to mention that bit?'

*There it is.*

What could she do? She had to tell the truth, she didn't feel there was any other option with this man. It was as if he could see into her soul. She gave a quick, barely perceptible nod and he sagged a little.

'Thought so,' he said, raising his eyebrows. 'Clearly, you are forgiven.'

'You might be right,' she said, 'but I don't think I can ever forgive myself.'

'That's not quite what I meant,' said James. 'You two obviously have some unfinished business.'

'I don't want to talk about him,' said Felicity, trying to steer things away from Adam and the whole ring palaver, but there had definitely been a shift in the atmosphere.

'Fair enough. Shall we get the bill?' said James, and before she could answer he was already turning away.

# CHAPTER SEVENTEEN

Driving home, the car was full of thick, uncomfortable tension. So thick you could almost reach out and touch it. There was silence, mostly, to start with and then things became even more awkward when Felicity started fiddling around with the buttons on the radio to break the atmosphere. It quickly became clear the entire universe had a vested interest in what was going on between them. On every single channel – or so it seemed – there was a cringeworthy love song with words that spoke right into their situation.

When 'Careless Whisper' by George Michael started up, she turned it off altogether. Cringing as she did so of course. Because you never turn off 'Careless Whisper'.

*Oh God. Sorry, George.*

She had to find a way to pull this back.

'So,' Felicity blurted out when they were almost back at her place.

'So,' he said, and, although she didn't dare look at him, she could hear a slight smile in his voice. Her heart leapt.

'Thanks for a lovely night, Mr Penguin Man. I absolutely loved that restaurant. What an incredible place. I can't believe you went to all that trouble. And you really didn't need to pay but... but I really appreciate it. Best non-date ever.'

'No problem.'

'I just hope I didn't ruin it.'

James pulled into the parking spot opposite her block and switched off the engine. They both stared straight ahead for a moment into the darkness of the night, which was lit only by an insipid orange street lamp, and then turned to look at each other at the same time and giggled.

He turned away again and spoke to the windscreen in front of him. 'You didn't ruin anything. I'm honoured you told me. I'm just a bit more cautious around women these days and, well, you know the reason why.'

She studied the side of his lovely face.

'I do,' she said, solemnly.

'And... date or not,' he continued, turning to look at her with such intensity this time that Felicity drew in a breath, 'it's complicated. For both of us. Like I said before, whatever it is that's still between the two of you, whatever's between you and this Adam guy, sort it out, okay? Just talk to him, spend some time with him, do whatever you need to do to work out if it's really over.'

She opened her mouth to object and then shut it again.

'No, don't argue with me. I know it's not your fault, I'm guessing he's the one who is wanting to be back in your life, not the other way round, but you owe it to yourself to find out for sure. Trust me, you'll regret it if you don't.'

She looked at him, his blue-grey eyes half hidden in the shadows cast by the street lights outside, his lovely brow furrowed as he stared at her, his Brad Pitt lips. *What did he mean?* She knew it probably wasn't the right moment and they were both so full of pastry... but despite what they had *just* been talking about, she found she was longing for him to kiss her.

He seemed to want it too. He was looking intently at her lips. In fact, he was leaning in. *This is happening*, thought Felicity, as he moved towards her, the air crackling between them and then, at virtually the last moment, he seemed to change his mind. He brushed her cheek softly with his lips, she got a waft of his aftershave, and her stomach did another little flip. He stayed close for a moment or two longer, his face right near hers, and then he seemed to collect himself and moved away and that was the end of the non-date or whatever it was. Felicity took a deep breath, her heart pounding.

'As far as I'm concerned, it's long over,' she said quietly, hating herself for even articulating this. 'But you're right when you say that I probably need to make sure Adam knows that...'

Her voice tailed off. He nodded curtly in agreement, or thanks, it was hard to tell, and she opened the car door and told herself to leave even though her body didn't seem to want to. Eventually she sighed and forced herself to clamber out in what she hoped was not a completely ungraceful manner. As she wobbled her way across the car park in her moderately high heels, she could feel his eyes on her. Burning into her.

*Be sexy.*

*Wiggle your hips or something.*

*Don't look back.*

*And whatever you do, Felicity, don't fall over.*

But even as that last thought popped into her head, the worst happened.

One minute she was upright and wiggling for all she was worth, the next she had a face full of grass.

*Well, that's that then.*

## CHAPTER EIGHTEEN

Felicity lay there for a second. Or was it an hour? It felt like an hour.

She was praying fervently that maybe James had already driven off before it happened or, *please, God*, she'd fallen so far that she'd managed to end up in Australia where he couldn't see her. But no. No, he was there, of course. He was still there and had seen the whole bloody thing and now he was getting out of his car and running over to her, and Felicity just wanted to die of shame. Her elbow and knee were on fire, but she hastily pulled herself up into a sitting position before he had to help her up like an old lady.

'What are the chances that you didn't just see that?' she said, spitting out mud and grass as he approached.

James was standing over her now. He wasn't laughing his head off, at least. 'Um. Sure, okay. Yeah, I didn't see anything.'

'Liar.'

'Are you okay?'

'What, apart from the fact that I can never look at you again?'

James laughed then, but gently. 'Yes, apart from that.' He sat down beside her on the grass. 'Are you hurt?' he said, after a moment.

'Just my pride. And my knee. My knee hurts.'

Felicity wanted to cry. She bit back the tears. She felt mortified.

*What an absolute tool. Messed this right up, haven't you?*

James put his arm around her, and they sat for a moment like that, her head hovering just above his shoulder.

'I can't believe I did that.'

'Don't worry about it, we all fall over.'

'Do we? Really? I mean, honestly... have you ever fallen over in front of a–?' She nearly said 'date'. 'In front of someone else. Or is it just me? I'm so embarrassed.'

'Don't be, honestly.'

'But have you though?'

'No, no, I haven't. But I could. So easily.'

'I find that hard to believe.'

She shivered with cold, suddenly, and James pulled her closer.

'Do you want me to take a look at your knee?'

'No, no, I'll be fine. Thank you though. It's just my pride. I'd prefer it if you could somehow turn back time and forget this whole evening.'

'After the night we've had? No way. I never want to forget this evening. Fall included.'

As if on a silent cue, they stood up, and turned towards each other. Felicity ached all over and desperately tried to straighten herself so he wouldn't guess how much it hurt.

'Thanks for not laughing your head off,' said Felicity, looking up at him, knee throbbing, face burning. *Oh, the actual mortifying horrendous shame.*

James chuckled. 'Oh, I will later, don't worry about that. And I'll be telling everyone I meet. Starting with Andrea.'

'You total git.'

There was a long pause. She knew she should probably make a sharp exit. The embarrassment was still so raw. Her knee was getting worse by the second. Her face was probably one big grass stain. She could feel blood running down her leg.

*Just go. Walk away. You've done enough damage for one evening.*

'See you on Monday, then,' she said, looking into his handsome face.

James was looking down at her, smiling into her eyes. And then he was bending towards her, his lips brushed hers, gently at first, as if he didn't want to hurt her. He drew back for a moment, and they blinked at each other in the dim orange light, and then they were kissing with an intensity that made Felicity's entire body light up like a firework.

*Well, hello there, Mr Penguin Man.*

Finally, finally, her hands were in that tousled blond hair, and as his tongue touched hers she let out an involuntary moan of pleasure and all the trauma of the evening just melted away. James responded instantly, wrapping his strong arms around her, and pulling her close as they kissed more and more urgently. When his hand crept underneath her coat and caressed her back through her dress, lightly and deftly, her nerve endings sparked, boom, boom, boom, in succession. It was all a wonderful, delicious blur and she had the strangest sensation of falling, as if she could just fall right into him somehow.

As if she'd found the place she was always meant to be.

Just as she was about to let herself go completely, she felt him hesitate, and by some instinct she moved away from him, just an inch or two, so she could look right into those eyes. His pupils were huge, his eyes a sparkling blue now.

'Everything okay?'

James was breathing hard.

'Sorry. I don't... I didn't mean to do that,' he said, running his hands through his own hair and making it stick out at all kinds of bizarre angles. 'Watching a woman falling over just really turns me on.'

Felicity laughed and hit him on the arm lightly.

'It felt like you meant to do it,' she said, after a moment.

'Okay, fine, I meant to do it, I meant every second of it... but I didn't mean to make things even more complicated.'

'I think it was already pretty complicated.'

'It was, you're right. It is. And I don't just mean with you and your hundreds of exes turning up out of the blue.'

Her heart gave a lurch. 'What does that mean, exactly? And it was just the one ex, may I remind you?'

'Ha ha, you say that, but I bet you've got hundreds out there, all lurking, waiting for exactly the right moment to turn up out of the blue and beg you to take them back.'

'Hardly. Trust me. And you're avoiding my question.'

James dropped his eyes and kicked at the ground with one foot. 'Am I? I suppose I am. I'll explain another time, don't want to ruin the moment and all that.'

*What does that mean?*

'Please just tell me.'

'Don't worry. It's nothing.' He put his hands on her shoulders and lifted his eyes to look her square in the face. 'Felicity Brooks, thank you, it's been a lovely night.'

'It really has.'

They stared at each other and, God, she wanted him to kiss her again. More than that. She never wanted to be without him again. Wanted to run off to the Bahamas with him and live in a wooden hut by the sea.

It was so tempting to invite him upstairs.

She nearly did. So nearly. The words were right there.

But, deep down, she knew he was right, that kiss hadn't

changed the fact that she needed to get her head straight. Oh, how badly she needed that. And now she had some serious alarm bells. *What had he meant by 'even more complicated'?*

Besides, she needed a plaster and a bath. She was absolutely jam-packed full of Trinity cream and vegetable pie and onion soup and although it had been a fantastic meal, it perhaps wasn't the sexiest preparation for a night of passion.

*Mental note: Next time you go out for a non-date with Penguin Man... eat fewer carbs. Oh, and try not to fall over and make a complete tit of yourself.*

She gave him one last lingering look, and then with great reluctance she turned and hobbled her painful way across the grass towards her building.

*At least it hasn't completely put him off. He's still watching me walk away.*

# CHAPTER NINETEEN

THE NEXT DAY WAS SATURDAY. It was just Felicity and Andrea at the shelter and Felicity was very grateful for the quiet and the space and the lack of men hanging about the place with their manliness and their delicious smell and their general ability to mess with her head. It was almost boring, in fact. How things had changed! Just a few weeks ago she was seriously contemplating crazy cat lady spinsterhood and wondering if she should purchase a footbath and day robe but now... now what? A world of possibilities.

The memory of The Kiss danced in her head all morning as she – somewhat gingerly – went about the familiar routine with the animals and fussed over the new arrivals, and every so often her phone buzzed in her pocket with another message from Bex or Sophie trying to get some – any – juicy details. So far, she hadn't replied, but she was enjoying mentally writing replies in her head as she cleaned out the cat cages. Never mind the awkward conversation about Adam, never mind the fact she'd gone arse over tit in front of James just when she was trying to be sexy; never mind that he clearly had his own complications going on; still, that kiss had to be a good sign, surely? *On some level, he must... want me*, she thought, and even just thinking those words made her tingle all over.

Every few minutes though, memories of the falling over situation would pop into her head unbidden, and – bingo – she was back to total mortification. Or her grazed knee would throb in an accusatory fashion, and after a few moments of shame she would have to remind it firmly that he *had still kissed her*.

As she moved gingerly around the cat nursery after coffee break, there was a chirrup from the table behind her. She looked around and to her surprise it was Mummy Gennaro who was giving her a little cat-greeting and rubbing along the side of the cage, demanding attention. Felicity was touched. That was the first time Gennie had ever made a noise of greeting that she was aware of, she had generally been very quiet since she arrived, other than that horrendous howling when they first caught her, of course. She gave her a little tickle through the bars and Gennie chirruped again and started purring at her touch. She couldn't resist glancing over at Holly curled up in their basket and her heart constricted. Just a ball of fluff. So tiny still. She was getting stronger by the day, but Felicity knew it would be a long time before they could be sure she was well enough to rehome.

'You two,' she whispered, shaking her head fondly. 'You were the ones who started it all, you know that?'

'Started what?' said Andrea, coming abruptly into the room with a mop and bucket for the floors.

Felicity blushed. 'Started, well, making me feel better,' she said hastily. Andrea's eyes narrowed slightly but she didn't question this response.

'You have been more cheerful lately,' she observed in her brisk way. 'I'm glad.'

Andrea seemed about to say something else and then clearly

thought better of it. Instead, she walked to the sink and began filling the bucket with soapy water.

'So,' she said, mock casually, over the sound of the tap. 'How was the date?'

'It wasn't a date,' said Felicity, quickly.

'Whatever,' said Andrea. 'Whatever you two want to call it. How did it go?'

'It was... good. I think.'

'You think?'

'Well, I had a great time. He took me to that Victorian place, you know, on the high street?'

Andrea turned the tap off and looked at her. 'That place is seriously fancy. I thought you said it wasn't a date?'

'It wasn't. I mean, I don't think it was.'

'It was,' said Andrea. 'A man doesn't take a woman to a place like that because he wants to be friends. That was a move. Mark my words.'

She lifted down the bucket and began mopping the floor methodically.

'Maybe,' said Felicity.

'Definitely. So... what's the problem?'

'He's a lovely guy... as you know.'

'But...?'

'For starters – and please don't tell anyone this – I fell over in front of him. And I do mean right in front of him. Like an absolute pillock.'

Andrea guffawed, just as Felicity knew she would.

'Bloody hell,' she said when she'd stopped laughing.

'I know, right? Mortifying.'

'I wish I'd seen that.'

'I'm very glad you didn't.'

Andrea stopped mopping and tried to look serious. 'That wouldn't put him off though, would it?'

Felicity couldn't stop the smile that sprang to her lips. 'No. No, I don't think so, amazingly...'

'So, what's the problem?'

'Well, I think he might have a girlfriend. Or at least, he's not completely free.'

Andrea sniffed. 'A man like that? I'm not surprised. There's bound to be some woman hanging around hoping he'll notice her. Doesn't mean he's not free though.'

'I guess not. I hate not knowing. But I don't want to know at the same time. Does that sound crazy?'

'I get it. He'll tell you in time, I'm sure. If you need to know.'

'I hope you're right. Oh, and as if all that wasn't crap enough, let's just say that Adam got in the way again.'

'Bugger.'

'That's one way of putting it.'

'What is it between you two, anyway? You and Adam I mean?'

'Nothing. There's nothing between us.'

'Well then, don't you think it's time you made sure Adam knew that?'

Felicity nodded. Andrea was always bloody right.

Irrationally, she hoped Andrea might go back to the James topic, tried to think of ways she could steer things back around to him, but the conversation was clearly over. They worked merrily away in silence for the rest of the morning and when break time came, Felicity checked her phone and smiled to herself as she saw all the questions from Bex and Sophie that she knew would be there.

As she scrolled further down, the blood rushed to her ears when she saw Adam's name.

> Dinner, tonight? Please. I really need to talk to you about something.

She replied before she could think about it too much.

Busy tonight, sorry.

She knew she needed to see him. Knew she needed to sort things out. She had promised James after all, and she'd promised Andrea, too, in the end; but tonight was classic movie night on Netflix and, besides, two dates/non-dates in two days with two different men? After a kiss like that? It just wasn't her style.

Two dates every few years, that was really more what she was used to.

His reply was immediate.

Coffee then?

Maybe next weekend?

That sounds like a cop out to me.

It is.

That shut him up for a bit.

When she'd returned to her flat the previous night she had stared at the ring for a long time. She had even contemplated putting it in the bin or putting it in the post to Adam or, hell, maybe just taking it to a pawn shop. God knows she could use the money, but something had made her hesitate and she just couldn't put her finger on exactly why that was.

Her head was mostly full of James of course, how could it not be after that kiss? That evening? It had been magical. Mostly. He had been so considerate and kind when she told him her sad story. And even when she fell over. *Cringe.* So why couldn't she just take him at face value? He was so kind and so gentle with the animals; he was volunteering at an animal shelter for goodness' sake, didn't that speak for itself? But, but,

but (went her mind), was it really possible to find a man who was genuinely kind and also really sexy? There had to be a catch, didn't there? He had to have some kind of terrible flaw. What was it going to be? Extra toes? A hairy back? A wife and three kids? Or worse, a deeply entrenched fear of commitment? She was petrified of finding out.

But, of course, there was a niggle there. A sense of unfinished business with Adam – annoying as that was. He had that way of getting under her skin but James was right. She had to get it sorted one way or another. Get it gone. Whatever *it* was. She hastily sent another text before she changed her mind.

> Okay, fine. Next weekend. Just a coffee. I'm free Saturday.

This time his reply took a little longer and she sipped her drink and tried to stop herself picturing Adam at the other end of the line, looking at his diary perhaps – he was usually so busy, she thought, yet lately for some reason he seemed to have time on his hands – or trying to craft some kind of masterpiece response to make her go weak at the knees.

Her phone buzzed again.

> 11am Saturday. Costa Coffee in the town centre. See you then.

So, not a masterpiece then. Still, the scene was set.
Just coffee.
That was safe, right?

On Monday, she waited for James. She was working, of course, but she had one eye on the door, and it felt like a repeat of New Year's Eve, except this time they had kissed and now the stakes seemed way higher. At break time, she caved and asked Andrea where he was.

'Oh, yes,' she said vaguely. 'Something came up for him at work. He said he was very sorry, but he can't help out this week after all.' Then, presumably seeing Felicity's face drop like a stone, she added, with fake breeziness, 'He said he would try to be back next week. Don't fret.'

'I'm not fretting.'

'Well good. So long as you're not fretting.'

There was a hint of a smile as Andrea put her mug on the side and headed back out into the corridor, which for some reason Felicity found deeply irritating. She stared at it, Andrea's stupid *The Cats Rule: I Just Live Here* mug, with its grubby handle and its tattoo of tea stains, for a long moment, the back of her neck prickling uncomfortably with a sudden heat.

Felicity hadn't for one moment anticipated that he might not come. That wasn't on the agenda. Truth be told, she hadn't thought about much else all weekend except seeing him. Not after that amazing non-date. That kiss. Bloody hell, maybe the fall had put him off after all? Or the confession. Or Adam. Any one of those things could put someone off, to be fair. Unless he really did have a Kardashian-style girlfriend or a wife and three kids, and was just trying to find a way to let her down gently.

'Felicity!' Andrea called from somewhere in the building, and she tried to compose herself. It was time for lunchtime feeds, and she could hear the animals getting restless and, in some cases (Bobby Charlton), demanding their dinner quite vocally. She knew she should mentally park the James situation to think about later.

'Coming,' she shouted back, jumping down off the desk where she had been perching and resisting the temptation to take her phone out of her pocket and text him immediately.

She did, of course, text him as soon as she got home that night.
*Act casual.*

> Hey. Just checking in as Andrea said
> something came up for you. Hope all okay, F x

James (an hour later – a whole hour!):

> Hey yourself. Yes, sorry about that, hope it
> wasn't too busy today, so you had time to miss
> me. PM x

> Sorry, who is this?

> Ha. Cheeky bugger.

> They call me, Man. Penguin Man. And you are?

> Lady. Crazy Cat Lady. At your service.

And then hastily, before she could regret it:

> Fancy a drink?

*In for a penny and all that.*
James (three minutes later, as if three minutes didn't feel
like a bloody lifetime):

> No can do this week, I'm afraid. And anyway,
> didn't you have a little something to sort out?

> Yes, damn your eyes. Okay, fine. But next
> week you are taking me out again.

> Fine, but next time I'm kissing you properly.
> You have been warned.

Felicity (basically on fire at this point):

Fine.

> Fine.

Goodnight then.

> Goodnight yourself.

xx

> XXX

Felicity (wondering how long this might go on for):

xx

Felicity: quickly turns phone off before this gets out of hand.

Felicity: lies back on the bed and wonders how she got herself into such a pickle... and also can't wait for next week. *What did he mean by 'properly'? That was a proper kiss, wasn't it? Oh God, what if he didn't think that was a proper kiss?*

Felicity: turns phone back on to check if he's replied again. He hasn't.

Felicity: realises she still doesn't know his last name so she can't practise her newly married signature in the back of her exercise book like she used to at school.

Felicity: realises she needs to sleep quite badly.

Felicity: sleeps and dreams she's in a labyrinth with red velvet walls and handsome men round every corner and she doesn't really want to find her way out.

# CHAPTER TWENTY

COFFEE WITH ADAM.

It sounded straightforward but turned out to be a logistical nightmare. Who arranges coffee on a busy Saturday morning in town during the January sales? What kind of sociopath thinks they can just drive in and find a parking space five minutes before the allotted meeting time? *Me, that's who,* thought Felicity grimly, as she circled the car park for the third or possibly billionth time. Finally, an elderly lady with a purple Mini Clubman and what looked like a fuchsia pink top hat on her head let Felicity take her (freakishly tiny) space and she edged her battered old Toyota Yaris into the gap and squeezed out of the door trying not to scratch the much nicer car next to her.

'You're late,' came an amused-sounding voice.

'You're meant to be at Costa,' she replied, as she extracted herself awkwardly from the tiny gap between the two cars and looked up at Adam, who was blinking at her in the sunshine.

'I saw you drive in. Besides, it's rammed. Do you want to try somewhere else?'

Felicity wailed. 'But... caramel latte...?'

'Okay fine,' said Adam, miming rolling up his sleeves. 'Let's do this.'

Twenty minutes later, they were successfully huddled in the corner of Costa next to the window, lattes in hand, flushed from their triumphant foraging expedition and only slightly battered and bruised from the experience. Felicity gave him a sideways glance. He looked back at her and they giggled like a pair of teenagers. She had forgotten how much fun they had together.

Adam was dressed for success as always, today in a pair of cream chinos and sky-blue shirt which set off his brown skin and big brown eyes beautifully. He looked rather pale, she thought, but that may have been the cream jacket he had on which wasn't really appropriate for the season but looked bloody expensive. She glanced down at her go-to jeans and hoodie combo and wondered vaguely if she should have made more of an effort.

'So,' he said.

'So...?'

'So, I've been wanting to talk to you.'

'I'm not sure what exactly we have to talk about, Adam, but I'm here, and I have caramel-flavoured coffee, so it's as good a time as any. Go for it.'

'Okay,' he said, but didn't continue. Instead, he seemed to be collecting his thoughts. 'Okay.'

Felicity was tempted to say something facetious, but she kept quiet, sipping her sweet, sweet coffee, just waiting.

'The thing is,' he said, 'I miss you.'

'You already told me that. When you turned up at my work out of the blue. Remember that?' She shifted on the uncomfortable café stool.

'Yes, I know, I know, but then that blond titan turned up and I got distracted.'

Felicity tried to keep her features neutral.

'Who is that guy anyway?' he added, as if the question had just occurred to him.

'That's none of your business, actually,' said Felicity. 'Anyway, he's not a titan. Fair enough he's pretty tall but I wouldn't say titan, exactly.'

Adam took a sip of coffee and looked up at her. 'Whoever he is, he's really into you,' he said.

Felicity flushed. She brought her cup up to her face to try and hide the involuntary smile at the thought of Penguin Man being into her.

Adam caught it though and leaned in towards her. His dark eyes were serious. 'He's not the one for you,' he said, and put his hand on her knee.

'Is that so?' she replied, looking at his hand but making no attempt to remove it. She wasn't going to admit it to him, but his touch felt good. She felt a stirring in the pit of her stomach.

'That's so.'

Felicity studied his face, which was inches from hers, and her heart started to thump. That handsome face was so familiar to her, so dear. She knew every inch of it, every inch of him. He had been there practically since her childhood, by her side. He had supported her through some very dark times. And, in return, she had broken his heart.

'Felicity, I...'

'Oh my God!'

At that moment a squeal from the doorway nearly sent lattes flying everywhere. Felicity's friend Bex was making a beeline for them. Felicity had a sudden urge to hide under a cushion, but it was too late and all the cushions in this place were freakishly small. A trend, presumably.

Bex – all stunning six feet of her, water bottle in hand – was pulling up a stool and dumping many, many expensive-looking bags on the floor and then looking from Adam to Felicity, Felicity to Adam expectantly, as if trying to read their thoughts. Felicity's thoughts were *Oh, bugger*. She had no idea what Adam was thinking – okay, that's not true, she knew exactly what he'd be thinking. He had always had a soft spot for Bex but she could be, well, a lot.

'Darlings! How wonderful to see you both,' said Bex, not adding the word 'together', though she clearly wanted to.

'Rebecca,' said Adam, nodding, with a rueful grin.

'Bought the whole town, I see,' said Felicity, indicating the bags. 'You do know it's not even lunchtime, right?'

'What? Oh, yes, just can't resist a sale, darling, you know me!' replied Bex, tossing her beautifully dark, glossy hair over her shoulder. Her voice seemed a bit more plummy than usual. Was that for Adam's benefit?

'How have you been?' said Adam, glancing at Bex. *Good of him to make her feel included*, thought Felicity.

'Fine, darling, just fine. It's wonderful to see you,' she said, giving him a long look up and down.

'Don't sound so surprised,' said Felicity, a bit more strongly than she had intended. 'You and Sophie were the ones who told him where I was!'

'Oh, rubbish,' said Bex, flapping her hand dismissively at her and taking a sip of water. 'He would have found you eventually.'

Felicity was already plotting all the messages she would send her traitorous friends later.

'You make him sound like a stalker,' said Felicity, trying to keep her voice light as she glanced at Adam.

He looked back at her intently.

'Oh my goodness, you were stalking me?' she said, eyes widening.

Bex giggled again, louder this time and some of the

customers crowded around neighbouring tables looked sharply over at her.

'I wasn't stalking you,' said Adam, spreading his hands wide and smiling nervously. 'I was... I told you, I wanted to keep an eye on you, that's all.'

'He was watching out for you. That's what he told us,' said Bex. Adam shot her a look.

'Watching out for me?' said Felicity. 'What does that even mean?'

Adam looked uncomfortable. He ran his hand through his hair and a memory stirred.

'Felicity, it's not what you think. I...'

'Yes?'

Adam wrinkled his brow. 'I just had to know you were okay. I told you I missed you.'

'Aw,' said Bex. And then, as if she'd only just realised the situation, 'Maybe I should leave you two alone.'

'No,' said Felicity. 'It's fine. We're done. In fact, I might do some shopping while I'm here.'

She found she was standing up without realising how it had happened. She was squashed against the window which meant the edges of the tiny table were cutting into her legs and she had to lean forward in a rather awkward manner so she could shuffle sideways. All in all it wasn't quite the dramatic statement she had hoped for. But she was standing, nonetheless.

Adam looked up at her.

'What are you doing?' he said, grabbing her hand and giving it a squeeze. 'You can't go yet.'

He pulled gently at her and she sat down again with a bump. Her stool seemed to be closer to him than before. Their knees and thighs were touching. How had that happened?

'Sorry, I... you're right, I'll just drink some more latte,' she said, reaching for her cup, and trying to ignore the closeness of him, never mind the uncomfortable feeling in her chest.

'So,' said Bex, leaning forward. 'Have you heard the news?'

She proceeded to tell them at great length a disappointingly scandal-free story about a *Carry On*-style misunderstanding between Sophie and her father-in-law, which Felicity had already heard from Sophie herself, in actual fact, but she was very grateful to Bex for the distraction. Felicity tried to concentrate on listening and resisted the urge to glance at Adam, although she was suddenly very aware of his presence next to her. His thigh on hers. The simmering static between them. It all felt so natural, like old times. In her (probably rose-tinted) memory they had always been such a great couple. It had just *worked*. And they'd always been great in public, in front of people. Having Bex here was certainly adding to the sense of nostalgia.

The look in his eyes when she had mentioned stalking, though. That part was new. He wasn't the stalking type of course, that was ridiculous... but something weird was going on, that was for sure. *What was that all about?* He'd definitely been about to say something important before they were interrupted, and while some part of her wanted to hear what he had to say, another part was more than relieved that Bex had arrived when she did. Had he been about to tell her he loved her? If he did, Felicity just didn't know how she would feel.

*What was the old saying about two buses declaring their undying love at once or something?*

As if to prove the point, on the following Monday morning, James was back.

He sauntered into the office just as Felicity was drinking her morning coffee. The atmosphere in the room became instantly electric, like a Van de Graff generator, and Felicity wondered for a split second if her hair was standing on end.

*Thank God.*

'Morning,' he said, giving her a flash of his blue eyes. There was a moment when he clearly thought about leaning in to give her a peck on the cheek but must have thought better of it and did a kind of ducking motion to try and cover it. Felicity stifled a giggle. *He does look like a blond titan.*

'Morning yourself,' she said, smiling over the top of her cup. 'We missed you.'

'*She* missed you,' said Andrea, barging into the room behind him. 'That's what she means. *She* missed you. The rest of us all got along just fine without you.'

James laughed. 'Thanks a lot,' he said to Andrea, then glanced at Felicity in a way that made her arms prickle with heat. 'How was your weekend?'

'It was... weird, actually. I mean, fine. Honestly, it was fine.'

James raised his eyebrows at her. 'Is that so?'

'Yeah, it was... quiet, I guess. What about yours?'

James shrugged. 'Boring, mainly,' he said. 'I missed this place. Is that sad?'

'No, not sad at all. I often miss it on my days off.'

Cue a long lingering look between them.

'You've only got him for one more week, you know, so you'd better not get used to this,' said Andrea, wagging her finger in Felicity's face and spoiling the moment somewhat. James raised an eyebrow at her.

'I'm sure I don't know what you mean,' said Felicity curtly, feigning offence, but she knew neither of them was buying it. How strange that as soon as she saw James, as soon as he was anywhere near her, all thoughts of Adam disappeared completely. All she wanted to do was be near him. Well, kiss him, all she wanted to do was kiss him.

The week proceeded in a reasonably orderly fashion. Andrea had assigned them different rooms, Felicity the cat nursery – obviously – and James the puppy room, which was full to bursting. She was quite strict about it too, presumably to maintain some sort of decorum. But every so often their paths would cross, and they would grin at each other like a pair of fools, or one of them would make a joke and the other would giggle or, mostly, James would give her a look that made her feel all wobbly. Felicity was starting to wonder what might be happening if Andrea wasn't on shift.

On Wednesday morning, Felicity was washing up the bowls at the sink when James came and stood right behind her as if he was going to put his arms around her.

'What are you doing here?' she said, under her breath, without turning round. 'Andrea will murder you if she catches you.'

He didn't reply but only moved closer, until he was right behind her, and she could hear him breathe-laughing in her ear. She shivered at his nearness and the shiver travelled all the way down her body. He edged closer and the shiver turned to a full-on body tingle. She felt him move to one side and just as she thought he was going to kiss her neck... a hand came down into the murky water. The next second, he had flicked dirty lukewarm water all over her.

'Yuck!!!' Felicity wiped her eyes with her polo shirt. 'You bloody... man,' she said, pretending to shake her fist as he disappeared out of the door.

As soon as he'd gone, though, she had to have a little sit down.

As the week progressed, Felicity found she was particularly enjoying watching him with the animals. He was so careful with them, as if they were precious treasures. When he thought no one was watching, anyway.

In particular, little Holly. Whenever he was actually allowed in the cat nursery, he would find an excuse to get the kitten out for a cuddle and Felicity would pretend not to watch him, being so tender, whispering to her as he stroked Holly's head with one finger, the tiny kitten looking up at him adoringly and purring her little heart out. It was all she could do to stop herself just grabbing him right there and then. She tried valiantly to distract herself with cuddles from Bobby and some of the new arrivals – including a pair of youngish tabby cats who looked like miniature tigers – but in truth she couldn't wait for the end of the week to see what might happen.

What happened was that she found him lingering outside the front door on the Friday afternoon. He was kicking at the stones in the patch of wasteland that served as a driveway for the centre.

*Is he waiting for me?*

'All right?' he said, looking sideways at her.

Felicity hugged herself with her arms. 'All right?' she said.

'So... I was wondering what you might be doing now?'

'Er. I was planning on taking a shower,' she said, indicating her clothes, which were covered in cat fluff from head to toe.

'I'm back for an evening shift later. Andrea's got another date with the mysterious Spanish man.'

'Oh, okay. No worries.'

'But... I've got a day off tomorrow if you wanted to do something?' she said, sounding braver than she really felt.

'I said I'd help Andrea,' he said. 'I felt so bad for letting you all down last week. And she'll be on her own otherwise.'

As if by magic, Andrea emerged from the doorway. *Magical nosey-parker powers*, thought Felicity suspiciously.

'Oh, hi, you two,' she said, casually.

'How long have you been there?' said Felicity.

'Never mind that.'

Felicity rolled her eyes. 'So, I guess you heard...?'

'About tomorrow? I may have.'

'So...?'

Andrea looked between them both, and then smiled. 'I'll be fine. You two go have fun. I'll call you if I need you. Oh, and his name is Javier, by the way. In case you were wondering.'

They weren't. After a few seconds, Andrea melted away into the doorway, not very discreetly, leaving them to stare at each other again.

James spoke in a low voice. 'So... Crazy Cat Lady.'

'Yes, Mr Penguin Man?'

'How about I meet you here at eleven tomorrow and we'll go... do something?'

Felicity nodded. 'You're on.'

'Good.'

'Good.'

'Okay then.'

'See you tomorrow then.'

'Okay.'

*Ooh. Fireworks.*

# CHAPTER TWENTY-ONE

Her stomach was doing somersaults by the time 11am came the next day.

It had been fizzing so much in anticipation, in fact, that Felicity hadn't been able to face any breakfast and now she was empty and hungry and excited and a bit tired from her evening shift, all in equal measure.

After an unnecessary amount of deliberation given the size of her wardrobe, she had settled on her favourite 'casual' outfit – her best jeans and her trusty Joules floral shirt that was now mercifully shaving-foam free. For a fleeting moment she had even contemplated wearing some smart shoes but it was only fleeting; she quickly saw sense and threw on her familiar trainers. They were comforting, somehow. Safe. She didn't want to look too eager, that was the thing. It still wasn't an official date, was it? Their status right now was 'unclear'. Felicity knew enough to know these were crucial times. *Be casual. Act cool. Wear the trainers.* Still, when the time came, she stood shyly outside the centre, cursing her choices and praying Andrea wouldn't come out and interrogate her even though she must have known she was there.

Her phone buzzed.

> Bex: Darling, are you free today? I've got
> something to tell you. Amazing gossip. Get it
> while it's hot!

*I'll reply later*, thought Felicity, after a couple of minutes of trying and failing to concentrate successfully on composing a simple text.

She waited. She looked up and down the road. She looked again.

She checked her watch. 11.15. That was cruel, she thought. The time had dragged so slowly that morning and now it was flying past. 'Slow down,' she told her watch. 'I want to enjoy this day.'

Hang on. 11.15?

And then from nowhere a familiar bad feeling flew down and lodged itself in her chest. The fizzing in her stomach turned to full-on nausea. He had been late before, of course, but this time it was different somehow. This had been a proper arrangement, after all, and something felt... off. She began to pace backwards and forwards, just for something to do.

*Please come. Please come. Please come.*

At 11.30, Andrea popped her head out from behind the door. She looked grave and Felicity stifled a sob and then tutted at herself. It was fine. Everything was fine.

'James has been held up,' said Andrea, brusquely. 'He said he's sorry and he'll text you later. Sorry, love. Do you want to come in for a cuppa?'

Felicity shook her head, already turning away and waving a hand vaguely so Andrea wouldn't see the tears rolling down her cheeks. *He could have called me himself.*

Her phone buzzed again as she walked slowly back to her flat.

> Bex: We could do lunch?

She sighed and quickly tapped out a response.

> Sorry, bit busy today, but soon, I promise. F x

And then, another buzz.
Heart in mouth time.

> James: I'm so sorry, something came up. See you soon though I hope. PM x

Felicity let herself in, slipped off her shoes, climbed onto her bed and lay back despondently, feeling like an idiot for letting herself get so excited.

*Maybe he's had a better offer.*

Felicity lay there for some time.

So much time, in fact, that she was getting really cold, but she couldn't be bothered to get under the duvet. It just seemed like too much effort. She could picture the action she'd need to do. It was so smooth when she ran it through in her head, like a movie ninja or crazy stunt woman – just one swift roll to the left, right hand pulls duvet out from under her body and then a smooth movement back to the right, with the duvet now in place above her, all warm and cosy. It was simple. It was the work of moments. But, somehow, she just couldn't summon the energy to actually do it. Plus, there was the fact that she'd probably end up on the floor in a heap.

She just shivered instead.

A whole hour passed like this, and then her phone buzzed again.

Another text. She thought about leaving it. Tried to ignore it. Tried not to check her phone. Tried to carry on staring at the ceiling but her brain wouldn't let her.

*It might be him. Things might have changed. He might be on his way. There's still hope.*

She looked. Of course she looked. And of course, it wasn't him at all.

> Adam: Please let me take you out for dinner tonight. We have… unfinished business. I know you know it too. A x

Felicity put her phone down again.

This was a dangerous time. She knew that from past experience. The pain of James' rejection, combined with the embarrassment of being stood up in front of Andrea, surrounded her with a familiar uncomfortable, prickly feeling, and she knew that in this state and with her legendary lack of willpower, she was liable to comfort eat, binge drink or do some other reckless thing she would later regret.

*Why did you let yourself trust him? Idiot.*

And she also knew this was the time that Adam in particular could get to her. He was like her kryptonite, as if he knew that she was always vulnerable to his advances. He also seemed to be a teensy bit psychic. Always knowing the perfect moment to strike. She still couldn't believe he'd come back into her life at all, let alone the same week that she met someone new.

Another message popped up on her phone, and her traitorous brain had read it before she even had the chance to clear the notification.

> Adam: Just dinner. No strings. I think we have some things to work out. I'll take you to that pub you like near the forest. I wonder if they still do that sloe gin? A x

Instinctively, Felicity glanced at the ring box, her mind whirring. She could practically hear James' voice, telling her to work things out with Adam. She could still feel the sting of him standing her up. And she could remember how it felt to be near Adam again after all this time.

Deep breath. Another deep breath. A third. And she typed:

Okay. Dinner. But that's all.

> I don't know what you mean 😉. See you tonight.

*Ugh. Winky face. What am I doing?*

# CHAPTER TWENTY-TWO

THIS WAS SURREAL. She was in a pub. With Adam. On a Saturday night. How had this happened?

They were sequestered in the corner of the White Lion, just as he had promised. Felicity kept thinking how sneaky and cunning it was of him to suggest this place, which had been their favourite, back in the day, even though it had now gone all up-market and bistro-style.

*Adam never does anything that isn't calculated*, thought Felicity. And then she chastised herself for being so cynical. *Try and enjoy it*, she told herself. *Try and relax.*

They were sitting in a small, dark oak booth. It smelled of stale beer and woodsmoke from the fire roaring away nearby, and the buzz of people chatting around them was just loud enough to make it feel like they had their own little bubble of privacy. It was only punctuated occasionally by the young, dark, and very attractive waitress who had clearly taken a liking to Adam and seemed to be coming to check on their table rather more often than was strictly necessary.

As they chatted, Felicity watched a bead of condensation making its way down her icy glass of sloe gin, served just as she liked it over plenty of ice. She was used to Adam being flirted with, and she was long past feeling jealous. It was more of an irritation really, which – she realised – must mean she wanted to hear what he had to say rather more than she had expected to. Weirdly, at the same time she also felt guilty about James. Nothing had been agreed, nothing had been discussed, they'd only ever managed one non-date and he had let her down badly today, but she still felt guilty for being out with Adam. Like she wanted to check for hidden cameras and was utterly convinced her phone microphone was going to switch itself on and somehow convey this whole conversation to him through the ether. Which was ridiculous on so many levels. Besides, it was James who had encouraged her to sort things out with him in the first place. Right?

The waitress finally moved off, but not before she'd touched Adam on the arm, Felicity noticed, with a hint of admiration. *Classic technique that.* Adam didn't seem to notice. He took a sip of his gin and tonic and gave Felicity a long, meaningful look. He did look good. She'd give him that. Not as tired as the other day. And the firelight was doing wonders for his chestnut skin and chiselled features. Her cheeks grew warm as an unwanted and rather X-rated memory flashed into her mind.

'So, you've opened the box, I take it?' he said, breaking into that chain of thought.

'Eventually,' she said. 'It's really beautiful.'

She found herself digging it out of her bag and handing it over. Was that the thing to do? Clearly not.

He waved it back towards her. 'It's for you,' he said. 'Please, keep it.'

She stared down at the little blue box. 'But, Adam, I... I just don't get it. Why would you show up out of nowhere and give me a ring like this? I mean, you nearly gave Andrea a heart attack, she thought you were bloody proposing!'

He laughed then, a little too hard.

'Well, even if that was my intention, you've put paid to that one, haven't you!'

*That doesn't exactly answer my question.*

'I've put paid to it? You were the one who showed up at my work, with a ring. On New Year's Eve. Talk about a weird vibe.'

Adam shrugged. 'It was meant to be romantic.'

He took another sip of his drink and Felicity followed suit, mainly so she had something to do other than stare incredulously.

'So,' he continued, and she looked up sharply. 'If I had proposed, what would you have said, exactly?'

Felicity's chest tightened.

'I would have said, "What the hell are you playing at?" I would have said, "You've got to be joking," that's what I would have said. Don't you remember how we left things? What I said? How I behaved? You can't just pretend that didn't happen.'

Shame washed over her at the memory, and she held the cool drink against her cheek.

'I can hardly blame you,' he said. 'I was bloody cheating on you, after all.'

The blood rushed to her ears in that moment as if she'd been ruthlessly hurled off the top diving board. Backwards.

'Wait – what?'

Adam shifted in his seat. 'I mean, I was cheating on you, Fliss. I deserved whatever I got back then. I can hardly blame you for reacting the way you did.'

Felicity's mind was racing and for a moment she felt like she might faint.

'What the hell are you talking about? What do you mean you were cheating? You've always denied it. You made me... you made me feel so terrible!'

Adam looked around furtively, his face panicked. Felicity,

meanwhile, found she was halfway to standing up, fists clenched, adrenaline pumping.

'Come on, Fliss, sit down. Let's talk about this. We can talk about this.'

She dropped into her seat; fists still tight.

'Don't call me Fliss. You were cheating on me? You actually were cheating that whole time?' Her voice rose as the emotion slammed over her like a wave.

'I thought you knew that?' he replied nervously. 'Hell, I've been with her the whole time since. How could you not know that?'

'You what?!' It was out before she could stop herself. A couple on a nearby table gave her a sharp look and she waved her hand in apology.

'Let me get this straight,' she hissed across the table and Adam looked like he wanted to be anywhere else in the world. 'You *were* cheating on me that Christmas and you've been with *that person* ever since? Have I got that right?'

Adam looked sheepish. 'I honestly thought you knew.'

'No. No, I did not know. Isn't it obvious from my reaction that I didn't know? Is this the face of a person who knew this information, Adam?'

'But... surely you did? When you saw that text message and put two and two together, I knew the game was up. You always were so clever, Brooks.'

'Don't you bloody "Brooks" me either,' she hissed. 'Now is not the time. You let me feel bad all this time, like I'd treated you so unfairly. You let me believe it was me being the bastard, when you knew it was something I would never ever want to do to anyone. Oh, I'm so mad at you.'

She was. As she said it, half in jest, she realised how furious she really was. Her hands were shaking. And then something else dawned on her and a cold sensation prickled her spine.

'When I saw you at the shelter the other day, you didn't set me straight. Why not? Or when we went for coffee for that matter.'

'I tried, honest. I was trying. And then your bloody designer-glasses-air-kissing friend turned up.'

'That's no excuse at all. You should have tried harder.'

And then as clear as if it had been whispered in her ear, an ominous thought arrived. Her palms were sweating. She virtually spat the words at him.

'And this? What was this ring for? My birthday, I suppose. Or was it never meant for me at all?'

Adam went pale and looked down at the box. She could see his mind doing some very rapid panicky calculations. *Let's see you smooth talk your way out of this one.*

'Tell me...' she said slowly, unable to look at him now, '...tell me you didn't buy this ring for someone else.'

Adam actually squirmed in his seat like a small boy and Felicity's stomach fell through the floor.

'I didn't... I mean, I did but not in the way you think. I made a mistake. I...'

Felicity felt more and more cross with every word. Beyond cross.

'Adam, tell me the truth.'

'I'm trying. Really, I am. I don't know what you want me to say. Whatever I say is going to be wrong here, isn't it?'

That old chestnut. Felicity was ready to throw something at him.

Instead, she drew breath into her lungs and then, very slowly and very clearly, enunciating every word, fingers and thumbs pressed together for extra emphasis like an Italian nonna, she said: 'Just. Tell. Me. I'm. Not. Your. Back. Up. Plan.'

Adam looked pained but, unbelievably, he still didn't seem to be able to find the words. She didn't need him to. All the pieces were thudding into place, like iron weights. How could she have been so stupid? The girls were going to have a field day with this.

Felicity stood up sharply, so sharply that the table flipped upwards and what remained of their drinks ended up in Adam's lap. He leapt up with a cry of indignation as the ice soaked his crotch, but she was already halfway out of the door.

# CHAPTER TWENTY-THREE

FELICITY'S FATHER walked out when she was six years old.

On Boxing Day.

Right between the cold cuts and the leftover Christmas pudding, to be exact.

Her memories are hazy, of course. She was only tiny, but in her mind's eye when she thought about it now, it was like something out of a surrealist French film. She supposed there must have been more to it but it felt to her – if she ever permitted herself to think about it – inexplicable. The kind of moment that makes your brain hurt if you try to make sense of it.

One minute, the family was sitting around the table together, munching away in (relatively) companionable silence, and the next – the very next minute it seemed – the atmosphere had altered in a flash. A black shadow had passed across her dad's face, that much she would swear to, and then he stood up without a word and walked out of the front door. In her memory, he was still wearing his Christmas jumper and the partly ripped yellow paper hat from his cracker.

Perhaps there was more to it that she didn't remember.

Perhaps her mum had said the wrong thing, done the wrong thing. Perhaps she didn't buy the right brand of piccalilli, or she hadn't made the bubble and squeak the way Nana used to. Perhaps she'd glanced at him wrongly or not glanced at him at all. Whatever it was remained a mystery. Her mother never spoke of it directly, but Felicity had gleaned enough over the years to assume that was just what he was like. Unpredictable. Always on edge.

Mainly, though, Felicity just knew him by his absence, by the dad-shaped hole he left not only after he physically walked out on them but also in The Before, when he was present but absent. When he 'forgot' to go to her first nativity play. When he 'forgot' to collect her and her brother from nursery and left them sitting on the drive with the nursery manager for over an hour. More than once. When their first-ever family holiday ended up being just her, Tristan, and her mother because something had 'come up' at the last minute.

But they had always thought he loved their mum more than life itself. They'd never dreamed he would walk out and leave her. And despite his many failings as a father, her brother Tristan (not Tris, never Tris) had doted on him. It was inexplicable, really, looking back, but at the time no one had been surprised when, as soon as he was old enough (or not quite), Tristan had walked out of the door, too. Sought out his father. Begged his new woman and their new children to let him into their new, shiny life. Begged them to let him stay. Presumably never even looked back or wondered what had become of Felicity, now eleven, or her mum, who was by this time working very hard at pickling her insides and not much else. The bloody traitor.

Tristan always had been a terrible judge of character. Their father was a case in point. There was no way to sugar-coat it. And while Felicity knew – in her head, at least – she was not like him, still deep down there was always the cold hard fear that her dad's flightiness, his propensity to run and run hard whenever things got difficult... that those things lived in her too. That they formed part of her identity in some way.

Was it possible to escape your own genes? Could someone with a father like hers ever do anything other than let people down? Was she doomed to be just like him?

Certainly, it was true of Tristan. He was an absolute disaster area, currently on his third serious boyfriend in as many years, as far as she could glean from Facebook. Reputedly leaving severely damaged and broken hearts in his chaotic wake. They didn't talk. Hadn't talked since the day he left, in fact. But she had learned enough to know that he had made a monumental mess of several relationships and friendships too. 'Toxic Tris', that's how one of his ex-boyfriends described him. The words had sent a cold shiver down Felicity's spine.

This was all buzzing round and round in Felicity's mind for the millionth, gazillionth time as she stormed home after that dinner with Adam. She had never felt so cross in her entire life. No, not just cross. She was livid.

At Adam, of course at him, but even worse, at herself. To think, she had spent three whole years feeling guilty for how she had behaved. When, in fact – and it was obvious now, of course – the fault was not hers at all. Adam was the bringer of doom in this situation. Of course, he was. How had she not seen it?

It was almost funny, except it really wasn't funny in the least.

She marched up the stairs to her flat and threw open the door with unnecessary force, then felt the need to apologise. It wasn't the door's fault, after all. The cold night air and having to apologise to a door managed to dissipate a modicum of rage but only a modicum, and when the march continued into the bedroom, and she remembered the ring in its stupid blue box it was all she could do to stop herself hurling it from the nearest window. But she didn't. It was Tiffany after all. There was probably some kind of law against throwing a Tiffany ring out of a window even if it was only the second floor. Instead, she took it out of her bag and proceeded to march round and round her flat with the ring gripped in her hand, until her knuckles were white, and the ancient old carpet was starting to develop a groove.

*How could he?*

Her phone buzzed.

Adam: I'm so sorry.

For just a fleeting moment, she contemplated sending both ring and phone to their doom.

# CHAPTER TWENTY-FOUR

FELICITY DIDN'T GET out of bed for two days straight. She told Andrea she was sick, but she knew the excuse would only last for so long and Andrea would need help with the cats at some point. So, on the third morning, she hauled herself out of her pit, opened a window to let in some fresh air and picked up her phone for the first time in forty-eight hours.

Six unread messages.

> Adam: I can explain. Please let me try.

> I'm sorry. I really am. I thought you knew.

> Please, please, Felicity Brooks, please can we talk? Please? Is that enough apologies yet? Please let me explain.

*Ugh*, she thought.

Delete, delete, delete with a jabbing finger.

> Sophie: Just checking in. How are things with James after your date? Fancy a coffee? X

Delete, with a sob.

> Bex: Darling, I absolutely insist you let me take you for lunch, I've got something super important to tell you.

Save, to deal with later.

> Andrea: The cats are missing you.

I miss them too. So sorry. I'll be in shortly.

Nothing, of course, from a certain Penguin Man.

With a sigh, Felicity hauled herself into the shower. She had come to a decision.

'I'm taking a week off,' she announced somewhat brusquely when she arrived at work. Andrea-style, if you will.

The real Andrea looked rather stricken, but Felicity was ready for this eventuality.

'Don't panic, I've asked my friend Sophie to cover for me. It'll all be fine.'

(She hadn't but she had made a mental note to do it later, which was almost the same thing.)

Still Andrea didn't speak, so it was time to administer the final blow.

'Besides, I haven't had a proper holiday since I started working here. I'm sure you don't need me to tell you that's actually illegal or something. Probably.'

There was a pause, and then Andrea threw back her head and laughed heartily, her plait bobbing.

'Fine,' she said, when she'd recovered. 'Fine. Bloody employees and their bloody tricksy ways. Your "friend" better be halfway sensible.'

'Oh, she is,' said Felicity.
*Sort of. Not really.*

The next thing to do was get on a plane. Only a very small plane and only for a very short distance but for Felicity this was a mammoth step forward.

'You're doing what?' said Sophie, when she called her that night to explain. 'How exciting. Can I come? I'm dying to get away.'

'Um, no, not really,' said Felicity. *Deep breath.* 'I need you to look after some cats and dogs and such with Andrea. Can you do it for me? Please? I'll love you for absolutely ever and ever.'

Another pause.

'You want me to do what?'

'I want you to, well, I need you to "be me" and do my job for a week. Sophie, I can't tell you how much I need this. I absolutely have to get away. I've got some... stuff to sort out. And I desperately need someone to cover my shifts because I can't leave Andrea in the lurch. I know it's such a lot to ask but please, pretty please, I'll love you for ever and ever and ever. Please?'

Sophie chuckled. It was a deep, throaty chuckle that didn't quite fit with the rest of her, that was what made it especially attractive.

'Oh, for goodness' sake, all right. What else have I got to do?'

She was being genuine, too. Sophie had no job and a live-in nanny for the children and a very rich father and even richer husband. Felicity didn't have a clue how she filled her days to be honest, but she knew it must involve a lot of 'wafting about'. *How the other half live.*

Deep breath. Here was the crunch.

'Great! Thank you! Er... and can you start tomorrow?'

'So, I mean, that's quite sudden, isn't it really?'

There was a pause. Felicity waited anxiously, picking at the scab on her arm and making it bleed again.

Then: 'But I can confirm I have checked my diary and I have nothing to do at all except for my spin class on Thursday night.'

Felicity let out a squeal. 'You cherub. I love you. I mean it. Thank you so much.'

They discussed the details quickly and Felicity came off the phone feeling suddenly excited. She hastily threw some things in a bag. If she didn't go now, she might never do it.

At East Midlands airport the next morning, the queues were pleasingly small.

'One return to Guernsey, please,' she said timidly, putting her driving licence down on the counter when it was her turn at the desk.

A tall, red-headed border control officer inspected her licence rather closely and Felicity felt a stab of panic.

'It's domestic. I don't think I need a passport, do I?'

The officer looked up at her with a severe look on her face, and then spotted Felicity's ginger locks and seemed to soften in the way VW campervan drivers always wave at each other, like they have a special club for vehicles that look cool but are impossible to drive.

She even smiled. Sort of.

'No, you don't need a passport. This is fine.'

'Oh, that's a relief, thank you,' said Felicity, scooping up her ticket and licence with trembling hands. *That's a relief because I don't have one.*

'Enjoy your flight,' said the lady with another appreciative nod at her hair (if that was possible, was that possible? Maybe it was just her anxiety talking, but it definitely, definitely felt as though the scary and slightly creepy officer lady had been staring at her hair).

'Thanks!' said Felicity and hastened through the barrier before the officer could start up a conversation.

It was only when she got on the plane and sat back in her seat that it became clear she had managed to get toothpaste in her hair during her super quick bathroom visit that morning. Quite a lot of it, in fact. It was massed in a clump behind her right ear. So much of it was stuck in her hair that it was almost as if she had squeezed an entire tube of toothpaste behind her ear. When and how had that even happened? And why today of all days had her body decided to forget the subconscious and relatively simple action of squeezing the correct amount out of a tube of toothpaste?

As they were about to take off, she wasn't allowed to go to the tiny aeroplane toilet, so Felicity did her best to clean it up with the only thing to hand, the sick bag in the seat pocket in front of her. It wasn't pretty. When the flight attendant came round, there was toothpaste absolutely everywhere. The whole row stank of Sensodyne, original mint flavour, and she could see the attendant's nose wrinkle as the smell wafted towards her. Felicity sheepishly handed her the crumpled bag and ordered a gin and tonic only to be told the flight was so short there would be no drinks trolley coming through. Tea, coffee or water was all that was on offer. Felicity gave a deep sigh and put her head back on the hard and rather scratchy headrest, trying to ignore the overpowering wafts of minty freshness.

Not a great start to the day, was it? She tried to relax and channel her inner cat. *What would Bobby Charlton do?* she thought. *He definitely wouldn't get toothpaste in his fur. Other things, maybe, but not toothpaste. He also wouldn't feel guilty about this trip. But then, he's a cat. Do cats ever feel guilty about anything?*

Felicity was just about to fall into a shame and guilt cycle for the umpteenth time when her stomach gave a lurch. The plane had jerked into life and her head was pinned to her seat as the pilot put his foot down – metaphorically or actually, she had no clue how this all worked. *Do planes have accelerators?* All she knew in that moment was she was suddenly having even more regrets about her rather rash decision.

The air hostess smiled reassuringly at her from the little fold-down seat three rows in front. In fact, there were only twenty rows in the whole plane and only about ten people on the flight, so it felt rather like a set-up for an unfunny sitcom. Or maybe a disaster movie, she thought, feeling a bit sick as the plane lifted into the air and gave a shudder.

*Please God, don't let me die. And also, if I do die, please don't let there be any more toothpaste in my hair when they find me. Although, I suppose I'll smell minty fresh for the rescue team.*

When Felicity first made the decision to do this, all of – *what was it?* – two or three days ago, it was on condition that she did not allow herself to feel guilty. This was her time. Something she needed to do. She had resolved to throw caution to the wind. Live recklessly. Spoil herself. All that jazz. Except that she did. Feel guilty, that is. It seemed to be a permanent state of mind these days. Shortly after her arrival on the island, a shockingly beautiful and apparently very tiny pile of stones in the middle of an expansive blue sea, the guilt set in in earnest.

For starters, amidst all the extremely last-minute.com

preparations, Felicity had blown more than £1,000 on a luxury hotel room for the week, an act of extremely un-Felicity-like behaviour. But then again, what on earth was she saving for anyway? She had everything she needed for the life of spinsterhood that was once again beckoning and a lifetime supply of rescue cats at her disposal, after all. What was a rainy-day fund for if not to blow a grand at the gorgeous Bella Dame Hotel in Guernsey?

Perhaps she was having some kind of breakdown. Who knew?

Anyway, when she walked into her beautiful room and saw the four-poster bed and roll-top bath and chocolates on the pillows, the guilt left her alone for a bit, presumably struck dumb in awe and wonder or something.

Felicity had chosen this hotel deliberately. It was far enough from the places that made her heart stop but close enough to the places she loved, and yet not somewhere that triggered any memories itself. In fact, she thought, as she put the tiny kettle on, she could happily spend a week here and not do any of the things she knew she really had to. She ran a bath and ate the tiny chocolates and wondered how long it was until dinner, and tried to pretend she didn't know full well that she would need to get on with things tomorrow. For now, she decided, it was only fair to enjoy herself. It had been an eventful few weeks, after all.

She checked her phone. Still no message from Penguin Man. Her heart clenched at the thought of him. His blond hair. His twinkly blue eyes. *A blond titan.*

*He might forget me while I'm away*, she thought, suddenly. And then immediately cursed herself for being such a sap. *Get up, Felicity! Go and do what you have come here to do.*

First stop was the gin bar downstairs, where a rather attractive Irish waiter served her a delicate bowl-shaped glass full of the special gin brewed on site, mixed of course with the finest tonic water and all the trimmings. Not that the in-house gin distillery was the real reason she had chosen this hotel, of course.

She was just contemplating a second drink when a waitress – who looked about twelve years old – arrived and led her through to the dining room, politely egging her on while she stuffed her face with the most divine lemon linguine and sticky toffee pudding and tried to look like she belonged in a place like that. No one seemed to think it odd that she was alone. In fact, dotted amongst the elderly couples and one or two families in the room there were a couple of other ladies who looked to be staying there on their own. Although they were wearing rather more pearls than Felicity.

'What brings you to Guernsey?' asked a very smiley elderly man later, when they were all being served coffee in the lounge, satiated, and glowing from the gin and the roaring fire.

Felicity hesitated.

*Oh, what the hell.*

'I was born here,' she said, simply.

'Is that so?' said the man, raising his glass in salute. 'How long since you've been back?'

Felicity took a gulp of her third G&T of the night.

'Twenty-five years. It's good to be back.'

And as she said it, she meant it. Sort of.

# CHAPTER TWENTY-FIVE

THEY HAD LEFT the island when she was seven. One day, after school, Tristan and Felicity had returned home to find all their things in boxes and a removal company loading a huge lorry with their furniture.

'We're going to a hotel tonight,' their mother had said, with false brightness, 'and then tomorrow we start a new life.'

Felicity and her brother had exchanged nervous glances. Their mother was smiling but it was that strange, fixed smile they knew all too well. Felicity started to cry.

'What about my friends, Mummy? I told them I'd see them at school on Monday. It's our prize-giving next week and we're all getting a prize, Mrs Taylor said.'

'We're going to England. We're getting the hell out of this place. And you're going to make some new friends so don't you worry about that.' She wagged her finger in Felicity's face. This was a voice you didn't argue with.

Tristan was crying now, too. He was a bit older and had been much quicker to fully grasp the implications of this strange announcement.

'I don't want to go to England! I want to stay here. I want to see Dad! I am not going! You can't make me!'

'It's lovely, you'll love it,' drawled their mother. She was slurring her words. 'We're going to Derbyshire. It's really beautiful.'

Neither of the children could have cared less about what it looked like.

They cried all the way to the hotel. Then they cried and complained most of the night while their mother just sat on the bed with that same fixed grin on her face, rocking ever so slightly back and forth as they screamed and shouted around her. By the next morning, Felicity and Tristan were so strung out and exhausted that as soon as the hire car rolled off the ferry at Poole, they fell asleep. They slept all the way up the country and they didn't wake until they heard a strange man shouting at their mother as she tried to park their old car at the bottom of what looked like a ravine. They had made it safely, which was a bloody miracle in itself, one they only really appreciated as adults. At the time, the fact their mother had been drunk at the wheel hadn't even been on their radar. The much more pressing issue was that the lorry had got stuck across the road, there was nowhere for them to pull in and the removal men had to trundle all their worldly possessions half a mile vertically up the hill. In Felicity's memory, it was all just a blur of fury and tears and rain.

Felicity had grown to appreciate it, as an adult, not just surviving the journey of doom but the beauty of the place they had arrived at. As a child all she could remember of her introduction to Derbyshire were those hills. Their aching leg muscles as they walked up and down, up and down, up and down, usually in the wind and rain and fog, all the way to their tiny terraced house perched on the side of the valley – although it felt more like a cliff – near Matlock Bath.

The town was usually grey and wet, and the rented house was grotty and cold and smelled of mushrooms. She had to share a room with her brother for the first time in her life. The absolute pits, that was. Until he decided to leave too, anyway. They had to walk two miles to school each morning and the other children looked down on them. She wanted to tell them all about Guernsey, about the life she had left behind. But no one ever asked her or showed the slightest interest. Not until high school, anyway. They had travelled halfway up the United Kingdom and now they were all alone in this strange new place, with just their gin-soaked mother for company.

The next day, Felicity put on her ancient and yet still slightly uncomfortable hiking boots and walked south towards the first stop on her self-imposed itinerary and the one she hoped would be the most straightforward. Ease in gently, that was the idea anyway.

It was less than a mile to Icart Point, a small headland on the southern coast of Guernsey, which had been the setting of the only decent holiday she'd ever had as a child. Her grandparents had taken pity on her in the summer after their father walked out, and they had treated her and her brother to two weeks in the lovely old hotel just along the footpath.

Sitting there now, perched on top of the cliffs on the newly painted (and still somewhat sticky) green bench, she could almost hear their voices carried on the tide as it swept and rolled around the rocks below. Every so often, the navy-blue sea would send up a plume of salt spray, soaking her in its fine droplets. Gulls sailed overhead and the winter wind rushed past, burning her cheeks. It was all jolly idyllic.

Felicity pulled her coat tighter around her and strained to

remember that holiday. Forced herself even. There were happy memories somewhere deep down if only she could bring them into focus. She waited patiently... and slowly, slowly, slowly they came.

First, there was a stout blonde waitress from Scotland who loved to swim slow lengths in the hotel swimming pool, which was heated like a bath. Even in the height of summer you could see the steam rising off its surface. Then, she pictured a dessert trolley heaving with sweet pavlova and thick chocolate mousse and sticky caramel apple granny and remembered how she'd once been allowed to have two ice creams for tea. The simplest things brought them joy back then. And there was that glorious day below the cliffs in Saint's Bay when they had sculpted a perfect little boat in the sand and rowed to the Caribbean and back in an afternoon, dodging pirates along the way. It was all jolly idyllic and wholesome.

But there was one thing about that holiday she had no memory of at all. Before she'd died, her nana told her that Felicity had spent hours during that holiday sitting on this same bench, staring out to sea. Eyes wide. Face stern. Hands clenched.

Sometimes, apparently, she would bring a small picnic, or her beloved toy rabbit, Mr Higgins, or even her granddad's binoculars (although they were usually held back to front or the wrong way up). She would set up camp on the bench with her precious items and it would take all their ingenuity to persuade her to leave when it was time for tea.

'Waiting for your daddy, you were, I'm sure of it,' her nana had said.

*No use waiting for him anymore*, thought Felicity grimly, but all the same she couldn't tear her eyes away from the sea. She stared down into the waves as they chopped and swirled in the cove below and, as she did so, the image of that tiny figure with her cuddly rabbit and her granddad's binoculars threatened to break her heart wide open.

# CHAPTER TWENTY-SIX

THE FOLLOWING DAY, Felicity drove slowly round the island in her hire car – with a maximum 30mph limit everywhere, even 20mph in some places, slow was really the only option. It was restful, mostly, unless you encountered a local coming the other way on one of the tiny roads. They really did not like tourists. Not one bit. And when they spotted her telltale number plate most of them seemed to speed up towards her instead of slowing down. Several of them had already attempted to barge their way through a 10cm gap between her tiny hire car and the low drystone walls they seemed to love so much. She'd already lost two wing mirrors and a headlight.

Still, in between all the low-speed crashes and minor road rage incidents, trundling along at that slower pace had allowed her to get her bearings and marvel at the strange Franco-English beauty of the place. Her memories of the island were so hazy but this was properly like stepping back in time. You could almost imagine horses and carriages trip-trapping along amongst the houses, except for the fact that, despite the low speed limit and narrow wobbly stone-lined lanes, every other car seemed to be a Ferrari or some other kind of sports car. *Rich people are peculiar.*

She had already made a mental note to visit the neighbouring island of Sark, where cars are banned completely and only horses and carriages, and tractors and bikes, are permitted. Or Herm, a tiny island with the most incredible sandy beaches, according to the sexy Irish barman, where there are barely any vehicles at all. *Do they still hate tourists?*

Felicity bought herself a crab sandwich and a portion of chips and drove to Jerbourg point, the most southerly and easterly point of the whole island. On a clear day you could see both Herm and Sark from here, but she mostly just looked at the sea. Two hours, just staring out at the Channel. Watching the birds wheel overhead and listening to the sound of the waves crashing against the cliffs below. It was a kind of healing and a grasping, trying to get hold of something, memories perhaps, that were just out of reach. Somehow in the middle of all the staring, she was crying again. Who even knew where the tears were coming from at this point? But the whole place had made her so nostalgic for a sense of home or family, in a way she just hadn't expected. Deep down inside her, her heart ached.

And it wasn't over yet. There was one part of the island she had avoided, even though she knew it was also the one place she really needed to be. She had told herself that Saturday was the day.

When it was time for bed that night, Felicity felt as though she'd run an actual marathon, she was so emotionally drained.

*And that was supposed to be me easing into this gently.*

Supremely grateful to be back in the safe, warm cocoon of her hotel room at last, she had caved and texted James.

Hey, Mr Penguin Man, play a song for me x

Silence.

Hmmm. Should she risk it and call him? Felicity had a mortal fear of speaking to people on the phone but, like a tax return or jury service, she knew it was something that occasionally had to be done. What if he didn't answer though? That would be mortifying. Had she messed it up completely with him this time? She was still confused and reeling from the brush-off he'd given her at the weekend. She'd spent the remainder of the journey here trying to work it out, making her brain ache from the effort. It had been a long time since she'd dated anyone but surely things hadn't changed that much. He had liked her, surely? He still liked her. She was (almost) sure of it.

So, if it wasn't that, then what? What could have possibly happened in less than twenty-four hours to change things so utterly? She knew it was a risk, going away like this, right at this moment, but if he really liked her then maybe whatever was going on at his end would have sorted itself out by then too. *Absence makes the heart grow fonder. Doesn't it?*

And then there was Adam of course. The cheating bastard. Three years of guilt and shame, for nothing. She felt robbed. Like he'd taken her prime years away from her.

The thought of Adam and the daylight robbery of her best years made her feel so wretched she got up off the bed and paced around the room. Her window overlooked the hotel's courtyard and, although it had been dark for hours already, they had strung fairy lights from every tree, so it looked like a miniature Tivoli Gardens. Or so she imagined anyway. In her adult life Felicity had never been further than Nottingham (before now of course) but she did a lot of travelling in her head.

A lot of googling and a whole lot of reading the *Lonely Planet* guides. Copenhagen was definitely on her list.

Just then, her phone made a kind of mechanical squeaking noise. James was replying. There they were – oh joy – the three dots! He was typing a reply. He was taking his time about it though.

Felicity eventually got fed up with staring at the screen, and wandered through to the bathroom to run a bath, flicking on the kettle on the way through. Her eyes felt bruised and swollen from all the crying she'd been doing. Very attractive. She splashed cold water on her face without looking in the mirror and went back through to the main room in time to pop a tea bag in the mug and pour the water in just after it boiled, a small but satisfying moment. Finally, her phone buzzed again.

> I'm only moderately sleepy and it's not like there's any place I'm going to… fa la la… x

> We missed you at work today. Holly and Gennie are missing you too. Andrea is… well, Andrea x

Hurray! A reply. But how did that take him so long to type? And also, he was at the centre? He wasn't meant to be. Felicity felt a twinge of anguish at missing a day spent with him, then remembered she was meant to still be mad at him for standing her up. She was all too aware that he had yet to explain.

Felicity (play it cool, she told herself):

> Aw, love them so much. How's Sophie getting on?

> She's no Felicity. A bit chaotic. But she's getting on okay. How are you doing?

> Just taking some time away, be back soon xx

*Two kisses this time. Not that cool then.*

> Andrea said you were. I think that's great. You
> so deserve it. Where are you staying? xx

Felicity (after a pause to consider):

> It's a secret! By which I mean, I'm having an
> adventure! I'll tell you all about it when I'm
> back xx

> How mysterious. Okay, I'm counting on it. I
> need to explain a few things. Sleep tight x

She smiled at the sign-off, but still couldn't help worrying that something had changed between them. Having started the conversation, she somehow wished she hadn't as now she just wanted to see his kind face and be in the room with him and tell him what this 'adventure' of hers was really all about. No amount of messaging could really cover it. If her tear-swollen eyes didn't look like two tiny pinholes poked in a marshmallow, she'd be resorting to FaceTime right about now.

Her phone buzzed again.

> Adam: Hey. I went to your work, but they said
> you'd gone away. Hope all okay. Please call me
> when you can, A xx

*Ugh*, thought Felicity. *Bloody cheating bastard.*

And then she felt guilty. Again. Before he was a bloody cheating bastard, Adam had been the person who got her through some of her darkest days.

She pulled the plug on the bath without using it and climbed straight into bed, her mind awash with so many conflicting emotions. Despite the exhaustion she could feel in her bones, despite the sea air and the long walks, despite the squishy, squashy pillows, and the cosy downy duvet, sleep was a long time coming that night.

Saturday arrived before she was quite ready.

Still, she told herself over the enormous indulgent breakfast, she had come all this way. Might as well see this thing through.

Le Manoir was, as the name suggests, an imposing Georgian manor at the end of a long, curving driveway. It was situated in the St Peter's (proper Guernsey name, Saint Pierre du Bois) parish on the west coast of the island, just a few hundred metres back from the coast road.

Even from her viewpoint through the property's high iron gates, Felicity could see it had fallen into disrepair. The striking white walls were no longer pristine. There were broken panes of glass in the lower windows and crumbling plaster just below the roof, which was missing some tiles. In the expansive garden there were huge ancient trees that looked to be surviving, except for one solitary oak just to the right of the building that had clearly been hit by lightning and was cracked and shattered right through its middle.

'Hello, my dear,' said a friendly voice with a French lilt.

Felicity started and turned to find an elderly lady in a roll-neck jumper and walking boots standing beside her.

'Good morning,' she said, trying to look as if she hadn't just been contemplating the crime of trespass.

'Such a shame, no?' said the stranger, nodding her head towards the house. 'It so desperately needs someone to love it.' (She pronounced it 'eeet', of course, very elegantly.)

Felicity nodded, her heart thumping.

'Do you know who owns it?' she said, cautiously.

The lady made a Gallic gesture of dismissal.

'It is still owned by the bank, I think,' she said, with a dramatic shrug of the shoulders. 'The family left, oh, perhaps twenty years ago. Maybe more.'

Felicity flushed. 'Do you know why?' she said, feeling her voice catch in her throat. She held her breath.

'*Non*, I am sorry,' said the woman. 'I only came to the island a few years ago. But my husband might, he was born here. Would you like me to ask him?'

'Oh, no, I couldn't possibly trouble you, but thank you,' replied Felicity.

The woman regarded her for a moment.

'That's fine, my dear, of course. Well, don't tell anyone I said this, but you can probably go in if you like. No one will stop you.' She waved her arms again in the direction of the gates and turned to go.

'Thank you!' said Felicity, feeling an irrational desire to beg her to stay.

*Don't leave me alone with The House.*

But the older lady had already waved her hand in farewell and was trotting along the road away from Le Manoir at a surprising lick.

Felicity turned back towards the entrance. Did she dare go in? Was it really allowed? She peered around her as if the police might be lurking nearby. If they even need police on Guernsey. Now that she thought about it, she hadn't seen any beyond the one solitary individual at the airport. Maybe he was the only one for the whole island, which would make the odds of her getting caught, well, pretty low.

Felicity walked up and put her hand on the cold iron gate. It opened easily under her hand, but she wasn't sure if that was good news or bad. With a deep breath, she slipped between them and began a slow walk along the driveway.

Up close, it was a mess. What had appeared as gleaming white walls from the pathway were really cracked and crumbling in more than a few places, and lumps of broken plaster and tiles littered the gravel sweep in front of the door.

Her chest felt squeezed with pain even though she had so few memories of how it had once looked on the outside. She'd never really seen any photographs and it was hard to believe this was the place she spent her early childhood. The place she lived when all had been well with the world. Virtually impossible, really, to believe it had ever belonged to her family.

The large Georgian front door was covered in badly faded and peeling pink paint, and as she ran her hand over it gently a memory stirred. A red front door had been her mother's dream. A cherry red front door, in fact, bright and glossy. Suddenly she could see them as if they were right in front of her, like a still from a home movie, frozen in time. Dad, paintbrush in hand, kneeling on the cold stone doorstep. Mum, standing over him, hands on hips, face angry. It wasn't a happy scene, as such, but Felicity smiled with joy.

*We looked just like a normal family. Who knew?*

She could remember it all now. Her mum had been blathering on at her dad about the front door, over and over again, until he had finally relented and painted it for her one weekend, getting more on the surrounding stonework than he did on the door. Then her mother had been beside herself with fury that he hadn't bothered to pay for a professional. And her father, in turn, was so cross at the suggestion that he was incompetent that even more paint went in all the wrong places.

Felicity ran a hand thoughtfully down the door frame, where a hint of red still remained. She pushed on the door, wondering if it would swing open like something out of a spooky gothic horror novel but no, no give at all, and no joy when she turned the grubby brass handle. Instead, she walked a circuit of the house on the outside, peering into the windows as she went. Perhaps it was just her imagination, but there was an air of foreboding lingering around the place somehow, as if Mrs Danvers might appear around the next bend at any moment, scowling.

From what she could make out through the grubby glass, it was in an equally sorry state inside. There were leaves all over the wooden flooring and bits of broken furniture could be seen in every room, where there was furniture at all. Nothing, really, that would indicate it had ever been loved. And yet she supposed her mother and father must have loved it, once. Surely, her father must have been pleased to inherit such an incredible place. She could almost imagine them crossing the threshold for the first time with such excitement, such hope for the future. Back when they were happy. Back when they could tolerate each other.

She walked past what must have been the dining room, and on impulse pressed her face to the glass and tried to remember what their dinners had been like, when they were all together. But all she could remember was that Christmas. *That* dinner. That awful, awful black day. She shook her head hard as if to shake the memory out. It had no place here. It belonged to a different time.

The house today was so peaceful. Felicity gave a deep sigh, closed her eyes and turned her face to the weak January sun. And as she waited, feeling a hint of warmth on her face, something else stirred. She only had a collection of impressions, nothing concrete, but she could sense a more definite image, lurking nearby, just out of her reach, like a dream that fades on waking. Felicity knew better than to try to grab it. Knew that would make it vanish altogether. Instead, she took a breath and tried to relax, to let more of the memory come. A tiny thread of it was just taking shape when a forceful voice cut through her thoughts and she was jolted back to the present.

'Ah, there you are, my dear.'

The old woman was marching towards her up the drive with unnerving speed, waving her arms. Felicity gave a weak smile. At least now there would be two of them to get caught by the police.

'My dear, my dear – phew,' said the woman, stopping to catch her breath and clutching at Felicity's sleeve. 'My dear, I asked my husband, and he found something for you.'

'Oh honestly, you didn't have to do that,' said Felicity, although she was intrigued immediately, of course.

The woman waved away her protestations.

'I knew he'd know more about this place,' she said, pointing at the house with an elegant finger. Felicity's face flushed with heat. 'But, well, when he gave me this, I honestly couldn't believe it! Look who it is!'

'Who?' said Felicity, the possibilities whirling around her head.

'*C'est vous*!' said the woman, thrusting a newspaper clipping into Felicity's hands. 'It's you!'

# CHAPTER TWENTY-SEVEN

FELICITY UNFOLDED the paper slowly and gasped.

There, right in the middle of page 3 of the *Guernsey Free Press*, was a picture of her and Tristan as children, smiling like a pair of Cheshire cats. Standing either side of a very large pig, of all things, and dressed in identical dungarees and sun hats, as if they were twins. The headline read, 'The sun gets his hat on for the Guernsey Show' and, underneath the photo, a bland caption. Nothing more than their names and ages in italics.

Felicity's hands were shaking as she stared at the image. She couldn't believe she'd never seen this photo before. She touched the spots of glue in the corners of the paper, which were past their best but still tacky.

'Look at that!' she gasped. 'How funny! Wherever did you find this? And how on earth did you know it was me?'

'It's the hair.' She shrugged, then went on, 'As I said, my husband has lived here a lot longer than me. When I told him you were asking about the house, he got out one of his old scrapbooks. He always said he thought it might come in handy one day. And you haven't changed a bit. It is Felicity, no?'

'It is, yes. That's me there, holding the ice cream. Wow. I can't believe he still had this.'

'Ah, that's not even the best bit,' said the woman, looking at her intently. 'Turn it over.'

And sure enough, there on the other side, there was a picture of the house itself.

There was no story with it, just a small caption. 'Le Manoir welcomes guests for annual garden party.'

Felicity was stunned. It was Le Manoir, of course, but it looked completely different. The paper it was printed on was faded and old, but the photo popped off the page. The house popped off the page might be more accurate.

It was shining like a bright white beacon even though it was effectively the backdrop. In front of the house, on the gravel where she was standing right this very moment, there was a long trestle table covered in white tablecloths and heaving with plates and cake stands piled high with all kinds of party food.

All around the gravelled area were poles strung with lights and bunting and there were ridiculously stylish-looking people everywhere, in every conceivable pose, some seated at the table, some standing chatting, drinks in hand, and all, every single one, appeared to be laughing or at least smiling. One very slim, elegant-looking lady on the left-hand side of the shot in a pale jumpsuit had her head thrown back, cackling exuberantly.

There were children running, playing in the grass, climbing the beautiful old oak tree next to the drive, which at that point was still standing strong. Some were sitting in the grass, making daisy chains and giggling. One little boy was hiding behind the oak, peering out with his finger over his lips like he had the best secret.

But it was a character in the middle of the shot that took Felicity's breath away.

It was her mother.

There she was. Right there.

Someone had folded the clipping down the middle right next to her. Felicity tried to smooth it with a cold and shaking hand.

Her mother was sitting in a chair in front of the table staring defiantly at the camera, arms folded. Hooded eyes, long dark hair in two plaits like Pippi Longstocking. She was wearing a kind of playsuit, faded denim and bum-skimmingly short, showing off her long pale legs and slim strappy sandals. Her legs were crossed, and one sandal dangled delicately from her raised foot. So beautiful, heart-stoppingly beautiful, and yet always so serious.

Next to her, his chair reversed at right angles to hers, was her father. Handsome, charming and slightly dishevelled, with thick dark hair, like a young Dean Martin, people always said. He had his legs astride the back of the chair, arms across its back, very close to her mother, smiling broadly and gesticulating as if he was trying to make a point, or perhaps get her attention. Mansplaining something no doubt. Meanwhile she looked as though she was stoically ignoring him, too busy posing for the camera or lost in a world of her own. Was that a hint of a smile? Perhaps.

Felicity traced her parents' image with her finger fondly. *Just look how happy we were once. Or they were, anyway.*

The date on the newspaper was 8 July 1992. It was almost impossible to believe this scene could have happened just months before her world fell apart. Almost.

Without a word, the woman handed her a delicate lace handkerchief. Felicity hadn't even noticed she was crying. She put a hand against the wall of the house to steady herself. It felt cold and rough under her fingers.

'Thank you,' she whispered. 'I can't tell you how much this means to me.'

The old woman made another of her dismissive gestures. '*Pah*, it's nothing, no problem. You were meant to have it,' she said.

Then she handed her a crumpled slip of paper.

Felicity unfurled it to reveal their name, Bisson, and a phone number.

'When you are ready to come and talk,' she said simply, 'we will be waiting.'

That night, Felicity skipped dinner. It was very unlike her to pass up the opportunity for a meal, especially one that came with gin and the opportunity for a little look at the barman, but she felt as though she might never have an appetite again. Instead, she lay amongst the fluffy pillows and stared relentlessly at the newspaper clipping. She felt that the secret to all the mysteries of her life might be revealed if only she could see it.

Of course, she had known visiting the house was going to be difficult, but this was next level. It had unlocked something inside her. Something she had hidden for a long time. Something she had forced herself not to remember. With time to study the picture of the house more closely, she had managed to pick out herself and her brother from the group scene. There was clearly a very elaborate game of hide-and-seek going on, and if you squinted you could make out a little girl just visible to the left of the house – her, of course – and there was Tristan, hiding under the table, peering out and giggling. He actually looked quite cute. The whole scene was so sweet it made her heart ache. Felicity wanted to shout, to warn them, to tell them what was coming. As if it would have made a difference. Those poor children.

And there in the middle, her parents, in that astonishing tableau. Frozen in time, yet so expressive. Alive somehow. You could almost feel the heat between them. She stroked the image with one finger. Her parents had been so obsessed with each other, so self-absorbed, in many ways, Felicity realised now. Such a weird feeling but even at such a young age she could recall the sense of being a third wheel whenever they were around, regardless of whether they were in love or at war, it didn't seem to matter with them. What a strange thing for a child to feel about their own mum and dad – like a gooseberry, they would have called it at school – but that's how it was, as if the children were intruding, first on their romance and then on their drama.

As she stared at the photo, she felt like she had missed something else and was just sensing it about to burst into focus like a bubble when her phone buzzed.

> Bex: Hi, lovely, Soph just told me the news! Are you really in Guernsey? How jolly exciting and rather random! I do hope you have a brilliant time. Can you give me a shout when you get back? I MUST tell you something really important. Mwah!!

Felicity cursed. She had lost her train of thought. Bex tended to have that effect on people.

She texted a hasty reply:

> Sure, will do xx

Then she rolled herself lazily off the bed and flicked on the kettle. Perhaps she should phone James. Tell him what she'd found. Or maybe Andrea? Or Bex? She felt a twang of guilt that she had been such a rubbish friend lately, so conscious Bex was keen to talk to her, and she wondered for a moment whether confiding in Bex about her family might at least show she still valued their friendship. But would she – could she – understand?

Her stomach rumbled and she idly opened one of the tiny packets of biscuits on the side table. Chocolate chip shortbread. This really was a good hotel. As she munched, she turned her attention back to the photo while the kettle popped and fizzed behind her on its slow journey to boiling point.

And then she saw it.

There, in the bottom corner of the picture, in tiny capital letters. BISSON. The photographer's name was Bisson.

The shortbread ended up in a small heap on the carpet.

# CHAPTER TWENTY-EIGHT

'THANKS so much for seeing me, especially on a Sunday afternoon,' blurted out Felicity, as soon as Madame Bisson opened the door. *Slow down*, she told herself, *be cool*... and promptly tripped up the step on the way in. Madame Bisson caught her in surprisingly strong arms. Felicity caught a scent of lavender and white musk.

'We knew you'd come eventually. Just maybe not this soon!' she said, laughing lightly.

'I'm only staying for a few days,' said Felicity, apologetically.

'It's fine. Honestly. Come on through.'

Felicity followed her along the hallway anxiously and there, sitting in a small but very comfortable-looking lounge, with the fire blazing and an ancient chocolate Labrador asleep on a rug, was, presumably, Mr or Monsieur Bisson. His face looked rumpled, as though he may have been napping. The dog raised its head and wagged its tail in greeting but didn't get up. The room smelled of elderly dog and Old Spice.

'Have a seat, my dear,' said the man in a clipped British accent, waving his hand, and she took a seat opposite him. He gestured towards a teapot and cake stand on the table between them, encouraging her to help herself. *Oh God help me*, she thought as she lifted the heavy pot and poured the rather stewed tea carefully into a delicate china cup on their beautifully white tablecloth. She could feel Bisson studying her face intently. Her hand was shaking just a little but she managed not to spill it.

When she looked up, he smiled easily. He had crinkles around gentle brown eyes, a balding greying head and shoulders that were slightly hunched against the back of his armchair. He was resting his slippered feet on a carpeted foot stool. She would have guessed he was about ten years older than his wife.

'So, my dear,' he said when she was settled and had recklessly begun munching on a piece of Battenburg without anticipating that, of course, they'd be expecting her to speak.

His wife ('*Cherie*') seated herself on the large sofa next to Felicity.

'Tell me what you want to know,' he said, gently.

Felicity hastily swallowed a mouthful of somewhat dry pink sponge, and said, 'Tell me everything you know about Le Manoir, please.'

Mr Bisson ('Albert,' he said, 'but everyone calls me Bertie') told her what he knew. He told her the history of the house, when it was built, how it had housed a minor royal for a few years, how Queen Victoria had once visited for tea during a tour of the area. All things she already knew from her own research. She listened patiently, nodding politely, and let him speak. His words washed over her, they had a lovely, poetic quality, and she felt a bit sleepy in the warm room. It occurred to her how safe she felt with these people. She didn't find that often. *Whatever you do, Felicity, don't fall asleep in this random stranger's house. That would be terribly bad form.*

When he finally finished, she thanked him and then took a deep breath.

'Can you tell me why the family left, monsieur?' she said,

tentatively. 'Your wife mentioned that it's owned by the bank now? Is that correct?' She picked up another piece of cake without thinking about it, then decided it would be rude to put it back on the plate and shoved it into her mouth in one go instead.

'It's Bertie, my dear. And one question at a time, if you please,' he replied, not unkindly.

'Yes. I'm sorry,' she managed to mumble, trying not to spit pink crumbs all over the carpet.

'It's okay, my brain just works a bit slower than it used to, that's all. Yes, it's owned by the bank. It was repossessed about twenty years ago when they could no longer afford the bills. Family break-up, as I understand it. I suppose it was an expensive place to keep.'

Felicity nodded. She swallowed the last bit of cake and opened her mouth to respond, but no words were available to her, suddenly.

'I heard they moved to England,' he continued, studying her closely. 'Somewhere up north, I believe. I'm afraid I can't be more specific.'

She nodded again as a single tear escaped from her eye and wandered down her cheek. *Keep it together*, she told herself sternly.

'And you were the photographer, right?' she said, thrusting the newspaper clipping towards him, wiping her cheek with the back of her hand.

Bertie took it but didn't look at it. 'Yes, I was the photographer.'

'And...' She trailed off, her voice catching in her throat. 'And did you know the family at all?'

'A little,' he said, nodding his head slowly. Then he looked at her with solemn eyes. 'You look just like her, you know. Except for the red hair, of course. That's all yours.'

Felicity's heart started to flip and bang against her rib cage.

'Really?' she said, not able to say more.

'Indeed.' His cheeks flushed. Could it be the heat of the room? 'She was very beautiful. Incredibly beautiful,' he said, fondly, looking down at the clipping for the first time. 'I loved to take her photograph.'

Felicity glanced at Cherie, who was staring down at her hands fixedly.

Then suddenly it all became clear.

'She was looking at you,' she said, before she could filter it. 'In the photo. She was staring at you.'

Bertie looked at her steadily for a moment, and then nodded.

'They were lovers, for a time, yes,' came the voice of Cherie from her right, quiet but very firm. 'It was a long time ago.'

Felicity nearly stood up but controlled the impulse. She considered reaching for her cup – just for something to do really – but she didn't trust herself not to spill it this time. Instead, she grabbed a nearby cushion and hugged it tightly against her lap. Bertie and Cherie waited patiently.

*Things just got weird.*

'Sorry, can you just say that again?' she finally managed.

Bertie laughed then, and it was a light and lovely and unexpected sound.

'I can say it now, I suppose,' he said, smiling at her. She could see how handsome he must have been, still was, really, with those lovely deep brown eyes. 'I was in love with her. Your beautiful mother. Jocelyn.'

It had been a long time since she'd heard anyone say that name. The tears began rolling in earnest down Felicity's cheeks and Cherie put a gentle arm around her shoulders.

'She was beautiful,' she said, quietly.

'That was the day we met,' he said, his eyes on the clipping.

'I thought it was the most boring assignment on the island. "Go cover the garden party at Le Manoir," they said. I nearly didn't go. But the moment I set eyes on her... she was just captivating. The most perfect subject. Look at her. Just look at her.'

Cherie shifted slightly in her seat, her arm dropping from Felicity's shoulders.

Felicity cleared her throat.

*What the hell have I stumbled into?*

'And you... you're the reason my father walked out?' she said slowly, as realisation after realisation washed over her.

'I'm the reason,' he said, serious then. 'I knew she had a family, and I should have just stayed away. But I couldn't help myself. I sent her a present for Christmas, left it on the doorstep, that's all, but your father found it and somehow he knew straight away what was going on. Must have already had his suspicions, I suppose.'

'What did you give her?' said Cherie, a little more sharply than perhaps she had intended. She visibly checked herself and then got up and started busying herself clearing away the tea things.

Bertie gave a little smile.

'It was a paperweight,' he said. 'Just a paperweight.'

Felicity let out a little gasp. 'It wasn't just a paperweight.' She almost shrieked. 'I bet it was a red glass heart. I still have it.'

Bertie looked at her, astonished.

Felicity nodded.

'She kept it,' he said with a secret smile.

'Yes,' said Felicity. 'She kept it.'

The paperweight was the thing.

In fact, the paperweight was the only thing Felicity really had of her mother's these days, apart from a few scarves and a couple of her old books. For as far back as she could remember it had taken pride of place on their mantelpiece, in their tiny mouldering cottage. It was a deep ruby red and perfectly shiny and flawless, or at least most of it was. Ominously, it had an almighty crack down the middle that at some point had been fixed with amber-coloured resin. Felicity had always assumed it was a flaw in the glass but now she wasn't so sure.

'Can I see it?' said Bertie conspiratorially, as Cherie bustled out of the room to put the kettle on.

'I don't have it with me, I'm afraid.' *It would be a bit weird if I did.*

'Oh. Oh well, that's okay. Anyway, your father was so furious he walked out the very next day. Dreadful, really, to leave you children like that.'

'It really was.' She paused. 'At least it makes a little more sense now,' she said, conscious she sounded a little pointed.

Bertie looked tired. 'I was young and very, very stupid. I'm so sorry, Felicity.'

'It's okay,' she said, not sure if it was okay or not. It was a relief, in some ways, to find out there was a reason. It had been her mother who was cheating. Of course, it was. It made so much more sense. Their father had walked out on them because *she* was cheating.

Bertie was staring at the photo again. He seemed sweetly unashamed of his love for this lady, despite his wife being present.

As Felicity looked at him, something dawned. She realised she knew him. Had seen him before.

'You came to our house for dinner!' she said, suddenly.

Bertie looked up at her in surprise.

'I did. Fancy you remembering that. You were so tiny. I came for dinner not long after the garden party. I brought my girlfriend at the time, actually. I don't even remember her name, isn't that dreadful? I thought that would serve as a good cover because, really, I just wanted to see your mother again.'

'I remember, you brought her flowers and she looked so happy. We got to stay up late that night. We got the leftovers, always our favourite.'

'Your mother was a terrible cook,' said Bertie, fondly. 'But the caterers were bloody fantastic.'

Felicity laughed. She couldn't remember the food from the caterers. All she remembered was helping her mother make the hors d'oeuvres. Early 90s style, of course. Prawns on Primula on Ritz crackers and mushroom vol au vents. Classic.

'And my dad?' she said, cautiously. 'Do you think he caught on at that point?'

Bertie looked thoughtful. 'I don't know. I could never work your father out. He looked like a movie star, such a handsome man, but he always seemed cross. Like maybe your mother didn't love him like he wanted her to. He seemed so...'

'Unpredictable,' said Felicity, feeling treasonous.

'That's it,' said Bertie quickly. 'You could never tell what he might do.'

'Yes,' said Felicity. *You have no idea.*

'He came to see me after that Christmas.'

Felicity went cold. 'What did he do?'

'Oh, nothing, nothing exactly. He came to see me, to look me in the eye, I think. He was so furious. He threatened to "make the lights go out", if I recall. I stood up to him. I was braver in those days. Later on, it turned out, he was cheating on your mother too. We only found that out when he moved in with his bit of stuff and her children.'

So, her father was still a bastard, just as she had always suspected. But he hadn't been a completely mad bastard. At least he'd had his reasons. Even if walking out on Boxing Day was still an unbelievably horrific thing to do, he actually had his reasons for doing it, and – weirdly – that meant a whole lot.

# CHAPTER TWENTY-NINE

THAT NIGHT, Felicity ordered the second biggest dinner she had ever eaten. She was ravenous. Stale Battenburg at the Bissons' was the only thing she'd consumed since Saturday morning's breakfast, and she felt as though she'd lived an entire lifetime since then.

She sat in the opulent dining room in her hotel and tucked into a massive veggie burger with a mound of chips, followed by two helpings of decadent chocolate mousse just like she remembered from that wonderful holiday. She declined the gin tonight, though. It wasn't called Mother's Ruin for nothing.

As she ate, she hid her tear-ravaged face behind her trusty copy of *Ulysses* and pretended to read while she thought about everything she had learned, trying to avoid conversation with her fellow guests. And the hot barman, for that matter, although she had definitely felt his eyes on her as she walked past him earlier. She wondered idly if he'd still look at her that way if he could see what she'd just put away. And then she decided she didn't care. She was officially 'Felicity Two-Puddings' now but, today of all days, she deserved it.

*What an afternoon.*

Felicity had ended up curled in a ball on Bertie and Cherie's comfortable old floral sofa, sobbing her heart out, with Cherie patting her arm at intervals and the stinky old dog ('Moses, thirteen years old, likes ice cream and orange Fanta') nuzzling her hand. It had felt good in a strange way. The questions she'd had for so long, the gap, the reason for her father's bizarre behaviour, all were becoming clearer.

She couldn't help feeling a tiny bit vindicated. If her mother... if Jocelyn *had* been cheating on her father just as Bertie said, then he at least had a reason for doing what he did, rather than being a completely unfeeling monster which, Felicity thought with a twinge of guilt, is kind of how she had him pegged. Even better, it meant she wouldn't necessarily have inherited the unfeeling monster genes after all. It wasn't necessarily in her genes or her make up or her nature or any of that nonsense. It felt something like freedom.

Of course, cheating on people might still be in her genes. If that was the sort of thing that could be coded into them. Felicity wasn't sure and made a mental note to do some googling later. Because she suddenly knew, and with frightening clarity, that Bertie hadn't been the only man to visit the house. Her father was often away, travelling to the mainland for his work as a surveyor, and her mother had never let her social life suffer as a result. As children they had assumed these mysterious 'visitors' were just friends, had pictured them sitting around in the 'smart dining room' with their mother, elegantly dressed, playing cards or embroidering cushions or some other Austen-like activity.

*Oh God.*

Felicity felt uncomfortably hot and uneasy at the thought that those innocent soirees might have been something Other... but she had to admit there were a lot of men. A lot. A whole lot of single men. Visiting late. Leaving early. She could see some of their faces if she concentrated hard enough. Not that she wanted to.

Even in Derbyshire, there had been visitors. She remembered them coming now, knocking on the door for a late 'supper' with their mother. They were sent to bed early on those evenings, but it was such a small place they could always hear the murmurings from downstairs. And other sounds too, laughter, sometimes crying, the sound of glasses chinking and strange, animalistic noises coming from their mother's bedroom on the other side of the rickety stairs. Funny, thought Felicity, how she had managed to block this all out until now. The metaphorical equivalent of sticking her fingers in her ears.

She had always found it a strange dance, the mystery of other people's sex lives. How on earth did anyone ever know who was sharing a bed with whom? Or who had an 'understanding', as it were? And how did it come about? It was like a card game she had never learned the rules for. These nightly goings on always seemed so separate from the mundane day to day of living; ethereal, somehow, and yet so base at the same time. Was that a British thing? Perhaps. It seemed inconceivable, in particular, to think that Felicity's incredibly beautiful and poised mother had ever been naked in the presence of a man. Blimey, no. Let alone multiple men. No wonder Felicity had blocked it out. She wondered if Tristan knew and had kept it from her all these years.

That night, her sleep was filled with lurid images of her mother in the arms of a succession of naked strangers, and even an elderly Bertie, complete with carpet slippers and a pipe. It was not a pretty picture. She woke up in the early hours in a cold sweat, her heart racing, and wrapped her arms around herself. *Jocelyn, what a hot mess you were.*

After a while, her heart slowed but she couldn't sleep. Instead, she lay in the dark, cocooned in luxurious sheets and the complete darkness and silence of the hotel. Of the island, for that matter. And as she lay there, she wondered exactly how many other latent traumatic memories she had buried deep inside her. It was time, she thought, to get some help.

But Felicity still had two more days on Guernsey. And despite everything, she was determined to make it feel like a holiday.

It wasn't that hard. The place was just so beautiful. On Monday morning she got up early and walked and walked and walked and, as she did so, she rolled all this new information around in her mind like savouring a new flavour of ice cream. And as she wandered, she found fields that would soon be drifting with rare orchids, watched birds of prey wheeling overhead and got deliciously lost exploring the 'green lanes', cliffs and footpaths that were supposed to be reminiscent of Devon and Cornwall. There were stunning coves and beaches and ancient architecture all over the island, it seemed, and all with a delightful French flavour, a little like the Bissons, in fact.

In the afternoon she finally managed to catch a boat to the nearby island of Herm. Her face nearly froze off during the short and deserted boat ride over, but she found peace and solitude on the tiny island rumoured to be a favourite of Cliff Richard, of all people, and she walked the entire circumference from high cliffs to low beaches in a couple of hours. Halfway round, she thought she saw a seal bobbing and disappearing amongst the waves. Puffins and dolphins could be seen here too, at the right time of year, and in the spring and summer it was awash with wildflowers. Perhaps old Cliff wasn't so bad after all.

# CHAPTER THIRTY

By Tuesday, she was even starting to feel a little bit relaxed.

After breakfast – *smoked salmon and scrambled eggs, if you don't mind, thank you very much* – she decided to head to the north side of the island. Sexy barman – whose name, she had discovered, was Colin – had advised her there was a great walk to Fort Pembroke right in the far north east where you could sometimes see gannets diving into the English Channel and where, usually, you had a beautiful stretch of coastline to yourself, and she was feeling peculiarly excited about it. She had even contemplated asking Colin if he'd like to join her.

Okay, total disclosure, she had actually asked Colin if he wanted to join her, but he'd given a wry smile and flashed her his wedding ring. Felicity immediately resolved to pretend that never happened as she backed rapidly away from the bar, muttering something about a misunderstanding under her breath.

*Cringe.*

*Moving on.*

The morning was bright and fresh and she lingered in reception looking at all the leaflets for local attractions, pretending it wasn't nearly time to go home, before heading to her hire car. Her heart was feeling light with possibility as she skipped down the entrance steps, and then something stopped her dead in her tracks.

Leaning against the car, looking for all the world as if he owned the whole bloody island, was Adam.

Felicity's jaw clenched shut. She was rooted to the spot.

'Hello, you,' said Adam, pushing himself away from the car with one foot as if this was a perfectly normal scenario.

'What the hell are you doing here?' said Felicity. Her voice had a definite wobble.

'Well, would you believe it? I've been meaning to come over for ages. The firm has a very – shall we say "worthwhile" – client in St Peter Port – and when I found out you were here at the same time, it was too good an opportunity to pass up. What a coincidence, eh?'

When her face started working normally again, Felicity raised an eyebrow to the sky.

'And you expect me to believe you've come all this way just for some property deal?'

'Oh but this is not just any property. This is Guernsey property.' Adam waved his arms around in the vague direction of the rest of the island, then grinned. 'Fine. I wanted to see you.'

'Yes, well, your timing couldn't be better. I booked this trip specifically so I could bump into you.'

'Ah. Sarcasm. There's the Brooks I love.'

He took a couple of steps towards her and she pretended not to notice how good he was looking in his white shirt and jeans combo against the expansive blue Guernsey sky.

Her fists clenched. *You're mad with him, remember?*

'Seriously, why are you gate-crashing my lovely restful me-time? Don't you remember what happened in the pub?'

He held his hands out and flashed her that Tom Cruise smile. 'That's why I wanted to see you. I wanted to apologise in person. I thought... well, I hoped you might have calmed down by now. But if you want me to bugger off, say so and I'll go. No questions asked.'

'Bugger off.'

'But before you do that,' he continued smoothly, 'will you let me take you for a coffee?'

'Because that worked out so well last time?'

'Look, I'm here now.'

'On *my* holiday.'

'On your holiday. Well, it's my holiday too. I mean work trip. It's a work trip, did I mention that? It's gone on expenses and everything.'

*Damn, he's good.*

'I don't care what it is. Will you kindly go back to your whatever it is now, please? *My* trip was going just fine without you.'

'It's just a coffee. I read about this great little place in St Martin's. And then I'll go, I promise, and let you get on with your, er, holiday or whatever it is.'

She was relenting. She could feel herself relenting, dammit.

Half an hour later, they were sitting at an iron table in the grounds of the impressive Saumerez Manor, armed with two enormous coffees and the thickest slices of Guernsey Gâche fruit loaf Felicity had ever seen.

'I thought you said this place was little.'

'I lied. It's meant to be great though. Best Gâche on the island apparently. Wait, that sounded wrong.'

'I think you'll find it's pronounced "gosh".'

He laughed knowingly. 'My mistake.'

A smile tugged at her lips but she was determined not to let him win her over, especially not over something so childish. She looked around her instead until she got her face back under control. The sun had come out and was warming the terrace pleasantly. Birds were nipping in and out of the greenery on the courtyard walls. It felt like being in the South of France, or so she imagined anyway. In spite of herself, she began to relax.

'I'm not sure if I've ever been here before.'

'Not even when you were a kid?'

'I don't think so.'

Adam put down his cup and looked across at her. His brown eyes looked hazel in this light.

*Stop that, Felicity.*

'Have you been to the house yet?'

'I went on Saturday.'

'And? How was it?'

'It's... sad. Run-down. There's no one living there even now and all the walls are losing their plaster.'

She began to spread the butter on her still-warm fruit slice, giving herself time to think.

'Ah that's a real shame.'

'It is. It's an amazing house but it's going to end up in ruins if no one saves it.' Felicity sighed. 'Much like my family.'

'I'm sorry.'

Adam took another sip of coffee and shifted in his chair.

*He'd better not be thinking about how much it's worth.*

'What are you doing here, Adam? I honestly can't imagine what else there is to say.'

He took a deep breath. 'I'm sorry for turning up like that. Please forgive me for hijacking your holiday.'

Felicity sat back and crossed her arms.

'I know how it looks but I genuinely do have to see a client tomorrow... honest. You can come with me if you don't believe me. You'd really like his place.'

He paused.

'But also... I had to see you.'

*There it is.*

'Why? What else is there to say, Adam? Seriously.'

'Well for starters, sorry. I'm so sorry for what I did. I know I've buggered everything up.'

'Yes, you have.'

'The truth is, Felicity...'

On reflex, Felicity took a bite of fruit slice. She chewed frantically without tasting.

*Talk about emotional eating.*

'What is the truth?' she said, mouth full.

Adam looked at her for a long moment. 'The truth is, I just don't think I can live without you.'

She stared at him. Waited. Chewed. Swallowed. Waited some more. Her heart was beating loudly in her ears, but she couldn't tell if it was with anticipation or fury.

'Please... give me another chance, Felicity,' he blurted out suddenly, reaching for her hand across the little table. 'I can be better; you make me better. I'm utterly crap without you, you of all people must know that.'

Felicity looked at his face, at his hand holding hers and she took a deep, determined breath. This man she had known so well, for so long. This man, who had steered her through so many choppy seas. This man, whose heart she broke and who broke hers right back.

'I... I'm not sure I can–'

He broke in, his face serious, brow furrowed. 'You can... it's easy. Just give me a chance.'

'I was going to say, I'm not sure I can trust you. Seriously. How could I ever trust you?'

Tears welled in her eyes out of nowhere, just when she was trying to keep it together.

Adam looked like he was about to deflate from the inside.

*Say something else.*

'Okay. Fine. Here's how it is. I can't believe I spent all that time feeling guilty for kicking you out on Christmas Day. Three years, Adam! I thought there was something wrong with me, like, pathologically!'

'I'm so sorry, Felicity. But it wasn't exactly a bed of roses for me either after you left. I was a wreck. I had to sleep in my car, for God's sake.' He paused. 'I guess I deserved it.'

'You think?'

Adam took his hand from hers and drained his coffee cup.

'Fine. Yes, I deserved it. I deserve a whole lot more than that, probably. It's just, when I fall for someone, I fall hard. What can I say?'

Felicity chose to ignore this.

'Tell me one thing,' said Felicity. 'This woman, you've apparently been with for the last... however long it's been. The one you were cheating on me with.'

'Tabitha.'

'Whatever. What happened to her? I mean, how come you broke up?'

He put his face in his hands, revealing a very expensive-looking watch on one wrist. Felicity was determined not to show him any sympathy. The watch helped.

After what felt like an eternity, while Felicity got more and more cross that he was ruining her break with this emotional shambles, he spoke through his fingers.

'Don't be mad,' he whispered.

'Oh my God.'

'I cheated on her too,' he said, the words tumbling out of him. 'I honestly don't know what's wrong with me. I knew things weren't right and I should just talk to her but instead I got drunk and met this girl in a bar and... well, you don't need to know the details.'

'Definitely not. I can't believe this. What the hell *is* wrong with you?'

'I don't know. Honestly. I have no idea.'

'And you were engaged.'

'Yes, we were engaged. God, I'm such a mess.'

He looked up at her, his dark eyebrows knitted together.

She *so* wanted to help him. She thought back over the years to all the times she had helped him, had made him feel good about himself when he was low, had stroked his ego.

*I am so not going there again. I just can't.*

'Adam, look, I know I like to rescue things and I think *you* think I'm going to rescue you in some way. That I'm the person who can prevent you from ending up alone. Because of course that's what you're afraid of. I can't believe I haven't seen it before.'

Adam visibly winced, as if he'd been struck.

'Yes, I know that's what this is all about. I'm not as dumb as you think. I know, we were each other's first love and everything that comes with that. And I always thought you were someone I could trust completely. But now? It's totally different now.' She was shaking with the force of her own words, her own truth.

'As much as anything else, you tried to fob me off with a ring you bought for someone else. Don't you realise that's verging on sociopathic? It's just not normal.' A tear rolled down her cheek and she wiped it away with the back of her hand. 'And the thing is. I deserve better.'

'You're right, you're right, of course.' He nodded. 'But I swear, the only time I've ever functioned properly in my entire life... was when I was with you.'

'Well, now you'll have to find someone else who makes you

feel like that. I'm sure you won't have any trouble. Girls seem to flock to you, after all.'

That last bit sounded more jealous than she had intended it to.

She stood up, her chair making a grotesquely noisy sound on the gravel, causing several heads to turn their way.

Adam reached for her hand again but she pulled it away.

'Wait. Can't I see you, sometimes, maybe? Just as friends? I miss you, Fliss. We've been through so much.'

'I don't think that's a good idea, do you?'

'Will you at least think about it?'

She sighed. 'I'll think about it.'

*What the hell is wrong with you, girl?*

'Thank you. And you're right, by the way,' he said. He was squinting at her in the bright sunlight, which at least meant his gorgeous eyes were not functioning at their full intensity.

'I know I'm right,' she said, arms crossed. 'About which part, exactly?'

'You do deserve better.'

He looked as though he might say something more. Then the moment passed. He gave a curt nod as she left the table and walked under the archway into the manor grounds. As she got halfway across the immaculate lawn she turned back, wondering if he might have followed her. Almost hoping he would for some twisted reason.

But no, she was alone again.

Alone, and confused.

*Nothing new there then.*

There were no more Adam incidents but she did spend the rest of the day wondering if he was going to show up again. Which was super annoying. And then most of the night running through their conversation over and over in her head.

*Bloody man.*

The next morning on her way to the airport, and still looking over her shoulder the whole time, she took a detour and knocked on the Bissons' door.

Cherie answered it. She looked tired.

'Oh, hello, my dear,' she said with a weak smile. She sounded tired too.

'These are for you,' said Felicity, handing over the flowers and chocolates she'd hastily bought from the petrol station on the way.

'Thank you, they are beautiful,' said Cherie, not looking at them.

'I just wanted to give you something...' Felicity tailed off. 'Um. Are you okay?'

'Me? Oh yes, my dear, thank you, I'm fine.'

'Thank you so much, for everything. You've changed my life. I mean that.'

Cherie looked at her for a long moment. Or past her, perhaps.

'You are welcome, my dear.' Then, after a pause, 'He's still in love with your mother.'

'Yes,' said Felicity. What else could she say? And then, 'I'm sorry.'

'It's okay,' said Cherie. 'I think I always knew he was, deep down. I suppose I asked for it really. I poked the bear. I could have just walked past you that day, couldn't I? You would have been none the wiser.'

'You were so kind to me, madame, I am just so grateful to you. I'm so sorry if it's caused problems for you.'

Cherie shrugged in a way that was already so familiar. 'You

coming here, someone coming for the house, it was always going to happen. I am glad you did. Honestly.'

'But you're also glad I'm going home?' said Felicity with a grin.

'Yes. Yes, I am also glad you are going home,' said Cherie gently.

'Will you be okay?'

Cherie gave her a tired smile. 'How do you say in English? We "rub along okay together". We'll be fine.'

# CHAPTER THIRTY-ONE

BACK TO WORK on Thursday morning, and an extremely grateful Sophie who looked like she'd worked for twelve weeks without a break, not just a few days. She threw her arms around Felicity's neck as soon as she walked in, chattering away about the animals and her experiences and how 'gorgeous' James was and how 'divine' Andrea was and being super enthusiastic about the whole thing, but Felicity could see and feel that she was exhausted.

And then she bumped into Andrea, who'd had to put up with Sophie's wafting about and general lack of common sense for an entire week. She looked tired too, and practically bear-hugged Felicity the minute she saw her, in a very unusual public display of affection.

The centre was a hive of activity. It seemed she'd picked the wrong moment to go away as they'd had phone call after phone call in her absence and the cages in the dog den and the cat nursery were now all completely full. It was bloody noisy in there too after her (mostly) peaceful time away, but she felt her heart gently warming as Andrea took her round and introduced her to some of the new arrivals. There were two bulldogs from the RSPCA, who had been neglected and starved and needed round-the-clock little-and-often feeding, three new cats including an ancient deaf white cat with only one eye –'Hit by a car, they think. She's super sweet. We've called her Little Miss Bump,' said Andrea, wryly – and four lop-eared rabbits who'd been left outside the front door in a cardboard box on Friday night ('Flopsy, Mopsy, Cotton Tail and Whatsit'). They were currently occupying a makeshift run in the corridor and seemed to be living their best lives as Sophie was absolutely smitten and kept sneaking them carrots.

She had missed her favourites of course, and they were delighted to see her too. Bobby Charlton leapt at the bars of his cage in his eagerness for a cuddle, Freddy didn't even growl when she walked in, and tiny Holly looked like she had grown three inches in the last week. Both Holly and Gennie were looking really strong, and Felicity was shocked at how much she had missed them.

'This is why I never take a holiday,' she whispered, nose to nose with little Bobby, taking in the digestive biscuit smell of his paws as he wriggled. She didn't regret it really, of course, but this place truly felt like home.

And when Andrea and Sophie asked her if she'd had a good time, she didn't quite know what to say. In some ways, yes, there was some healing, some closure. It had been very moving to see the house in real life after all this time. But the encounter with Adam had left her feeling peculiar. What had happened to him? He was a bit pathetic, and it was strange to see him in such a state. Had he really said he wanted her back? Was he serious?

She didn't even know where to begin with that. No sane person would ever contemplate going back to him, would they? Not after everything. Tiffany ring or not.

The ring.

There was a thought.

What happened to the ring? Did she leave it at the pub? When had she last had it? Did she throw it out of the window after all? Felicity couldn't remember. She made a mental note to search the flat when she got home. She felt a bit shocked that she hadn't thought about it for over a week but hopefully that was a sign of her impending liberation.

It was a nice ring. She might like to try it on again. But it wasn't on her nightstand, not behind the bed, nor down the side of the sofa, nor in any of the places she usually liked to drop important things. Maybe her subconscious had decided to 'misplace' it for her own good. Returning it would mean seeing him again, after all, which seemed to be becoming more and more dangerous.

She did manage to find her mother's paperweight in a shoebox at the bottom of her wardrobe and decided it was time it went on display. The ruby red glass was striking and when she placed it on her mantelpiece the shape of it refracted light from her lamp around the room like a rainbow. It made her smile.

Something else was missing too. There was still no message from James. No text, nothing, and Andrea hadn't even mentioned him. Felicity tried to tell herself this was perfectly normal but really his absence had been like a huge elephant – or penguin, maybe – in the room all day long.

What had happened? Where did he keep disappearing to? It was all very mysterious. She felt really guilty about letting Adam get into her head and so she'd already decided she needed to do something about the whole Penguin Man situation when she got back from her holiday – but now she couldn't quite put her finger on what or how to make it right. Instead, the worry just nagged, nudged and niggled at her insides, and when she finally slept her dreams were lurid and unsettling. She woke with a start at 6am and sent him a text message she knew she would probably regret later even though it was as breezy as she could make it under the circumstances.

> Hey you, just got back from the trip and I'd love to see you, hope you are doing okay, give me a shout when you are free, hope you're okay F xx

*Damn. Said 'hope you're okay' twice there. This is why you should never send an impulse text.*

When her alarm buzzed at 7.30am she immediately checked her phone but there was no reply.

*It's still early,* she told herself.

'What the hell did you do to Adam?' said Bex without preamble when they finally met for coffee a couple of days later.

Felicity slid gingerly into the booth beside her, clutching her huge mug of peppermint hot chocolate. Man, she loved the winter.

'What do you mean?' she said, blowing on its surface and poking at the marshmallows with one finger.

'Well, I saw him yesterday and he's in bits. Absolute bits. I was tempted to take him home and adopt him, I'll be honest.'

'You should,' said Felicity, wryly. 'He needs taking in hand.'

She looked up in time to catch a slight flush creeping across Bex's neck. Bex quickly moved her scarf to cover it, but she was a nanosecond too late.

'You want to take him in hand!' said Felicity, and as she said it, it made perfect sense. Bex and Adam. How had she never seen it before?

Bex looked down at her coffee. She tapped a sugar packet an

excessive number of times before she finally ripped it and tipped it into her latte. She stirred it ferociously, staring straight ahead of her. Felicity waited patiently, feeling faintly amused for some reason. When Bex finally spoke, though, it was little more than a whisper, and it shocked Felicity to her core.

'Been there, done that,' she said.

'I'm sorry, what?' said Felicity, leaning in.

'I said, I've been there, done that,' said Bex, a teeny bit louder, taking a sip of her drink and giving her friend a sideways look.

'You never...?' Felicity's eyes widened and her stomach dropped all in the same moment.

*What the hell...?*

'Just once, mind.'

'When?'

'Just after you broke up.'

Felicity shot her a look.

'No, not then,' said Bex hastily. 'The first time. When you went to university. It was a one-time thing. Never to be repeated.'

'Never?' said Felicity, raising an eyebrow.

'No! Never. I would never do that to you.'

'It sounds like you already have!'

Bex ducked her head, sheepishly.

'I actually wouldn't mind,' said Felicity, to her own surprise. 'Genuinely. In fact, you two would make more sense in a lot of ways. But I should warn you, he's a serial cheater.'

Bex looked up at her then, her eyes shining, but her voice steady. 'I know. And that's not even the main issue.'

Oh God, Bex was actually in love with Adam. This was... unexpected.

'Er, I know I'll probably regret asking this question, but what is the main issue, exactly?'

'Surely you know what I'm talking about.'

Felicity took a sip of hot chocolate and then shrugged.

*I don't dare guess.*

'Come on, Felicity. The main issue is that he will never get over you. He's obsessed. He always has been. Even when he was with that Tabitha girl. He never got over you completely. I could never compete with that.'

Felicity flushed in spite of herself.

'Oh nonsense. It's not me he's obsessed with. It's just the idea of me. Not even that. The idea of someone. Anyone. I think the truth is he's just scared of ending up old and saggy and alone.'

Bex giggled.

*Best not mention he came all the way to Guernsey to see me a couple of days ago.*

'He'll move on soon, he's only ever been in love with himself, truth be told.'

Felicity stared at her own reflection in the coffee shop window. She wondered why she didn't feel more upset.

This was their favourite bijou independent café – there wasn't a Costa or Caffè Nero or any such chain in sight on this elegant street – and this was their favourite spot, wedged at the front of the shop in a leather booth, their backs to the baristas, with a perfect view of the lane, just right for people watching. Today, though, she was seeing a flashback of sorts as she stared into the glass. Adam and her, his face when she told him she was going away to study. His all too frequent and sometimes surprise visits to her in halls of residence. The way Tom the handsome barman had stepped aside so quickly when Adam came to see her that weekend.

*They had always had something.*

Before she could take that train of thought any further, Bex decided to drop the bombshell of all bombshells. She did it ever so casually, didn't even look up, almost delivered it under her breath, but Felicity heard every word.

'I didn't know Adam and that lovely penguin guy knew each other, by the way.'

Palms sweating instantly.

'Who? What?'

'The penguin guy, the one you met on the doorstep. The one you went on that date with.'

'Yes, I know the penguin guy. Penguin Man, I mean. But how do you know him? I mean James, his name is James.'

'Oh, I met him once,' said Bex, vaguely. 'I popped into the centre looking for you one day and he was there. He's gorgeous, by the way, but I think you're missing the point rather, darling.'

'Fine, okay, we'll come back to that. Anyway, James doesn't know Adam. I mean, he has met him, but I wouldn't say he knows him.'

'Oh.'

'What do you mean, "oh"?'

'Oh, well it must be my mistake. I could have sworn I recognised him the other day.'

'And?'

'And...' And here, Bex took a long slurp of her latte, presumably to eke out the drama. She did love a drama. Felicity rolled her eyes in mock jest at her friend, but her heart rate had definitely increased.

'And what?'

'And he was sitting in the pub. With Adam. I have been trying to tell you this, darling. You do keep ignoring my messages.'

There was a pause in the space-time continuum as Felicity processed this.

'He can't have been.'

'He was. I'm sure of it.'

'But he can't have been.'

'I know. You've said that a few times now.'

'But he can't have been sitting in the pub with him. They don't know each other. I mean, they've met in passing but that's it. It must have been a mistake. You must have made a mistake.'

'Fine.' Bex lifted her hands in surrender. 'I made a mistake.'

'When was this, exactly?'

Bex gave a long sigh and drained the last of her coffee. She picked up her phone and started scrolling idly, her beautifully manicured purple and silver nails tapping lightly on the screen.

'Like I said, it was a while ago.'

'But. What. Day. Was. It?' said Felicity through gritted teeth.

'I have no idea, a Friday, maybe...' Bex said breezily, while Felicity contemplated throttling her with her own Liberty scarf.

She put her head in her hands. 'It's important,' she said quietly, through her palms. 'It's really important. Can you remember anything else?'

Bex stopped staring at Facebook and made a show of concentrating. She pulled up her text messages.

'Okay, um, I don't know... I guess it was probably about two weeks ago.' She scrolled for a moment and then poked at her phone with an elegant finger. 'Look,' – tap tap tap on the screen – 'here's the first time I texted you. That's what I wanted to tell you. I'd nearly forgotten about it, it's been so long.'

'Two weeks ago,' said Felicity, flatly. 'The Friday night, you say?'

'Yes. At least, I guess so.'

*The night before the Saturday no-show.*

'They didn't look friendly, that's what made me wonder. I didn't think they knew each other at all so it was surprising to see them together. And, well, James didn't exactly look comfortable.'

Felicity lifted her head and looked at her friend. 'How not comfortable?'

'Really not comfortable,' said Bex. 'Cross. He looked cross, to be honest, but then Adam does have that effect on people.' An attempt at another giggle which Felicity ignored.

'I have to see him.'

'You don't think... I mean, Adam wouldn't say anything awful, would he? He wouldn't do that would he?'

'He would,' said Felicity bitterly. She could feel the tears looming. 'And by the way, if you love Adam so bloody much, have him. You're welcome to him.'

She wrapped her coat around her and blundered out into the cold street.

*Let's try this again. Keep it light, remember.*

> Hey there, Mr Penguin Man, I'm back! How are you?

> Just wondered if you fancied meeting for a drink or something? Missed you at Saviours this week.

> x

James (two hours later – two hours!):

> Hey there CCL, great to hear from you, hope you had a lovely time away. We missed you at Saviours too! Sorry I didn't reply the other day.

> No worries at all, I know you're busy.

> A drink sounds great, but I'm swamped at the moment I'm afraid.

Okay, maybe another time.

*Ruined it.*

But how about a quick coffee next Saturday? Could meet you at that little place in town you're always going on about? 10.30?

Felicity (a little too hastily):

Sounds perfect, see you then.

*Thank God.*

But how was she going to wait another week? And why was he being so cagey? As if she didn't know. Bloody Adam had a lot to answer for. Felicity lay awake for a long time that night. At 3am and really just for something to do that didn't involve men, she emailed a local therapist to make an appointment.

*At least I'll have something to regret in the morning.*

# CHAPTER THIRTY-TWO

'Come in, Felicity. Have a seat.'

Felicity edged into the therapist's room and looked around.

It looked normal. Just what she had expected, in some ways. Potted plant in the corner: check. Leather-topped desk in front of the window: check. Comfortable chairs with a coffee table between them: check. Man-sized box of Kleenex: check.

No chaise longue or couch though. Not like you'd see in a *Times* cartoon. But then her therapist wasn't a cartoon dog, either.

'Just sit wherever you feel most comfortable,' said the therapist.

Her name was Hattie, of all things, and she had a friendly schoolteacher-ish look about her. She was wearing a mustard yellow cardigan over a long grey dress and a pair of kitten heels. Her dirty blonde-grey hair was piled on top of her head in a reassuringly messy bun, and she had a pair of glasses balanced in front of it. Felicity was dying to look to see if she had any pencils stuck in the bun, but she thought that might appear a tad rude. The room smelled vaguely exotic, like incense, but not too much, the scent was very faint and just wafted across the room every so often, conjuring up opulent images of faraway markets and peppermint tea.

Felicity sat – or rather, perched awkwardly – on the edge of one of the comfortable chairs, which was a lovely deep orange velvet and had upright wooden arms. After a few seconds, her hands began to cramp from gripping the arms rather too forcefully and with an effort she unclenched them, put them in her lap and tried to relax. Resisted the urge to march right out of the door again. *Deep breaths.*

Hattie sat opposite her in a matching chair and crossed her legs. She peered at Felicity as if already assessing her. Felicity concentrated on trying to look normal.

'So, Felicity,' she said. 'What brings you to see me today?'

Until she opened her mouth, Felicity didn't know what was going to come out. And then – wow – it all came out in a rush. So much so that after a couple of minutes Hattie held up a hand, a smile spreading across her face.

'I'm sure that's all very interesting and relevant, Felicity. Unfortunately, you're speaking so fast I can't understand a word you are saying,' she said gently. 'Take a deep breath and start again, can you?'

'Sorry.'

'And don't be sorry. I won't allow any apologies in my therapy room. Unless you were to stand on my foot of course,' she added, still smiling.

'Fair enough,' said Felicity. She sat back a little.

'So, let's start again, shall we? What brought you to see me today? Take your time.'

Felicity could feel her heart hammering in her ears. 'I'm here because I don't know who I am,' she said. And there it was. Tears prickled behind her eyes.

'Go on,' said Hattie.

'I thought I knew. I mean, I really did think I knew who I

was, Hattie.' She cringed at this familiar use of the therapist's name, but Hattie didn't seem to mind. She was listening intently.

'It sounds really angsty and childish, I'm sure, but I genuinely don't know who I am. I don't ever seem to know my own mind, what I want, how I feel about things. And I think it's probably because I've never really had anyone around me to bounce things off? Do you know what I mean? It's always been me having to work things out on my own.'

'I'm sorry to hear that,' said Hattie. 'Have you ever had any role models in your life, that you can think of? People you've looked up to?'

'I do now, I guess. I have friends. My boss, perhaps. She's pretty cool. But no, there was no one when I was growing up.'

'No one?' said Hattie, making a note.

'No one. And I do mean no one.'

'What about your parents?'

'They were completely useless.'

Hattie looked up from her notes, sharply. 'Define "useless".'

'Literally useless. Ineffectual. Ineffective. "An item having no use". They were non-parents, really.'

'Those are very strong words, Felicity.'

'In this case, justified.' Felicity could feel her jaw clenching.

Hattie nodded slowly, as if sizing her up. 'Okay. Do go on. What effect has that had on you, on how you live your life?'

'It's affected everything, I reckon. Mostly because I've spent my adult life being terrified that I might end up like them.' She paused. 'I say *them* but I really mean *him*.'

'Your father?'

'Yes. I've always thought I was like him. Or at least, that I could be like him. That I had that potential.'

'And that's obviously not something you wanted? To emulate him?'

'God, no.'

'And why is that? Can you be more specific than "useless"?'

*How long have you got?*

'He... hurt us badly when I was young. He hurt me badly when I was young, and I never quite got over it.'

Hattie scribbled something in her notebook. Felicity took a breath.

'But now – recently – I found out it wasn't just my dad who was... well, bad. My mum was too, she was just as bad as him. Maybe even worse. And so now I have a whole new parent trauma I don't know what to do with. Honestly, my parents are – wait, am I being a real cliché right now? I just heard myself then and I sounded like a proper therapy cliché.'

Hattie laughed gently. 'There's a good reason that parenting traumas are therapy clichés,' she said, simply.

'You could write a whole book about mine,' replied Felicity.

'Let's start with one session, shall we? Why don't you tell me a little more about your family?'

And so, she did.

# CHAPTER THIRTY-THREE

Felicity came out of that first session feeling lighter. Freer, in a way, although she was absolutely exhausted too. Hattie had said she might need to lick her wounds afterwards, that she might feel a bit bruised. And she was right. But it still felt brilliant to be able to tell someone about her mum and dad without feeling guilty about betraying them in some way. Well, she mostly didn't feel guilty. And she couldn't wait for her next session, which was sort of the opposite of how she had expected to feel.

But there was something else she needed to get out of her system. As well as lighter, she also came out of that session ready to do something a teensy bit reckless.

Tristan Brooks. What a name.

As Felicity scanned her brother's Facebook profile the next day for the umpteenth time, she tried to conjure up some feelings of sibling affection... some semblance of emotion or empathy, some glimpse of filial love, but truth be told, it was like looking at a stranger. He could be some random guy off the street for all he meant to her. It was sad... but then he was the one who had left, after all (she told herself).

When they were young, Tristan and Felicity were so close that people often mistook them for twins, which was understandable given they were both pale and ginger and skinny. But while her skin was clear and her hair was closer to auburn, Tristan's face was covered in freckles and his hair was bright orange, so that he was visible from streets away, and on a small island like Guernsey the two of them together were a rarefied sight. And that meant they were made a fuss of wherever they went, or so her nana had always told her. When they vanished off the radar it's a wonder more people didn't notice or alert the authorities, but as far as they knew, no one ever did.

They had jump-started their lives in Derbyshire the best they could, trying to fit in at school, scraping together money for the bus, for uniforms, for school trips, doing their best not to draw attention to themselves as if they could sense even at such a young age that someone paying attention would not be good for their little family unit.

Felicity had always looked up to Tristan in those days, especially at school, he was clever and sharp-witted and popular. The day he announced he was moving out to live with their dad something died, something deep inside her shifted and although outwardly she had been calm, cold even, inside a huge chasm had opened up between them. He felt it too, she was sure of it, and as he packed his suitcase, he wouldn't even look at her or talk to her. His pale face had been flushed with two red spots on his cheeks from... what? Shame? Guilt? Or just sheer determination? That's what had hurt the most, his bloody-minded determination to get the hell out of there and the fact he never thought to take her with him. Now more than ever it felt like such a turning point in her life. Where would she be now if she had insisted on going along, packed her tiny suitcase and sneaked onto the train with him?

Another life.

She narrowed her eyes and zoomed in. His profile photo never gave much away, usually an arty shot, all shadow and light and trickery. The odd glimpse of that signature red hair.

She opened the Messenger app and started to tap out a message.

Then she shut it again.

Then opened it again.

How the heck do you start a message like that? 'Hey bro...?' 'Hi there...?' 'How's life?'

She settled for Dear Tristan.

> Dear Tristan, I hope this message finds you well and I'm sorry for dropping you a line out of the blue like this but I feel awful that we've lost touch. It would be wonderful to have the chance to chat sometime. Let me know if you could stand to do that. It would mean a lot to me. Take care and love always, Felicity.

As she finished and prepared to send, the green dot beside Tristan's name appeared. He was online. He would see this immediately. Damn. He might already know she was messaging him. There was no going back now. She hit send and then clasped her hands together to stop them shaking.

His little icon moved down next to her message. He had seen it. She waited a few minutes, and then a few more... hoping against hope that he would respond quickly and put her out of her misery but no. Of course not. He had never been that kind of guy. He would make her suffer, she felt sure of it.

And she was right. There was no response that day. Or the next.

Finally, on the third day of hovering over the message every spare second she got, the words 'Tristan is typing...' appeared. And with it, a sick feeling deep down in her gut.

> Dear Fliss. It's good to hear from you. Chatting is what I do best. Love, Tristan.

*Thank God.*
Felicity (responding immediately):

> I'm very glad to hear it.

Tristan (after an hour):

> Good. That's settled then. I'm working tonight but I'll message you properly later, okay?

> Okay 😊

A bubble of hope swelled and popped in her chest.

Of course, he didn't message later that night.

He didn't message back the next day, either.

But he did. Eventually. Tentatively. Politely. Perhaps even apologetically.

It was a start, she thought.

# CHAPTER THIRTY-FOUR

AFTER A WEEK of torment from all angles, on Friday afternoon Andrea finally addressed the small matter of the penguin in the room.

'So, any news from our mutual friend?' she suddenly said during their lunch break, after a particularly busy morning doing meets and greets with potential rehomers.

Felicity feigned innocence. 'Our mutual what?'

'You know exactly who I mean. Tall? Broad?' (So broad!) 'Handsome? Blond? Am I ringing any bells yet?'

Felicity let out a giggle that she hoped sounded nonchalant. 'Oh, him!'

Andrea raised one eyebrow and peered at her over her glasses. 'Yes, of course, him. Penguin Man. James. Who else? Have you heard from him? Are you two getting it on or what?'

'I really don't think you're supposed to ask me questions like this during work time,' said Felicity, piously.

'Fine, I'll just ask you later.'

'Fine.'

'Fine.' She paused. 'Okay, no, we are not dating. No, I don't know if he's available. No, I haven't seen him, and no, I don't know what went wrong. Okay?'

She didn't mention the planned coffee. She was nervous enough about it without getting Andrea all wound up.

'Right,' said Andrea, her mouth twitching.

'What do you mean, right?' said Felicity, voice strained with the effort of appearing breezy about this thing that she was most definitely not breezy about.

'I mean, I don't entirely believe you, but I'll let it go for now.'

'How can you not believe me? Why would I lie? And also, I really like him.' Felicity hadn't planned on saying this last bit. 'I didn't mean to say that last bit.'

'I know.'

'You know I didn't mean to say that last bit or you know I really like him?'

'Both.'

'Right.'

'Well, if it's meant to be, it'll work out,' said Andrea.

'I think that's the most philosophical thing I've ever heard you say.'

'Yes, well, what of it? Get on with your work, break time's over.'

Felicity grinned. Andrea grinned right back. And with that, they both went back to work.

It was time.

It had only been three weeks since she last saw him, but it felt like way more revolutions of the earth than that. Things had changed. So many things.

Penguin Man was waiting in the Bex booth when she arrived, and he put his hand up in greeting and gave a little grin as she slid in beside him just as she had with Bex the week before. This time, her emotions were somewhat different. This time, she did spill some of her coffee on the table, which at least gave her an excuse not to look at him directly for a few moments while she mopped it up with her sleeve, the coffee smell soaking into the fabric and making her nose wrinkle.

He looked absolutely gorgeous. Of course he did.

He was wearing a cap, for the first time that she'd seen, which made him look more chiselled than usual, his blond hair slightly less unruly but still straying a bit at the sides. His blue-grey eyes looked super blue against his white Lacoste polo shirt, and as she squeezed into the booth she remembered just how, um, well-built he was. She could feel his huge arm pressed against her puny one and her heart started to pound furiously as if it intended to betray her. She was tempted to shush it, but she knew that would only make it beat faster.

'Penguin Man,' she said with a grin, staring down at her coffee and trying to remember that he had let her down a few times. That he had definitely cooled off for some reason. That she needed to play it cool at least until she knew what was going on. The barista had swirled an arty little clover leaf into the crema, which had now sloshed to one side of course and she tried to make her brain focus on the resulting messy swirl and hoped the side of her face wasn't blushing.

'Crazy Cat Lady,' said James, giving her a little nudge.

'How have you been?'

'Fine, fine, how are you?'

She could feel him looking at her, but his face was so close she found it impossible to raise her eyes to his. She stared straight ahead instead and then realised she could see both their reflections quite clearly in the window in front of them, partly thanks to the mist and fog that was hanging over the whole town. James' reflection was staring at hers quite intently.

'I'm okay,' she said slowly. 'I'm okay.'

'Well, you sound okay.'

'I am okay.'

'That's good then.'

They both giggled, and Felicity finally turned and looked him in the eye.

'Where have you been?'

'I might ask you the same question.'

'I asked you first.'

James looked pained. He stared down at his half-drunk cappuccino and for a second, she regretted asking him, afraid of what he might say.

'I've had some stuff to work out,' he said eventually.

'That's not an answer,' said Felicity. 'What kind of stuff?' *He's secretly married. He's secretly married to a man. He's fallen in love with Sophie. He's fallen in love with Andrea. He's moving to Bermuda. On and on and on went her brain.*

There was a long pause. His eyes dropped to her lips and despite all her doubts, a delicious tingling sensation ran down the back of her neck. Just as she was sure he was going to lean in to kiss her, he turned and looked down at his mug again.

'Something I said?' she said before she could stop herself.

'Ha. More like something you did,' came the reply.

'What's that supposed to mean?' she retorted sharply.

'Well, you're messing with a man's resolve. Coming in here, looking like that, when I was all determined that I was going to keep it together.' He was speaking in that low, suggestive voice of his and Felicity felt like her entire body was blushing.

After a beat, she replied in a bolder tone than she really felt. 'And why would you need to keep it together, exactly?'

James gave a long sigh. 'Because I promised I would.'

# CHAPTER THIRTY-FIVE

'Run that by me again,' said Felicity, tapping her fingers on the table rhythmically to try and keep herself calm.

'Your "friend" Adam, he came to see me a couple of weeks ago.' James was methodically taking all the sugar packets out of the bowl and arranging them on the table by colour as he spoke. Pink sweeteners. Brown demerara. White caster.

'To be clear, he's not my friend. Came to see you where exactly?'

'At my work. He came to see me at my office.'

Felicity made a mental note to ask him where he worked later. She had managed to glean that it was some kind of office job during their shifts together, but probably should have pried a bit deeper. Or, you know, a bit.

'And?'

'And he offered to take me for a drink.'

'And?'

'And I agreed.'

'Yes, obviously, you agreed, although I have no idea why.'

'The poor bloke was a mess. He wanted to talk, who was I to turn him down?'

Felicity had been making a mental list of all the questions this conversation was generating and it was already quite long. She rubbed her forehead with her thumb and forefinger and tried to focus.

'And so, you met him for a drink? Then what happened?'

'He said he was still in love with you, and he asked me to back off. Begged me, really. It was quite touching. He said I needed to end it now before it went any further.' James took a deep breath. 'He told me all about your story, how long you two were together, you were childhood sweethearts, all that jazz. He said it was destiny for you two to end up together and I would just be getting in the way.'

'And you believed him?'

James looked sideways at her from under the cap. 'Of course. Well, I mean, I didn't know what to believe but there's a code.'

'I can't believe that's a real thing.'

'Well, there is, it's a guy thing. You and I had only ever had one kiss and so I didn't really feel I had much claim over you or anything. I mean, it was a hell of a kiss...'

As he said this, he leaned forwards ever so slightly so she could feel his breath on her ear, and it made her whole body vibrate...

'...but it was just a kiss and I wanted, I want, you to be happy. I really thought that if I backed off then you two could have a chance, and truth be told...'

He sounded strained, and Felicity sneaked a glance at his face.

'Truth be told?'

'Um... yes.' James shifted uncomfortably in his seat. 'And *truth be told*... I wasn't exactly free.'

Felicity jerked in surprise, knocking her coffee cup properly sideways this time. There was a brief interlude while she mopped ineffectually at the resulting stain with a tissue she found in her bag. It bought her vital seconds to gather herself together.

Eventually Felicity stopped mopping and summoned the courage to ask the question she had to ask.

'When you say "not free"...?' she said quietly, staring at the table in front of her.

'I mean, I had a small obligation to someone. I don't anymore.' This last part was added somewhat hastily.

'A small obligation? I'm afraid, much as I'd like it to be, this is not the Victorian era. No one has obligations these days.'

'Okay but I did.'

'Okay. Who to?'

James swallowed. 'It was a girl I'd been seeing... before Christmas.'

'Oh, right.' Felicity's attempt at nonchalance came out like a high-pitched squeak. 'Did *she* know it was small?'

'She does now. Sorry, that was a bit flippant, wasn't it? The poor girl. She was nice enough. Olivia, her name was. I just meant it was small in that we'd been out a couple of times... it was obvious it wasn't going anywhere... but I hadn't exactly broken it off. Do you know what I mean? I probably should have said something sooner.'

'Maybe that might have been a good idea, yes.'

'Sorry.'

'It does explain a few things.' She was pouting, she knew, but it was impossible to stop. 'Before Christmas you say? You mean, you were still with her when you met me?'

James sighed. 'I had been seeing her before I met you, yes. Briefly. Honestly it was just a couple of dates. She wasn't really my cup of tea. I should have ended it straight away but...'

'But she was keen.'

'Something like that, yes.'

*Bloody Andrea was always bloody right.*

'I'm sorry. I thought I was doing the right thing.'

'And now?' she asked, gently.

He looked deep into her eyes and there was that lightning again, this time striking in the pit of her stomach. It felt delicious.

'And now I realise I've made a huge bloody mistake.'

'That's not even the half of it,' said Felicity. 'Shall we get out of here?'

They bundled out of the booth, leaving the fug of the coffee shop behind them, and set off towards the town centre. It was a pretty place on a sunny day but today, through the mist and fog, the buildings loomed close on either side of them, pressed together and taller than usual, it seemed. It was like something straight out of a Dickens novel.

As they walked, Felicity proceeded to enlighten James on a few things about Adam. By the end of it, it was James' turn to vibrate, this time with rage.

'The absolute bastard!'

'That's about the size of it.'

They had reached the park without really meaning to, and both automatically slowed as they entered greener environs. Trees and bushes with misty tops surrounded them on all sides and the air was damp and thick as if they were walking through a cloud. They wandered for a few more minutes in heavy silence, eyes trained on the ground in front of them. Then, as if they were responding to an off-stage cue, they both stopped at the same moment and turned towards each other.

'The thing is,' said Felicity, looking up at her companion, 'he never really wanted me, but he never wanted anyone else to have me.'

James looked down at her, his eyes wide, his fists flexing. 'The man's a bloody idiot.'

'Well, that's a matter of opinion. He's definitely a bastard, that's for sure. But I think, deep down, he's afraid of being left alone.'

'We're all afraid of that. I'm sorry but that's no excuse. He's a bastard for cheating on you and a bloody idiot for letting you go.'

Felicity suddenly felt a bit hot and bothered. She held his stare for as long as she could manage and then dropped her eyes to his shoes.

'So, I have a question,' she said. 'This obligation. This *Olivia.*'

'Yes...'

'Is it definitely over?'

'It's over. It never really began. She was a nice girl and all but...'

Felicity held up a hand. 'That's enough detail, thanks. So... was there ever a black-tie party? On New Year? Or was that just your escape clause?'

James looked blank for a second before realisation spread across his features and lifted his eyebrows just a fraction.

'Oh that. There was a party. There was definitely a party. I just found myself not particularly wanting to go to it.' This in a low voice.

'Oh.' Felicity was properly blushing now. 'Oh, that's good, I mean. I like that answer.'

'Good.' James began moving towards her but Felicity put up a hand and he stopped obediently, an amused look on his face.

'Can I ask something else?'

'Do I have a choice?'

'What do you do for a living, exactly?'

James laughed out loud. Actually laughed. 'How do you not know that?'

'I don't know! I think we went too far down the line and then it was too late to ask. Like, you know, if you've met someone three or four times at a party or something it's far too late to ask them what their name is so you just have to pretend to know it? Or wait for someone else to say it? Like that.'

'I feel like whatever I say is going to be a huge disappointment at this point.'

'You're right, it will be. A horrible disappointment. On second thoughts, don't tell me, I'll just make it up instead.'

'Go on then. Can we walk though? It's bloody freezing.'

'Fine, let's walk,' said Felicity, slipping her arm through his. It felt deliciously solid through his thick coat.

They walked down the central path towards a large ornamental pond. Despite it being a busy Saturday, the place felt as if it had been abandoned, apart from one nuclear family at the water's edge. They could just make them out through the mist. There was a young mum and dad shepherding a tiny toddler, who was wrapped in a thick body suit and hood. He appeared to be feeding the ducks or was he torturing them? It was hard to tell. Ducks were scattering in all directions, that much was for sure.

Surveying the scene, feeling the solidity of that arm under her hand, Felicity's face began to ache. She was grinning like an idiot. She sneaked a look up at James and saw he had a huge smile on his face too.

'So, go on then,' she said, feeling it might be helpful to exercise her face a little. 'What do you do, exactly?'

'Ah no, that's cheating, you said you were going to guess.'

'Actually, I said I was going to make it up.'

'Go on then, give it a go.'

'Spy?'

'No.'

'Astronaut?'

'Nope.'

'Um... mortgage adviser?'

'Ha, no!'

'Oh, that's the one you scoff at. Right, so I was obviously closer with astronaut, how intriguing. Okay, fine. Erm, hedge fund manager?'

'Do you even know what one of those is?'

'No. Do you?'

'Not a clue.' James laughed. 'But I'd guess I'm about as far from that as you can imagine.'

'How on earth am I meant to know what the opposite of a hedge fund manager is when I don't know what a hedge fund manager is?'

'It's a conundrum that's for sure. Why don't you stop guessing and just kiss me instead?'

And with that James somehow managed to extricate his arm from hers and sweep her in front of him in one motion. It was smooth and took her so by surprise that a ripple like static rolled down her back and into her legs and made her knees feel suddenly completely unreliable.

'Um, isn't this against your code?' she managed to squeak as she looked up at him.

'Oh, for sure. One hundred per cent,' he replied, with a grin.

And in that moment when James the Penguin Man wrapped his arms around her and looked deep into her eyes, Felicity felt like she never wanted to be anywhere else again.

As he bent to kiss her, she almost swooned. It was that good.

# CHAPTER THIRTY-SIX

THEY WENT BACK to her place, obviously. Did he even have a place? Was he even real? Perhaps he was just a fabrication of her mind that she had created to pass the time. Assuming he was, in fact, real, Felicity made a mental note to ask him about his place later. She didn't want to ruin the excitement of the moment with silly things like details.

And if she was completely honest, at that point Felicity didn't care at all where he lived or what he did for a living or any of that other stuff. She didn't even care if she'd just made him up. Whether he was real or imaginary, she just wanted to be held by him, like she had never wanted to be held by anyone before. As they walked arm in arm towards her flat through the fog, the tension between them felt thick and charged with electricity. Surely, she felt, it must be visible to the naked eye. Maybe even from space. The thought made her chuckle to herself as they walked. Or was that just the nerves?

As they reached her building and began to walk up the stairs to her flat, Felicity was slightly in front of James and she could feel his closeness, feel him just behind her. She was longing for him to touch her, tingling all over with the anticipation of it. It was thrilling.

The moment was ruined, however, when she arrived at the flat door to find the pale blue Tiffany box sitting on the doormat along with an enormous bunch of incredible yellow roses. Enormous, perfect yellow roses. Mind-blowingly beautiful and filling the entire vestibule with their heady scent. It usually smelled of far less savoury things.

They stared at the vision before them for a long, interminably long, excruciating time. Side by side. Neither saying a word.

'So, there's that,' said James, eventually.

'Yup,' said Felicity and she could feel her vision narrowing as if she was on the verge of a panic attack. *Stay calm.*

'Let's go in, shall we? No point standing around out here,' she said, briskly. There had been a profound shift in the atmosphere and she couldn't think how to pull it back. James nodded, not looking at her. Felicity unlocked the door, and then picked up the ring as if it was a bomb, holding it at arm's length as she navigated the threshold and then placed it carefully on the kitchen worktop. She decided to leave the flowers, there was no way to carry in such an enormous and beautiful bunch of flowers without looking a tiny bit pleased.

James hovered in the doorway, his face like thunder.

'Come in, if you're coming,' said Felicity over her shoulder, in a much breezier tone than she felt. She took her coat off and flicked the kettle on and sent up a silent prayer. *Please let him come in, please let him come in,* over and over like a chant. She'd had time to make two coffees and right-angle-tidy the lounge before he finally emerged from the hallway.

'Have a seat,' she said.

He sat, coat and shoes still on, face fixed in a combination of confusion and anger.

Finally, he spoke the question he had clearly been formulating since they got back to the flat. 'What does it mean?'

'I have no idea.'

He glanced at her, finally.

'Honestly, James, I had no idea he even still had it, he must have taken it when we went to the pub.'

'You two went to the pub? When, exactly?'

*Backtrack, backtrack.*

'Oh, er, way back before my holiday. We just, um, had a catch up, that's all.'

James looked like he was trying to calculate a complicated maths problem. Felicity, meanwhile, could hear a strange roaring noise in her ears. Another mild dose of panic on its way, presumably.

'And you needed to take the ring with you, did you? To this catch up?'

This conversation was getting worse by the minute.

*Whatever you do, don't mention Guernsey.*

'I was taking it back. Returning it to him. I didn't want it. Even if it is Tiffany and bloody expensive. Should have flogged it on eBay instead, now I think about it.'

James didn't even crack a smile.

'But, er, that's not what's important. The important thing here is, the ring means nothing to me. Adam means nothing to me.'

'I know that,' said James simply, looking at her directly now. 'How could he mean anything to you? He's a lying snake.'

'Yes, yes he is,' said Felicity, a little taken aback.

James was on a roll now. 'Never mind the fact that he used it to turn up out of the blue and "sort of" propose to you after a three-year separation. And then left it on your doorstep. That's a bit creepy, don't you think?'

Felicity felt a weird impulse to defend Adam. The fact that

she'd known him so long, that they had been childhood sweethearts and all that, wasn't exactly reflecting well on her.

'I'm sure he didn't mean it to be creepy. He's... lonely, I guess.'

James shot her a look.

'I mean, I know it looks bad, all this. But he's a good guy, underneath it all.'

'You're not defending him, surely?'

'No, no. Course not.'

*Maybe. A bit.*

She moved from the armchair to the sofa next to him and gently pulled his coat from his shoulders in a vague attempt to placate him. And maybe, just maybe, to discourage him from walking out of the door immediately. It was awfully cold out, after all.

*Please don't leave.*

'Look, I've told him how I feel. I've told him I'm not interested. I can try again, if that will make you feel better.'

James gave a sort of non-committal grunt and then slipped an arm around her shoulders. 'I know something else that will make me feel better.'

He pulled her into him and covered her mouth with a kiss. His lips felt so natural on hers, somehow, and she pressed herself against him, feeling her whole body respond to his, all thoughts of Adam immediately vanishing. Her blood thumped in her ears as his hand moved round to her back and slid up underneath her top. It felt firm but soft and so good on her skin. So right.

As his lips grazed her neck, she could bear it no longer.

'Stay,' whispered Felicity.

But that was clearly not the right thing to say, and she cursed herself as he broke off and looked at her.

'I want to,' he said, his voice husky. 'I want to... so badly. But

I've got your bloody ex-boyfriend in my head now, and I'm not letting him get in the way of things again. Give me a week. Next Saturday I'm coming to cook for you and then I'm going to get you naked. Trust me, it'll be worth waiting for.'

Under his gaze, Felicity felt all her clothes disappear in a puff of fire and smoke.

*But I'm ready now.*

# CHAPTER THIRTY-SEVEN

THEY MUST HAVE TALKED it up. The very next day the bloody ex-boyfriend himself came to visit her at work, looking sheepish.

'Hey, you.'

Adam hovered in the doorway of the puppy room where Felicity was cleaning the floor. Immediately Freddy the dachshund started growling. Adam jumped and moved back from the doorway, which just annoyed Freddy more. He started yapping even more ferociously and Adam gave Felicity an anguished look.

'Don't look at me. He hates me, too.'

They waited. Felicity silently counted the seconds, one thousand, two thousand, three thousand, wondering whether the little dog would eventually run out of steam. He didn't. As if on cue, Felix joined in. Then the bulldogs. Then suddenly, the whole room was at it.

'Is there somewhere we can talk?' shouted Adam over the din.

Felicity looked at him for a long moment and felt a new affinity with Freddy. A better judge of character than she was, clearly.

'Sure.' She shrugged, carefully navigating the narrow space between Adam on one side and cages full of yapping dogs on the other, and leading the former out into the corridor, trying to calm the dogs down as she did so. The noise was astonishing. She got a waft of Adam's expensive aftershave as she passed him, which she tried to ignore. 'But you've got five minutes. That's it.'

The door shut behind them and one by one the dogs quietened down. Mission accomplished. Every so often they could still hear Freddy giving a warning growl as if to prevent a recurrence.

'Woah, that little dog is really aggressive,' said Adam, clearly a bit shaken... or had he looked like that when he arrived?

'He's been through a lot,' said Felicity. 'Who can blame him for being a bit edgy? But I think we're slowly coming to an understanding, the two of us.'

Adam nodded and crossed his arms like he was feeling a sudden chill.

'So. Five minutes. Go,' said Felicity.

'Right, yes,' said Adam and then paused.

'Go on then.'

'It's not that easy.'

'Try.'

'Okay, fine. Erm.'

*What is this?*

'Okay. Look. I came to say I'm sorry, Fliss.'

'I think we've been over this.'

'I mean it, Felicity. Even now, even these last few weeks, I've treated you so badly and I just, I need to tell you I'm sorry. I need you to hear me.'

'And when were you going to tell me you'd slept with Bex. What the hell, Adam?'

He took a step backwards, his cheeks pink. 'Oh God. She

told you. Look. It never meant anything. She means nothing. You've always been the love of my life, you know that.'

There was a pause. Adam seemed to be expecting her to say something. Did he actually have tears in his eyes? The phone rang in the office and Felicity could hear Andrea picking up the receiver, then talking more quietly than usual. She wondered vaguely who it was.

*Am I on some kind of hidden camera show? Is that them calling to give me my prize and have a good laugh at my expense?*

She'd felt sorry for Adam for a second or two, but it was fleeting. Then she realised, perhaps for the first time in her life, she felt sorry for herself. He opened his mouth to say something more, but she cut him off sharply.

'I'm sorry too, Adam. I'm sorry I gave up on us but more than that, I'm sorry I wasted so much of my time on you in the first place. It feels like you've been hurting me in slow motion.'

'I don't think that's entirely–'

She held up a hand and he stopped abruptly. 'All these years, you've controlled me, manipulated me, cheated on me, and even now you won't let me get on with my life. You don't ever want me to be happy and for someone who professes to love me, that's a very strange state of affairs. You left a bloody ring on my doorstep. What the hell was that about?'

She was in full flow now and although she knew she sounded caustic, she didn't feel inclined to stop.

'I don't think I'll ever forget what you did, but I'm damned if I'm going to let it rule my life any longer. So, I forgive you, if that's what you wanted to hear. Will that satisfy you? I forgive you and also I'm not going to be the person who saves you from being alone. Or from your own stupid mistakes. In fact, I never want to see you again.'

As she spoke those final words, Adam dropped to the floor suddenly and with an almighty thump. It happened in a split second, and it was so shocking that Felicity let out a little scream. His eyes were wide open, and he had ended up sitting very upright, leaning against the rabbit enclosure, posed at rather an unnatural angle. Felicity ran towards him, hysterically shouting for Andrea to call an ambulance, convinced he'd somehow dropped dead in that instant, already running through what would happen if she'd killed him with her words.

'Adam? Adam! I'm so sorry! Adam, please be okay!'

After the longest five seconds in the history of time, Adam blinked once, and the relief was so overwhelming that Felicity dropped to her knees on the floor next to him and started sobbing uncontrollably. She grabbed his arm and felt for a pulse. It was slow and shallow, but it was there. His brown eyes were wide and staring into the distance, his pupils looked enormous, and he seemed to be struggling to breathe. Felicity could feel the panic rising in her own chest; somewhere that seemed very far away she could hear Andrea on the phone – loud this time – giving directions to the ambulance – and she told herself to stay calm. *Focus.*

Adam was scarily pale. Grey, even. As she watched in horror, he started clawing at his chest.

'Adam, can you hear me?' said Felicity, tears rolling down her cheeks. 'I'm so sorry, I'm sorry, I'm sorry.'

When the paramedics arrived, they had to prise her away from him.

He was alive.

That was something.

It had been dicey in the ambulance. The female paramedic riding in the back with them was deep in concentration for the whole journey and never took her eyes from the machines

Adam was strapped to. Felicity hadn't dared speak, she just held Adam's hand and prayed silently that she hadn't killed him. *Bloody typical, that would be,* she thought, *if I've killed him by saying what I really felt about something for the first time in my life. For Pete's sake.*

When they arrived at the hospital, Adam was whisked away through two sets of swing doors and Felicity spent an excruciating few hours pacing the floor of the waiting room, feeling weighed down by her own guilt and an overwhelming need to comfort eat. She walked backwards and forwards, drinking water from the dispenser and eyeing up the chocolate bars in the vending machine. *Exactly how many Mars bars is too many Mars bars? That's the question...*

At 6pm, a doctor finally came to update her. He was a very tall, slim man with glasses, who looked as if he'd had a rough day.

'He's alive.'

Felicity nodded, tears springing to her eyes without warning.

'He's doing okay, and it's all thanks to you.'

'I'm not sure about that,' said Felicity, shifting uncomfortably.

'I'm serious, are you a first aider? You must be. It was your fast response, calling the ambulance so quickly in the first place and keeping him awake, which probably saved his life. I mean that. Really, well done.'

Felicity's stomach had tied itself into a knot by this point. Um. *That's not exactly the whole story.*

'I'm not sure I was that much help, actually...' she started to say.

'You were, trust me. Now, the thing is, although he's doing okay, we don't know exactly what happened, so we'll need to run some more tests tomorrow. He's stable for the moment so I suggest you go home and get some sleep while you can. You've been through a serious trauma today, too.'

Felicity nodded, but she knew she couldn't possibly leave. Instead, as soon as the doctor left, she went outside and rang James.

'I know it's spectacularly awkward and I know I don't have the right to ask you for anything, especially when it comes to Adam... but...'

'I'm on my way,' said James, when he managed to gather what was going on between sniffs.

He arrived within the hour and wrapped her up tightly in his arms while Felicity sobbed and snotted all over his shoulder.

Mr Fix-it that he was, James had offered to pay for a hotel just down the road so Felicity could get some sleep but still be near the hospital, but she declined. Although she really wanted to run away and hide under a duvet, she couldn't bear the thought of leaving Adam on his own and they had no idea who to call. Felicity wasn't in touch with Adam's family anymore, and only God knew if he was still in contact with this Tabitha person. Or whoever it was he'd cheated on her with. Or whatever other woman might have been lurking around the edges of his life these days. A quick nosey on his Facebook profile had left them none the wiser, so instead, they settled in as best they could in the waiting room. James had even brought snacks and a change of clothes for Felicity, procured from somewhere or other on his way. In jollier circumstances, she would have been mercilessly mocking his appalling taste in women's clothes or asking whether he'd picked up any Percy Pigs. (He had, of course.)

'Jaaaaaaaaaames,' said Felicity, later that night, shifting position where she was curled up on the uncomfortable metal bench. The dodgy velour tracksuit he'd bought her – from what she could only assume was a low-price supermarket – was chafing in some awkward places.

'Hmmm?' said James, who had been nodding off next to her with his head leaning on his hand.

'Is it all my fault?'

'For the millionth time, I'm sure it wasn't. What did you say to him? I mean... I'm just asking. I'm not suggesting anything.'

'I blew my top. I have no idea why. It just suddenly all came out, all the anger I've been burying for so long. All the stuff about Bex, all of it.'

'I'm sure you weren't that bad. You can't have been... I mean, you never lose your temper.'

'You weren't there. It was seriously bad. I feel awful now.'

James patted her leg supportively while Felicity chewed her lip and tried to relax. His presence was definitely a comfort even if the nearness of him so late at night was also rather distracting despite the circumstances.

'Try and get some sleep,' said James. 'We'll talk to the doctor tomorrow.'

# CHAPTER THIRTY-EIGHT

THE NEXT MORNING came very slowly, as it so often does when you are wearing a tracksuit made of polyester and trying to sleep on an uncomfortable bed cobbled together from NHS-standard plastic and metal waiting-room chairs. They had spent the night surrounded by people shouting and doctors coming and going and generally just hospital noise and detritus. Felicity had eventually dropped off in the early hours, only to be roused abruptly at 7am, first by the extraordinary noise made by the canteen workers bringing breakfast round the wards, and then the tall, thin doctor looming over her, looking rather like Jack Skellington from *Nightmare Before Christmas*.

James had moved to a bench a few metres away at some point during the night and now, annoyingly, was still asleep as far as she could tell from the steady up-and-down movement of his back.

'I'm sorry to disturb you,' said the doctor in a low voice, 'but I'm about to go off shift and I wanted to update you first.'

'He's okay, isn't he?' she said, standing up and straightening her clothes as best she could.

*Please God.*

'Yes, yes, he's had a good night and seems to be doing okay.'

He hesitated then, and Felicity waited anxiously.

'Has he had some kind of emotional stress or trauma that you know of?' said the doctor, taking off his glasses and cleaning them on his green scrub top.

At that, Felicity must have gone even paler than she usually is.

She decided the truth was the only way forwards and explained what had been going on when it happened. A slightly edited version, of course.

'Did...? I mean, who...? I mean, was it me, is it my fault?' she said at the end, swallowing back fresh tears.

'Not exactly,' said the doctor, which wasn't all that reassuring. 'It does explain a few things though.'

He paused. For dramatic effect? Or was he trying to find the right words?

'I shouldn't really say any more. You're not his next of kin.'

But he really looked like he wanted to tell her. So, Felicity waited patiently, keeping her features as still and friendly-looking as possible.

*Come on, Jack Skellington.*

It didn't take long for him to crack.

'Okay, fine. But I didn't tell you anything, okay?'

'Okay.'

'Good. Well. Okay. Our initial scans seem to show he didn't have a heart attack. It presented very much like it, but I suspect this may be what's known as stress-induced cardiomyopathy or broken heart syndrome. We don't normally see this in men... it's usually women, I'm afraid to say, around ninety per cent of cases, in fact. Perhaps because you are generally more in tune with your emotions,' he added, with a weak smile. 'In any case, it can be brought on by a severe emotional trauma. Usually, the death of a loved one. Hence the name.'

Felicity's hands flew to her face.

'Oh my goodness. I did it. It was me. I nearly killed him.'

'Oh no, I shouldn't think so,' said the doctor. 'Even if your, er, argument was somehow a trigger, you couldn't possibly know that this would happen. It's not your fault.'

'I think you're just being kind.'

'No, honestly. It's not something we see very often, it's very unusual. Most likely he's got something underlying. We are doing some more investigations.'

'Oh my God.'

'He's in good hands, don't worry.'

'Can I see him now?'

James waited outside with the sports supplement while Felicity crept tentatively into Adam's room.

He looked terrible, which was hardly surprising, but Felicity still felt inwardly shocked. She was so used to Adam looking 'together', having it all 'together', and it dawned on her that in all the time they had known each other he had rarely been ill – or not that she could remember.

Now though, he looked ghastly. His cheeks were pale, his face gaunt, and his bare chest was covered in electrodes. There was a large cannula in his hand, something that always made Felicity wince. He looked tired, but he smiled as she walked in, and she felt overwhelmed with guilt yet again.

'Hey, you,' he said, his voice sounding hoarse.

'Hey yourself,' said Felicity, trying to keep her own voice light and airy. *Don't cry, don't cry.*

'How are you feeling?'

'Oh, you know, I've been better.'

'I would have thought being waited on by nurses would be your idea of heaven.'

*Don't mention heaven, what are you doing?*

'Well, I haven't had a bed bath yet and I don't know if they still do them but if they do, I'm definitely down with that.'

Felicity rolled her eyes. 'Glad to hear you haven't lost your sense of humour, if that's what you call it.'

'What do you think of my gaff?' said Adam, ignoring her and waving his free arm around the room weakly.

'Love what you've done with the place.'

'Knew you'd like it.'

They smiled at each other for a moment.

'So... what the heck was that about then?' said Felicity, mock punching him gently on the arm. 'Apart from scaring the living daylights out of me, that is.'

Adam winced and shuffled on his pillows. Felicity stepped forward and began to help him rearrange them behind his head. Too late she realised it was rather an intimate move – a girlfriend move, really – and she quickly retreated, bashing into the heart rate monitor as she did so and ripping two of the electrodes from his chest.

He let out a yelp and then tried to cover it with something a little more manly. As he jerked in pain, both his pillows fell off the bed and landed on the floor at Felicity's feet.

'Ouch!'

'Oh my goodness, I'm sorry! So sorry.'

Adam was rubbing the sore place on his chest with one hand and trying to reach down to retrieve his pillows with the other and something about the scowl of concentration on his face gave Felicity a sudden and irrational impulse to laugh. She tried to cover it by fussing around on the floor picking up the pillows herself but as she stood up, she could hold it in no longer and it came out in a guffaw. As she leant over him again to put the pillows back in place, Adam burst out laughing too and then winced in pain.

'What are you like?' he said when he could speak again.

'I really shouldn't be allowed out in public.'

'You're not kidding.'

He was still rubbing his chest and once he was comfortable – ish – and they'd both stopped giggling, Felicity picked up the ends of the electrodes and attempted to stick them back in place, batting feebly at his chest to get them to stick and trying not to think about the last time she'd touched that skin.

She had to get really close to him now, and let out a little cough to cover the awkwardness. But if Adam felt the same, he didn't comment. When it all looked reasonably similar to before, she sat down on the bed and patted his hand lightly.

'Ahem. Sorry about that. You were saying?'

'What was the question?'

'I was just asking you about, you know, the whole terrifying the life out of me thing. You remember that, right?'

'Oh yes, that. Well. I have no idea what happened, basically. I don't remember much about it. But my previous approaches didn't seem to be working on you... so I thought I'd try a different tack. Sympathy vote, you know.'

She flushed. 'Bit dramatic, don't you think?'

'You know me. Never knowingly understated.'

Felicity laughed. 'That's true enough.'

'So...?'

'So?'

'Did it work?' Adam shifted himself upwards in the bed. Then he held up a hand. 'No. Second thoughts, don't answer that. I don't think I want to know.' Still, his brown eyes flashed with hope. Or was it anxiety?

'I think it's best I don't,' she said, gently. 'It was all my fault. I'm so sorry, Adam, I never should have spoken to you that way.'

Adam waved a hand. 'Don't worry, honestly, I deserved it.'

'Maybe. A bit. But I was pretty cruel. And then I tried to bump you off again by pulling all those thingies off you. Sorry.'

Adam stared into her eyes for a long moment. 'I meant what I said earlier, Fliss. It's me who needs to say sorry. Please forgive me.'

'Of course, I forgive you,' said Felicity, and in that moment, for the very first time, she knew it was true. She had forgiven him. It felt like a huge iron helmet lifting from her head. Relief washed over her.

'Thank you,' he whispered.

She placed her hand on his and they just sat quietly together for what felt like an hour. Felicity's heart had started to thump. It felt so familiar. So comfortable. She was conscious that a certain particularly gorgeous Penguin Man was just outside the door and yet she suddenly didn't want to leave. How did Adam always have this effect on her? Even now. He was so irritating and also so confusing. And charmingly pathetic, right in this moment.

Adam looked as if he was about to say something more and Felicity's heart raced even faster – *calm down* – but just as he went to open his mouth, in bustled two nurses and asked Felicity – politely, but firmly – to let him rest.

*Don't look too closely at the electrodes, for God's sake.*

As she left the room, she looked back over her shoulder to see Adam staring out of the window and biting his lip. He never bites his lip, she thought, vaguely.

*What had he been going to say?*

Her head ached.

God, she needed to sleep.

# CHAPTER THIRTY-NINE

FELICITY WENT HOME and slept for twelve hours straight. She woke on the Tuesday morning groggy and still confused but slightly less headachy, at least.

She checked her phone immediately.

Four messages.

> Andrea: Penguin Man is a star. All well with cats and dogs. Hope A okay x

> James: Hope you slept well, CCL. I'm going to help Andrea for a couple of days so no need to rush back to work. Give me a call when you're awake and feeling a bit better. XXX

> Adam: Bex is here. No need for you to come back, I'll be fine. I'll give you a call when I'm home.

> Bex: Heard the news, I'm heading to the hospital right now, will come and find you xxx

*Damn.*

She also had a missed call.

Voicemail: 'Hi, darling, it's me, it's Bex. I wonder if you

might give me a call when you have a chance, please. Nothing to worry about but, well, yes just call me, please. Mwah.'

Bex sounded odd. As if she was calling from the bottom of the sea... although that seemed unlikely. Felicity tried returning the call but it rang out. She made a mental note to try again when she was feeling a bit more awake and headed for the shower, where the mental note immediately got washed away along with her tension headache and half a bottle of her best shower gel.

It was only the next morning that Felicity finally remembered to call Bex back. She really was a crap friend.

'Oh! My darling I'm so glad you called me. I really need to talk to you.'

'I'm here, what is it?'

'It's about Adam.'

Felicity felt a shiver. 'What about him?'

'I don't know if I should tell you like this. Are you free to meet me?'

The shiver turned into five cold fingers crawling up her spine. 'I can't – I have to get to work. What is it? Please just tell me.'

'I don't know... I'm not sure where to start...'

'Just say it.'

*Don't be dead, don't be dead, don't be dead.*

'Well, the thing is, well, basically, um, he's asked me to marry him!'

Bex shrieked so loudly down the line that Felicity dropped the phone in surprise. After a few seconds of fumbling, she managed to retrieve it from under the sofa and turn it the right way up, heart hammering, palms sweaty.

'Felicity! Are you there? Did you hear me?'

'Yes, yes, I heard you.'

'Did you hear what I said?'

'Yes, I definitely heard what you said.'

'Are you mad with me? Are you angry?' She sounded terrified.

'No! I'm bloody relieved! I thought you were going to say... something else.'

'What?'

'It doesn't matter.'

'Oh, well that's fine then. I was so worried what you might say!'

'I can see why. So run this by me again. Adam – my ex-boyfriend Adam, just to be clear – he proposed to you and you said yes?'

'Ha ha, didn't I mention that bit? Of course, I said yes. It's Adam!'

*Am I living in a parallel universe?*

'Yup. It's Adam.'

'Please say you're not mad?'

'I'm... I'm happy for you, actually,' said Felicity, although she felt a bit faint all of a sudden and sat down in her armchair with a bump.

*Was she? Maybe not happy as such. Shocked, mainly. But not jealous, that was for sure. Definitely not. Okay, maybe a teensy bit jealous.*

*Shocked. Jealous (a teensy bit). Mainly completely confused.*

*The sneaky little whatsit.*

Bex was still talking. 'Thank goodness for that as I was hoping you'd be my maid of honour. You'd be fabulous!'

'Woah there, Nelly. One step at a time.'

'I'm sorry, you're right. I'm so excited, that's all.'

'I can hear that.'

A pause.

'Fliss, are you still there?'

'I'm here.'

She was stalling for time while her mind whizzed back through the past few weeks, searching for any signs that this conversation was ever on the cards. She came up empty.

'Tell me something though...'

'Anything.'

'Aside from the whole, you know, "how on earth did this happen" thing... Did he propose in the hospital? I mean, like, while he thought he was dying or something?'

*Or the split second I left the building?*

'Ha!' said Bex, with a snort of laughter. 'No, not exactly. Well, yes, actually, although he knew what he was doing.'

'I wasn't suggesting he was delirious or anything. I just meant, well, you know it's quite weird timing.'

'Not that weird, as it goes.'

'Go on...?'

'Um. Look, why don't I come over tonight and I'll tell you all about it?'

'Okay. Deal.'

Felicity couldn't help calculating the number of days it had been since Adam had sort of proposed to *her* on New Year's Eve. Perhaps she'd best not mention that to Bex either.

That night, wine in hand, mind still racing, Felicity asked the first of many, many questions she'd been storing up all day.

'Did he give you a ring?'

Bex bit her lip and waggled an empty hand. 'Not yet, he hasn't had a chance to get one yet. He's been, you know, in hospital, after all.'

'Yes, I was there. Oh, well, maybe he'll get you one made out of tin foil or a Hula Hoop or something.'

Bex gave a hollow laugh. 'Oh yes. A Hula Hoop, ha ha.'

Felicity chewed her lip. 'I think I need to tell you something.'

Another hollow laugh. 'Is it about the Tiffany ring?' said Bex.

'Yes! How did you know about that?'

'Addy told me all about it. He said it was all a misunderstanding, apparently. He never meant to propose or anything, it was just a gift.'

'Yes, yes of course, it definitely didn't mean anything.'

'No, it didn't mean anything.'

'No, it definitely didn't mean anything.'

There was an awkward pause. Felicity tasted blood in her mouth and hastily stopped chewing.

'Can I see it?'

'Um... okay...'

Felicity stood up slowly and found herself mechanically walking through to her bedroom and retrieving it from its recently recovered spot in her bedside drawer, even though there were a million alarm bells going off in her head. *Pretend you've lost it. Pretend you gave it back. Maybe now's the time to actually throw it out of the window?* Instead, she handed the box tentatively to Bex and went to the kitchen to put the kettle on. Just to *do* something. She fussed around in the cupboards for some biscuits even though she knew there weren't any.

There was silence from the living room.

'What do you think?' asked Felicity, over the noise of the kettle.

'It's beautiful,' said Bex.

'What?' said Felicity. 'Sorry, I can't hear you over the kettle.'

'I said, it's beautiful,' said Bex a little louder.

'That's what I thought you said.'

Another awkward pause while they listened to the kettle finish bubbling.

'But it doesn't mean anything,' said Felicity, into the ensuing silence.

'No. It doesn't,' said Bex, still staring at it.

Felicity felt slightly panicked. She poured the water over two decaf tea bags – it was late, after all – and furiously stirred the milk in, buying herself precious seconds to consider what she might do next. As she carried the tea through to the lounge, she noticed Bex was still staring at the ring. She had silent tears running down her cheeks.

'Are you okay?' said Felicity.

Bex wiped one eye with an elegant finger.

'There's something else I need to tell you,' she said.

'Go on then,' said Felicity with a sigh. 'But you'd better not be pregnant.'

# CHAPTER FORTY

'ACTUALLY, IT'S TWO THINGS,' said Bex. She was still clutching the ring box.

Felicity sat forward in the armchair, holding her very favourite battered velvet cushion for comfort or protection, she wasn't entirely sure which. The fabric was soft and worn and she ran her fingers across its surface as she waited.

'Firstly, you know how you said this was rather out of the blue? Well, it's not really. I lied when I said it had never happened again.'

'You've been sleeping together?' blurted out Felicity.

Bex nodded and looked up at her friend. 'It's happened a few times. We've... well, quite a few times actually. I'm so sorry, Fliss. I never meant to deceive you. I just, well, I couldn't bear to lose you. And besides, he's always been so mad about you that I honestly didn't think it ever meant anything to him. Please don't kill me.'

Felicity nodded slowly. She felt as though she was watching this conversation at a distance. Neither the Felicity sitting on the armchair nor the one watching from a distance had any idea how they should react.

'You're the reason he split up with Tabitha,' she said, when she'd recovered the power of speech. 'Adam told me he met some girl in a bar. The lying little toad.'

Bex winced, then nodded. 'I was always the one he turned to, I guess. You know, his second choice. Sometimes third or fourth.'

It was Felicity's turn to wince now.

'I got used to it in the end. The sex was great and it just became a thing we did. Casual, like,' continued Bex, hastily. Then: 'I thought that was all I would ever be.'

'So, what changed?'

'Well, that's the other thing I need to tell you,' said Bex. 'Adam is sick.'

'I know, I was there.'

'No, I mean, he's really sick, Fliss.'

'Well, you don't get much sicker than collapsing in the middle of a conversation.'

'No, I know, and that's what I mean. The whole collapsing in the middle of a conversation thing is how they found the problem. They ran some more tests after you left and he has some kind of heart condition.'

Felicity felt a bit woozy. 'A what?'

'It's something he was born with apparently, but it was never picked up until now. I was in the room when they told him.' She sounded weirdly proud.

At least the Jack Skellington doctor had done his work. Her instincts were correct. Felicity felt both vindicated and terrified all at once.

'And can they... I mean, is there anything... er... what's the prognosis for something like that?'

'They can treat it – to an extent. It makes him breathless and whatnot, but they think he's had it for so long his body has learned to adapt. It probably wouldn't have been found if it wasn't for you... well, if you hadn't been... well, if it wasn't for your *candour*, shall we say? He's had a fright, for one, plus he got such a telling off from the doctors and from me that he knows he needs to get his bloody act together and take better care of himself.'

'Yeah, er... sure.'

'And I guess the hospital made him re-evaluate things.'

The two friends looked at each other for a long moment.

'Bex, I think I need to tell you something now.'

'Is it about Guernsey? He told me all about that.'

'Did he now?'

'It's fine, he explained everything. How funny that you both ended up over there at the same time.'

'I'm not sure that's exactly...'

Bex held up a hand. 'It's fine. Honestly.'

'If you say so.'

This may have been the weirdest night of Felicity's life. She moved across the room and sat next to her friend on the sofa. 'Bex. Honey. I have to ask. Are you sure this is the right thing for you? And by "this" I do mean Adam, by the way.'

Bex smiled and nodded, but she had tears in her eyes. 'Look, I know he'll probably always love you to some degree, but I think we could make this work. He's changed... I know it.'

'Yes but don't you think maybe he...?'

*How could she say it? How could she say she thought he was just scared of being alone? That her and Bex were his last hope?*

Felicity leaned forward and took Bex's hands. 'If this is what you want, I will support you one hundred per cent.'

Bex smiled and two huge tears rolled down her cheeks. 'It's what I want.'

'In that case,' said Felicity, 'I think you should keep the ring. If that's not too weird.'

Bex shook her head and started crying for real then and

Felicity put her arms around her and gave her a squeeze, feeling her headache returning.

No way was she going to be their bloody bridesmaid.

There had been long weeks before. Long, tedious weeks. Many of them, in fact, throughout her life. Weeks when life was just an endless routine of getting up, going to work, coming home, and going to bed. When time had been slow, interminable. Verging on unbearable. But not like this. Now, when things were finally happening in her world, when she was finally starting to live again, life chose to be particularly cruel.

Time flew when she was with James. Actually flew. That wasn't just a metaphor but a cold, hard fact. The minutes were like seconds. Just when you want life to slow down so you can appreciate every moment, that's precisely when it decides to speed up and whizz past at a million miles an hour. And then, when James and Felicity were apart and she was absolutely desperate to see him again, desperate for time to fly, that's when it slowed down so much it was like wading through thick, viscous mud. Or time still flew but it was full of nightmarish visions of her ex-boyfriend collapsing in a heap on the floor and having to spend the night in A&E and then meeting with her best friend for wine and revelations.

How was it possible that two measly days could feel like forever?

By the time Saturday finally (*finally, finally*) came around, Felicity was about ready to spontaneously combust. When James knocked on the door of her flat it was all she could do not to immediately fling the door wide and jump into his arms. She stood in the hall and counted to ten. Very quickly.

When she opened the door and saw him, she burst out laughing.

He was dressed as John McClane from *Die Hard*. Complete with dirty vest (very tight!), grey trousers, bare feet, police badge and (toy) gun holster. He had even smeared his face with what looked like army paint. The overall effect was funny, of course, but also incredibly sexy. Especially the bare shoulders. And the bare feet, for some reason. *Hmmm. Never thought I was a feet kind of girl.*

'Well, hello there, officer,' said Felicity, leaning against the door frame, trying to appear casual even though her whole body was tingling.

'At your service, ma'am,' he replied in a passably good New York accent. His blond hair was flopping over his eyes, and he pushed it back with one hand as he proudly presented her with a large bag of food with the other.

'I got pizzas and beer. What else would John McClane eat?'

'Twinkies!' replied Felicity. 'But I can live without those.'

'Check the bag.' James laughed, kissing her on the cheek and, pulling out his toy gun, he pretended to check the threshold, pressing himself against the wall of the hallway and then shouting 'Clear!' from the living room.

Felicity giggled and shut the door behind him. She peered into the bag. He had actually brought real-life Twinkies.

What else could they watch on such a night but *Die Hard 2*?

As they munched on stuffed crust pizza and cold Asahi beers, watching the 'real' John McClane attempt to take down an entire battalion of political terrorists in an airport with just his bare hands and a couple of flares, Felicity could not stop sneaking glances at James, who was sitting next to her on the sofa, apparently engrossed in the film. She was obviously trying to concentrate on the film too, of course, but he was just so damn close. She thanked the sweet Lord for her small flat – and even smaller sofa – and edged closer. Their hands were almost – almost – touching, and you could practically see the sparks flying between them. Felicity was just wondering if it was time to get naked yet when James turned to her.

'So,' he said, looking her right in the eye. 'I have a very important question for you.'

Felicity's heart did a backwards somersault. 'Go on, officer,' she said in a low voice.

'Vest on or vest off?'

She laughed and began grabbing at it with her hands. 'Definitely vest off,' she said, pulling it over his head and running her hands over his perfect, perfect chest. The holster was the next thing to go.

Felicity woke up the next morning and even though it was still only February, it felt like the first day of spring. Unusually for her, a starfish sleeper mostly, she had slept all night nestled in the crook of James' arm as if she had been made specifically for that spot. She cringed at how cheesy it all was, but she had even woken up with a smile on her face. An actual smile. James stirred as she traced a figure of eight on his bare stomach with her finger, idly.

'Mmmmm, that's good,' he murmured.

'Good morning,' she whispered, the memory of the night before suddenly coming back in a rush and making her squirm.

'Good morning yourself,' he said, turning to kiss her forehead.

'Let's just stay here forever,' she said.

He made an appreciative noise, moving his lips against her skin, and then leaned back onto the pillow, smiling a broad, happy smile. She took the opportunity to sneak another look at his Disney Prince chest and abs. Honestly, the man looked like Li Shang from *Mulan* with his clothes off. It had virtually taken her breath away.

'What are you looking at?' he said quietly, his eyes still closed, but his voice had a smile.

'You,' she replied guiltily.

'Fair play. But it's my turn next.'

Felicity playfully pulled the covers up to her chin and giggled as she felt his hands start to wander.

'Okay, okay! One more time but then we really must get up.'

'Sure, whatever you say, Crazy Cat Lady.'

They made love twice more that morning. And then once more for luck.

# CHAPTER FORTY-ONE

WHEN THEY FINALLY EMERGED FROM the flat, blinking in the sunshine and desperately in need of sustenance, it was practically lunchtime. Thankfully, 'Officer McClane' had brought along a change of clothes and was now dressed in a blue and white checked shirt and jeans, as if the whole dressing up as an 80s classic movie character thing had simply been a figment of her imagination.

The memories, though, were very real.

'Come on, I know just the place,' said James, and they jumped in a cab and ended up in a part of town Felicity had never been to before. It was leafy and quiet and, as they finished a ridiculously posh pie and chips lunch in a high-end pub called the Coach and Horses, something clicked into place.

'This is where you live,' said Felicity.

'Yes,' said James, with a gesture almost of apology.

'Is that why you didn't want to tell me? Because you live in Chelsea Downs?'

James winced at the nickname. The area was called Chancery Downs and, well, the nickname was not exactly intended to be complimentary.

'I don't drive a Range Rover, if that helps,' he said with a shrug.

'Very glad to hear it,' said Felicity. 'So, what do you drive?' *You can tell a lot about a man by the car he drives. That's what Bex always says. Not that her judgement could really be trusted anymore.*

'You'll see for yourself in a minute,' said James, thanking the waitress on the way out in a way that made Felicity feel inexplicably proud to be walking next to him.

She felt even prouder when he led her along the street to an enormous 1950s house with a huge bay window and modern sage-coloured windows. There was a vintage Mustang and a brand-new shiny Tesla in the driveway.

'Yes, I'm a hypocrite,' he said with a grin, gesturing at the cars. 'I only use the naughty petrol one when I really need to let off steam.'

Felicity nodded. It was so pretty she could see why. Red high shine polish with a white go-faster stripe. Like something out of a movie.

But it was when he opened the door of the house that she was completely blown away.

It was renovated on the inside to within an inch of its life, all wooden floors and modern, slightly uncomfortable-looking furniture – except, she was pleased to see, for the large and very squishy sofa in the living area. Felicity decided that from now on, she would always judge a man on his choice of sofa instead. It was as good a way as any, after all.

The kitchen area – for the ground floor was almost entirely open-plan – was grey marble with hand-crafted kitchen cabinets. The obligatory island in the middle had a very large, very expensive-looking hob built in. All the surfaces were clutter-free and sparkling clean.

'That's the dream,' said Felicity, before she could stop herself. 'Look at that island! And it's all so... clean! So neat!'

'Don't look too closely.' James coughed, looking embarrassed.

'I hadn't picked you for a neat freak,' said Felicity, head on one side.

'I'm more of a right angle tidier, if you get my drift.'

Felicity nodded. She did.

'I just go around adjusting angles and hiding things in cupboards. The rest... that's all courtesy of my lovely cleaner, Lorraine.'

'You have a cleaner. Oh my goodness I'm so jealous. But also, how very 1950s of you.'

James laughed. 'It is rather. I don't usually admit to it in public. It seems morally questionable somehow. But the simple truth is that this house would be in a state of disrepair by now without her. She's completely amazing. And I just don't get time to do any of it.'

Felicity raised an eyebrow.

'Okay, I don't get *much* time to do any of it. And when I do get free time... well I prefer to volunteer at cat sanctuaries and suchlike.'

'Maybe it's time you told me what you actually do for a living,' she said, conscious she was smiling like an absolute idiot.

James sighed. 'Come with me.'

Penguin Man opened a door at the top of the stairs, revealing a bank of computer screens in front of a huge black desk. Yet another thing in James' house that resembled a movie set. In one corner stood a large Ficus in a black and silver plant pot and there was an expensive-looking black leather chaise longue in front of the window.

*Hattie could do with one of those.*

'Well, this is a very fancy office,' said Felicity, immediately heading over to test the chaise longue. 'It's the sort of office James Bond would probably have, I imagine. You know, if he was real.'

'Okay, so the whole James Bond thing... it's not a million miles away.'

'It's not?'

'Not a million miles. But don't get too excited, remember?'

'I promise.'

*Too late.*

James paused.

'Are you going to tell me then, or what?'

'I work for GCHQ,' said James, with a shrug of surrender.

'You are a spy! I knew it!'

'Ha, no, sadly, nothing as exciting as that. I'm a software engineer. I work in their cyber security division. And that's pretty much all I can tell you.'

'Official Secrets Act?' said Felicity, leaning back against the upright section of the chaise in what she hoped was a knowing manner. Bex had worked for the Cabinet Office in London for a while, and she'd had to jump through all kinds of security hoops.

*Bloody Bex.*

James nodded. 'That's just the start of it.'

'Wow. It's like the geekiest job ever. No wonder you were a bit secretive about it.'

'Was I? I like to think I was being mysterious.'

Felicity raised an eyebrow. He was a civil servant, essentially. All the computer screens made her think of 24 with Jack Bauer even though she knew he wasn't that kind of government agent. Disappointingly.

And then a thought struck her. A somewhat worrying thought.

'James,' she said slowly.

'Yes?'

'I hate to mention Adam after, well, the day we've had.' James raised an eyebrow at that. 'But when you said he came to your office...?'

'Okay, I fibbed. He didn't come to my office. How could he? Unless he's a spy too, of course.'

Felicity laughed a little nervously. Not only had he omitted to mention this Olivia person he'd been seeing, but now he'd lied to her. For the first time that she was aware of, anyway. It wasn't a good feeling.

'So, I know I'm going to regret asking this question...?'

'I'm sorry, I shouldn't have said that he came to the office, but I didn't want to worry you.'

'What do you mean?' said Felicity, palms prickling.

James sighed and dropped down onto the chaise beside her.

'He tracked me down. I don't know how. He had got hold of my number and he called me. Asked me to go for a drink. And that's when he asked me – begged me, really – not to see you anymore.'

'And that's why you didn't come on that Saturday?'

James nodded slowly, a crinkle appearing between his eyes. 'I'm sorry, I know I completely messed up there, but I was trying to do the right thing. By you. By him. How was I to know how you felt? He made it sound so convincing. Like I'd be interfering with the love of the century or something.'

Felicity flinched at the word.

'You should have told me,' she said levelly, giving his shoulder a nudge. 'But I can understand why you didn't.'

James looked relieved.

He looked even more relieved when she told him all about Bex and Adam.

'Woah. I did not see that coming,' said James.

'Neither did I. And I've known them both for years. Does that make me a bad friend?'

'Not at all. We see what we want to see, I guess.'

'They were bloody sleeping together, and I didn't notice. I'd say that's pretty bad on my part.'

'Well then... she's not exactly friend of the year, is she?'

Felicity giggled. 'No, I suppose not.'

'So, what happens now? Do you intervene or leave them to it?'

*Good question.*

Felicity thought for a long moment.

'She thinks it'll make her happy. She says she knows all about how weird he's been with me lately and she reckons she's okay with it. That she'd rather have him like this than not at all. I know she's almost certainly going to get hurt but then she's already been causing herself so much pain over it – maybe this will be a step up?'

'Maybe. Or a car crash.'

'There is that.'

'But it might be the next big romance, who knows?'

'I have no idea. I need to talk to her but not just yet.'

James nodded.

'Anyway, in other news... I have one more question. And it's rather important, I'm afraid.'

'Go on,' he said, a smile playing around his lips.

'What do I call you, exactly? I mean, do you have like a oo number or something? Your name is James after all. It's not James Bond... is it?! I just realised I don't even know your bloody surname.'

'God, can you imagine if it was James Bond? That would be

beyond cool.' He laughed, pulling her towards him. 'It's James Taylor.'

She shot him a look.

'I'm kidding. It's James Cowley. But you can just call me James. Or Penguin Man. Or Officer McClane. I liked it when you called me that.'

He drew her into his arms and kissed her hungrily. As she pulled him down onto the chaise longue beside her, Felicity wondered for the umpteenth time if this was all an elaborate dream she was about to wake up from.

# CHAPTER FORTY-TWO

IT WAS BACK to earth with a bump on Monday. Felicity trundled to work with her head in a fog. She was exhausted, for a start. It had been a while since she had been that... um... active.

And now she had a – what was he, exactly? A partner? Too grown-up. A boyfriend? Too childish. A lover? Too eighteenth century. Whatever he was, she was down with it. After years of abject misery interspersed only rarely by the odd day of joy (usually the result of kitten cuddles rather than actual human interaction) her heart felt so light, as if at any moment it might float away out of the top of her head like a helium balloon. She felt as though finally, *finally*, someone had pressed play on the film of her life, after years of being caught, frozen in time, while everyone else passed her by. *Now it's my turn.*

There were some niggles, of course. You didn't go through as much pain as Felicity had in her life without learning to be incredibly mistrustful of happiness or anyone who seems to promise it, or even anything pertaining to the possibility of happiness at some point in the future. For a start, James worked for the government. It made some sense. No wonder he hadn't exactly been forthcoming in explaining his job. And it was a teensy bit thrilling, if she was honest. He was defending the country. With computers, not with a handgun or secret poison pens, right enough, but still. And yet there was a piece of the puzzle missing. How had he managed to get the time off to help at Animal Saviours, for example? Surely someone with a job like his couldn't just take a couple of weeks off to look after cats and dogs?

She made a mental note to ask him. They had been a little busy the previous day, Felicity thought, the pale skin on her neck betraying her as usual as it flushed bright red.

'What on earth happened to you?' said Andrea as she caught Felicity at the sink, lost in this reverie. 'Or should I say, who?'

'I don't know what you mean,' said Felicity, firmly.

'Well put it this way. If I come back in half an hour,' said Andrea, 'will you still be washing that same bowl up?'

Felicity stared at the yellow cat bowl in her hands. How long *had* she been washing it for? She had no idea.

She turned then, suds dripping on the floor, her face shining.

'I had a date with Penguin Man,' she said. 'A proper one this time.'

'I figured as much,' said Andrea, with a grin. 'Tell me everything.'

Andrea, it turned out, knew a little bit more than she had been letting on.

For example, annoyingly, she already knew what James did for a living. And she knew why he had come to the shelter. Other than to spend time with Felicity that is. He had explained that he was on sabbatical. That he had had a dreadful experience at work and that they had encouraged him to take some time off.

'That doesn't make any sense,' said Felicity. 'He told me he was a programmer, essentially. Unless he's lied about that too.'

'I don't know any more than that.' Andrea shrugged. 'Honestly, I don't,' she added when she caught Felicity's sharp look. 'Why don't you just ask him?'

'I'm sure he'll tell me when he's ready,' she said, but her heart constricted with worry. *Is he still lying?*

They had arranged to meet the following weekend and although she was desperate to see him again there was a small whisper of warning deep, deep down inside where only the cobwebs live.

The next session with Hattie was rather dominated by a certain blond man.

'Your eyes are shining,' said the therapist as Felicity dropped into the orange chair and crossed her legs. 'And you look a lot more relaxed than last week.'

'Do I?' said Felicity and yet again that telltale blush crept up her chest and over her face. 'I can't imagine why that might be.'

Hattie raised a sceptical eyebrow.

'I've had an... interesting week,' she said.

'Do you want to tell me about it?' said Hattie. 'Or would you like to talk a bit more about your family, perhaps?'

'Well... I messaged Tristan,' said Felicity. 'My brother.'

*It sounds strange to say that out loud.*

'Oh, that's wonderful,' said Hattie. 'How did it go?'

'Slowly. I messaged him on Facebook and he replied... eventually. He's still an absolute pain in the arse, and makes me wait for like days and days before he'll even reply but... it was good to hear from him.'

Hattie nodded.

'It's strange. There's so much to catch up on that I don't think either of us knows where to start. I've got the basics out of him. He's got a partner and it seems to be going okay for once, I think. He seems happy, I guess, as much as I could tell by the messages anyway. Of course, he patently doesn't want to talk about what happened. You know, why he left.'

'I'm sure he will in time.'

'I hope so.'

'Do you think you might meet up?'

Felicity took a moment to think. What would it be like to come face to face with her brother after all this time?

'I don't know yet.'

It was the truth.

'Good. Well, good progress. What else would you like to talk about this week, Felicity?'

What else could she talk about but Penguin Man?

She took a deep breath and told Hattie the whole story. Well, saga really. She didn't mention Adam though. *Too complicated, somehow.*

'And what is it that attracts you to James?' said Hattie when she had finished.

That was a good question.

'Wait. You're not going to tell me it's because I've got daddy issues, are you? Because I think it's a bit more complicated than that.'

'Of course it is. It's always more complicated than that,' said Hattie, with a sympathetic smile.

'I mean, he's very capable. And kind. And he has a grown-up job. He feels like a grown-up all round, to be honest with you. Isn't it funny how some people seem like grown-ups even when they are the same age as you? And others...' She tailed off when she noticed Hattie peering at her over her glasses. 'Sorry. I know, I'm dodging the question.'

'Somewhat.'

'Hmm. Okay. So, what is it about him?' Felicity was stalling for time.

'You said he was kind. That's a good start,' prompted Hattie.

'He *seems* kind. But me being me I'm still not sure whether he's real or not. You know? He's way too good to be true. And you should see him with the kittens, he's never really been around animals but he's so gentle with them and they just seem to take to him. I always think animals are a great judge of character, don't you?'

Her therapist nodded sagely. 'Let's see. He's kind, he's good with animals. He's attractive?'

'Oh yes,' said Felicity, rather quickly. She paused. 'But that's not it.'

'Not what?'

'That's not why I really like him,' said Felicity, and suddenly she knew the answer. 'When I'm with him, I don't want to run away and hide. He makes me feel calm and like I can trust him and I'm... I'm not used to that.'

'Which for you is...?' said Hattie gently.

Felicity nodded, swallowing the lump in her throat. 'It's a big deal. Yes. Since everything that happened with Adam, he's the first man I... well it's the first time in ages I've really trusted anyone. Recently, anyway...'

Hattie waited.

'So yes, it's a really big deal for me. I wasn't sure I would ever find someone who could make me feel like that again. These days I'm so used to getting on with my job, you know? Getting my head down and not having to think.'

'Is it just about not having to think? Or could it be more

than that in some way?'

Felicity thought for a moment.

'I guess it's more than that. It's about not, well, not engaging I suppose, in some way. It's easier to hide, isn't it? But when I'm with James... if I really concentrate, I can imagine having a life outside of the centre. I can imagine doing couply type things, you know, like normal people do, and I don't feel like my heart is about to be ripped out any minute.'

Felicity paused.

'And what about when you're not with him?' asked Hattie.

'Oh, when I'm not with him, that's a different matter. When I'm not with him, then I absolutely think everything is going to end up in flames and fire. Even today I've already decided he's lied to me about ten or eleven vitally important things.'

Hattie wrinkled her brow. 'Why is that, Felicity, do you think? Why might you be catastrophising this relationship already? What I mean by that is, foreseeing the worst possible outcome?'

'That's a great word.'

'Thank you.'

'Why am I catastrophising this?' Felicity rolled the word around in her head as she thought. Then suddenly: 'Because I don't deserve to be happy.' The words were out before she could filter them. 'Or that's what life has taught me so far. When things are going well, something is always just around the corner, about to bugger everything up.'

'Can you give me an example?'

'I... yes. I could give you about fifty, I reckon.'

Hattie pursed her lips. 'Well, let's start with one. You mentioned someone called Adam earlier. Who is Adam?' said Hattie, crossing her legs and leaning back in her chair.

'Ah... ' said Felicity. 'Now there's a good example right there.'

# CHAPTER FORTY-THREE

THE FOLLOWING SATURDAY, Felicity – a new, and improved Felicity, she liked to think, one who was quick to forgive and generous enough to donate an ex-boyfriend to her best friend; a Felicity who was free of the past and refused to carry the weight of three years of guilt around with her anymore; yes, *that* Felicity – elected to spend a luxurious Saturday morning in her PJs watching cartoons and eating cereal.

At lunchtime her phone buzzed.

> James: Hey you, what you up to? J xx

Felicity grinned on reflex.

> Hey yourself. I'm literally channelling my 12-year-old self. What about you? Xx

> Intriguing. I'm watching cartoons in my pants. Is that too much information? xx

> Me too! How funny!

> Ooh, in your pants? Want some company? ;-)

Pyjamas, sorry to disappoint. But sure. Come on over.

PS. Bring pizza.

I'm on my way.

Later, they lay side by side in Felicity's bed, looking up at the ceiling, hands clasped.

'Jaaaaaaaaaaames...?' said Felicity after a few minutes.

'Yeeeeesssss?'

'Can I ask you something?'

'Well, I imagine you're going to anyway.'

'Yes, well, it's just that I can't help wondering how someone who works for GCHQ gets to have so much time off to help at an animal sanctuary.'

'Ah.'

'I mean, I hope you don't mind me asking.'

'I don't mind you asking.'

Silence. A long pause. Felicity wondered if he'd fallen asleep. She was just wondering if she had time to sneak off to the bathroom when he began to speak.

'I had to deal with a very unpleasant case a few months back.'

Felicity sat up on one elbow and looked down at him. His jaw was set tight. She waited, hoping she hadn't completely ruined the moment.

'I can't say much about it... basically it started as an investigation into a hack but ended up something much darker. I was, well, right in the middle of it all.'

There was another long pause.

'I'm sorry,' said Felicity.

James ran a hand across his brow. 'Thanks. It was incredibly hard. It involved connections to human trafficking which we had no idea about when we started the investigation. I had to help the police go through a lot of extremely unpleasant websites and it was really, really tough.'

'I can imagine. Well, not really. I can't imagine at all... that's awful.'

'It wasn't good. I mean, it was successful in the end. We caught a ring of nasty individuals which was a huge result... but it took its toll on me and the rest of the team.'

He rubbed his eyes.

'The hardest thing is that you can't really tell anyone. We were given some therapy, of course, but they also told us to take some time off if we needed it. I hadn't taken any, I thought I could handle it, stupid idiot that I am, but then, when I met you – and, well, the cats – I thought it would be the perfect place to take my mind off things.'

'Cats are the best kind of therapy,' said Felicity, smiling down at him even though her heart was hurting on his behalf.

'They really are,' said James, turning to look up at her. 'And not just the cats. You're bloody great therapy too.'

She leaned down and kissed him, very gently and slowly, her heart thumping. She contemplated telling him about Hattie, but it didn't seem like the right time, somehow. Instead, she wrapped him in her arms, and they lay like that for a long time.

'Did it work?' murmured Felicity, a bit later.

'What?'

'Us? The therapy?'

'I'll tell you in the morning.'

## CHAPTER FORTY-FOUR

It had worked for Felicity, at least.

She felt like she was walking on air for the rest of the weekend, and it was by no means easy to get up on Monday and go to work knowing James wouldn't be there.

To take her mind off his penguin-shaped absence, Felicity spent the morning in the cat nursery, taking care of two tiny black and white kittens who had recently arrived. *Ah things are not so bad*, she thought, as she gave them both a stroke. *It's a hard life*, she thought with a smile, as she dangled a fishing line toy for Bobby Charlton. *I love my job*, she thought, when it was time for cuddles with Holly and Gennie who would finally respond to being stroked like normal cats. Tiny Holly even gave a little chirrup whenever Felicity was near her cage and flicked up her tail in greeting. It was heart-meltingly cute. *Things are looking up.*

'Felicity!' came Andrea's voice from the office.

'Yesssss?' said Felicity, swinging round the door frame with a big smile on her face. Then she stopped sharp. Andrea wasn't alone.

'Oh, hello there,' she said, to the very elegant, very tall Asian lady in a long expensive-looking wool coat, who was standing rather incongruously in the middle of the room.

Andrea was sitting behind her desk. She looked – what was that look? Apologetic? Whatever it was, it was not a facial expression Felicity had ever seen Andrea make before.

'Felicity, this lady is looking for James,' she said slowly.

Felicity's hands and feet started tingling as she realised who this person was. Of course. Nothing was ever straightforward, was it?

'Can I help you?' said Felicity quietly. She couldn't get over how beautiful the other woman was. Dark, flowing, shiny, oh-so-silky hair. Amazing dark eyes. And she looked like a grown-up, somehow. Felicity was suddenly ten years old again.

'I don't know,' said this person – who was obviously Erika – looking Felicity up and down with clear disapproval. 'Do you happen to know how I can get hold of him? I have something very urgent that I need to speak to him about.'

'Well, I can't just give you his number or anything, I'm afraid.' Felicity could feel her heart pounding out of her chest.

The person-who-was-obviously-Erika's beautiful dark eyes narrowed and she lifted her perfectly shaped chin in apparent defiance.

'I'm not some random stranger. My name is Erika. James and I are... old friends.' She was gesticulating with gloved hands. Expensive-looking leather gloves, of course.

'I don't care if you're his mum,' replied Felicity. 'I can't give out his number.' She could feel Andrea's eyes on her.

Erika's lips pursed sharply as if she had been asked to swallow something unpleasant. 'I think you're being rather unhelpful.'

Felicity clenched her fists. 'I think you should go.'

And with that, Felicity stepped aside. *Was that subtle enough?*

Erika didn't move, though. She threw a furious look at Andrea as if for assistance, but Andrea just spread her hands wide and shrugged.

'I know who you are, you know,' she said, looking back at Felicity. It felt like those incredible eyes were boring into Felicity's very soul.

Felicity crossed her arms over her chest. Her Animal Saviours T-Shirt felt grubbier and more faded than ever.

'Good for you,' she replied.

'Do you like the house? I designed that house; those interiors are all mine. That kitchen island is made of Italian marble.'

Felicity flinched. 'Not my taste,' she said, slowly.

Erika snorted. 'That doesn't surprise me.'

'I think it's probably because it's so soulless.'

Erika drew her breath in sharply. Out of the corner of her eye Felicity could see Andrea's head going backwards and forwards between them as if she was watching Wimbledon. She may as well have been munching popcorn.

'I think you'll find it's minimalist.'

'That's one word for it. I prefer "empty".'

'Well, yes, you would think that. Clearly you have no appreciation for interior design. I suspected as much.'

'Hey, we can't all be stuck up our own arses now, can we?' replied Felicity, her voice calm but her mind screaming a warning.

'What the hell is going on here?' came a familiar voice from the doorway.

James was leaning against the doorpost, looking impossibly handsome and also, somewhat cross.

*Immaculate timing as always.*

'Ah, there you are, darling,' said Erika, but James held up a hand.

'Don't "darling" me,' he said. 'And don't think I didn't hear what you just said to Felicity.'

Felicity did a little inward jig and put out a hand towards him, but he shrugged it off.

'I heard what you said, too,' he said, looking down at her with raised eyebrows.

'I can explain.'

'Save it for later,' said James.

'James, I need to talk to you,' said Erika, ignoring this little exchange and lifting her immaculate chin even higher.

*Any further, and she'll be looking at the ceiling.*

'Well, this is hardly the place, now, is it?' It was his turn to cross his arms. Felicity tried not to notice how his shirt fabric stretched in all the right places. She felt like a naughty schoolgirl again, but she was confident James would give Erika short shrift and then there would be plenty of time for her to make it up to him.

'It's important, James,' said Erika, with a sideways glance at Felicity, as if daring her to butt in.

James contemplated her for a moment and everyone held their collective breath.

'Okay, fine. But not here. I'll give you my new number and you can call me on the phone like a normal person. In the meantime, let's leave these lovely people to get back to their work, shall we?'

Erika nodded in satisfaction just as Felicity's jaw dropped to her chest.

*Wait, what?*

Erika swept out of the building so quickly she practically left cartoon swish marks in her wake. James lingered long enough to keep up appearances, long enough to drop off the lunches he'd bought for them and check on the cats, but then he made a sharp exit. He had flatly refused to listen to Felicity's explanations.

'I know she's tricky,' was all he said. 'But you are normally so kind. I'm surprised at you, honestly.'

That cut deep. She spent a couple of miserable hours that afternoon feeling like the worst person in the world as his words ran round and round in her mind like ball bearings. The logical part of her brain knew it wasn't entirely fair. Clearly, he hadn't heard the way Erika had spoken to *her*. She had only been responding, had only snapped because of the way Erika had been. Her attitude had just been so... horrible. Surely in those circumstances what Felicity had said was justifiable. Perhaps.

*What a stuck-up cow*, thought Felicity, and then felt shame all over again as if James could mystically hear her thoughts. She so badly wanted to talk it through with him properly, but knew she'd have to wait until later. In the meantime, she needed someone else's take on this. As painful as it was to admit, she might actually have to ask Andrea what she thought. She had been a witness, after all. But, knowing Andrea as she did, she'd almost certainly wish she hadn't asked.

*God help me.*

Despondently, Felicity lingered behind at the end of the day in hopes of probing Andrea on the whole incident while she was locking up. She wasn't expecting a great deal, as Andrea usually gave some massive generalisation or other, told you what you needed to do to sort everything out in no more than three short sentences and then got a bit bored of hearing about other humans' lives and returned to her animals.

So, she was surprised to say the least when Andrea leaned in conspiratorially.

'What did you think of that Erika? I thought she was a complete cow.'

Felicity let out an impromptu snort of laughter.

'A complete cow. Didn't you think?' said Andrea again, as if Felicity hadn't heard her.

Felicity shrugged and tried to think of something nice to say. 'I thought she was very beautiful.'

'Oh yes, sure, very beautiful but also a total cow and nowhere near nice enough to be with James, by the way.'

'Is that so?' said Felicity.

'*Nowhere near.* He's an absolute doll. The only explanation is that she's either got a really rich family and hooked him in with that or he was so blinded by her beauty he couldn't see her cow-like characteristics.'

Felicity was starting to feel a bit better. 'He was smitten with her,' she said. 'Totally smitten. He told me she walked out on him on Boxing Day. Broke his heart. I didn't know they were still in touch...'

'*She* walked out on *him?*' said Andrea. 'She must have had a stroke. Or some kind of aneurism. A funny turn of some sort, anyway. Nothing else makes sense. What possible reason could anyone have to walk out on a man like that?'

*That's for sure*, thought Felicity.

'So, what the heck was she doing here then, do you reckon?' she said out loud.

'Oh, she wants him back,' said Andrea, simply. 'She will have invented some excuse. A family emergency or something. But it's all a ploy to win him back. You mark my words. She's a conniving cow.'

Felicity laughed. 'It might be something completely genuine. Then you'll feel awful.'

'No, I bloody won't. And speaking of bloody, if she ever comes back here, I know a few activist friends who would happily come and throw red paint at her for those leather gloves.'

'You don't mean that.'

'I bloody do.'

'Okay, well, I'm sure that won't be necessary but, you know, I'll let you know.'

'You do that.' Andrea nodded as she locked the big door.

'Hey. How's things with Javier?'

Andrea turned and looked at her then. 'I can't believe you remembered his name. I thought you were too wrapped up in your penguin.'

'Ouch.'

'I didn't mean that to sound quite so bitchy.'

'I'm very glad to hear it.'

'Javier is a delightfully sexy man, as it goes.'

'Oh. Great. Um, not sure that's quite what I meant but okay.'

'Ha ha, don't be so squeamish. Old people have sex too, you know.'

'Oh sweet Lord. Yes, I'm painfully aware of that fact, thanks to you.'

'Cheeky minx.' Andrea was smiling from ear to ear.

'You like him, then?'

'I think I might keep him. Haven't decided yet. It depends if he actually gets his act together and gets a divorce.'

'He's married?'

Andrea's shoulders sagged a tiny bit. It was almost imperceptible to the naked eye. But it was there.

'Separated. It's not ideal but it's very complicated. His wife is... well, let's say I like to think of myself as the light relief.'

'Far, far too much information now. Thanks!'

Andrea was still smiling as she waved her goodbyes.

As she watched her walk away, bobbly old fleece in place, grey plait swinging from side to side in a jaunty fashion, Felicity had a sudden urge to run up behind her and hug her. Andrea was full of surprises.

That night, Felicity lay in the bath and ran through the whole encounter in her head. Sure, she hadn't exactly been friendly, but Andrea was right, Erika had been a cow, too. Still, she felt awful for her part in it. Jealousy was an ugly emotion, that was for sure. *Was it jealousy? Maybe it was anger? Possibly both.* Even though she didn't really have any right, even though it seemed a bit perverse, she still felt so cross at Erika for walking out on James the way she did, for hurting him so badly. When she was towelled and dried and curled up in her pyjamas on the sofa, she took a deep breath and called him. Engaged tone. *Hmmm, okay.*

She waited a few minutes and tried again.

Still, engaged.

*He must be calling her right now*, she thought with horror.

And then another thought whipped in like a dart.

Erika had said, 'I know all about you.' But how did she know all about her if James and Erika weren't in touch? And she knew Erika didn't have his number, which implied they weren't in touch. But then, it didn't make any sense, unless they were in touch. They must be in touch. The question is, how? And how often? And how much touching had gone on, exactly?

# CHAPTER FORTY-FIVE

THE PHONE RANG. Or at least, started drumming. Vigorously. The *A-Team* ringtone was usually a winner, but not when you've fallen asleep on the sofa, thought Felicity dully, as her sleep-addled brain scrambled to answer it before the 'duhhhhh duh duhs' kicked in.

'Hello?'

'Hello, yourself,' came that lovely deep voice.

'It's you.'

'It's me.'

'I thought you hated me.'

'What? Why would I hate you? Don't be daft.'

Felicity let out a long exhale of relief.

'I was a bit cross with you, though,' he continued.

'I'm sorry. You weren't meant to hear that. I mean, er, I'm sorry you had to hear it. It wasn't my finest hour.'

'You really upset her.'

'Who?'

'Who do you think?'

'Well, she upset me too.'

'I'm sure she did. She can be... spiky. I'm sorry about that. I had no idea she was just going to turn up out of the blue like that.'

'No kidding. Is that who you were just on the phone to?' The words were out before she could filter them.

'Have you been stalking me again, Miss Brooks?'

'Yikes. No, I just tried to call you a couple of times, and you were engaged.'

'Yes, that is who I was on the phone to. We had some things to discuss.'

'Some things?'

James sighed. 'Yes, some things.'

Felicity waited.

Another sigh. 'Erika's dad passed away. She asked if I would go to the funeral. Her dad and I were always close, even after... everything. He was a wonderful man.'

'I'm sorry,' said Felicity, meaning it. *Bugger.* Now she felt terrible. She felt particularly bad about her conversation with Andrea. Not as bad as Andrea probably would, mind. But still pretty bad.

*No wonder Erika was so on edge.*

'Thanks. Yeah, it's a shock, he wasn't that old. So, we had to sort out the logistics. Looks like I'll be away for a few days at least.'

'You'll be away?'

'Yes, I knew him really well. I'll need to be there anyway, so I said I'd help with the arrangements. He did loads for me, back in the day. I owe him that much.'

'And you'll be away for a few days? For a funeral? I mean, sorry that wasn't very sympathetic, was it?'

'It's okay. Yes, it'll be a few days at least. Well, maybe a couple of weeks. The funeral is in Japan.'

'Oh.'

*A couple of weeks?*

She waited. No invitation was forthcoming.
*What just happened?*

He got on a plane a couple of days later and Felicity was left literally and metaphorically holding the baby (kitten).

It was an agonising wait.

First, she spring-cleaned her flat.

It wasn't very big, so it didn't take long. It was messy but not dirty. Usually. But as she cleaned out her kitchen cupboards for the first time since she moved in and collected up junk for the charity shop, she could hear Erika's sneer about her lack of taste reverberating around her head. It was true, her décor wasn't a patch on the fancy house in Chancery Gardens, but she liked it. It was homely. Cosy. Lots of cushions. Cushions made Felicity happy. She got a few more out of the linen cupboard just to make a point.

Then she met up with Sophie for coffee, something she tried to do as rarely as possible, but she still felt guilty about the whole 'friend who covered her job for a whole week while she swanned off to Guernsey' thing.

And it wasn't as if she didn't *like* Sophie per se. She was perfectly nice and great company. And, as she proved time and time again, really caring and kind and supportive. It was just that her life always made Felicity feel so inadequate. Not to mention jealous. When you'd had the kind of upbringing Felicity had had, it was extremely difficult to really feel empathy for someone who still had both her parents, plus a loving husband, two gorgeous children, an electronically opening triple garage *and* a car port.

And to top it all off, Sophie was so 'together', somehow, so 'managed', that it always made Felicity feel like an emotional pile of old knitting. So much so that she usually preferred it when the three of them were together – for balance. She thought of Bex now, the three of them together at Christmas, giggling, teasing each other, and something twanged in her chest at the thought it may never be that way again. And then, right in the middle of their conversation, the seemingly always together Sophie suddenly wasn't together at all. Felicity was shocked to see tears in her eyes. She edged closer to her in the familiar coffee shop booth and tried to look supportive.

'The thing is, Felicity darling, I've been feeling kind of, well, actually, I've been feeling *really* lonely lately. I wasn't going to say anything but I thought you might understand. A little bit. I mean, oh God, I hope that doesn't sound bad. You know what I mean.'

Felicity put a hand on hers. 'I do. Understand, I mean. And I had no idea, Soph. I'm so sorry. I feel awful.'

'Don't be sorry. You guys have had a lot going on.'

'That makes me feel even worse.'

'Honestly, it's fine. I just want to get back to how things were with us, you know? Before.

"I'm not sure they ever will now. How can she be marrying Adam of all people?'

Suddenly it was Felicity's turn to have tears in her eyes.

Sophie put her head on one side. 'Are you okay with this? Really?'

'Yes. I'm okay with it. I mean, I think I am. They can do what they like, honestly. But I did think she might have felt a bit bad about sleeping with my ex.'

'You know what Bex is like. She's a narcissist. Always has been. I'm not sure she knows how to be a friend in the normal sense... but I know she loves you a lot.'

'I know she does. In her way.'

'But it still hurts, right?'

'Right.'

They paused while they both drank their coffee and tried to get their respective heads around Bex spending her life with Adam.

'They'll have beautiful babies,' said Sophie, suddenly, and Felicity burst out laughing.

'Oh God, you're right. All glossy hair and amazing skin. How irritating.'

'It is rather.'

Felicity took the last gulp of her drink and felt anxiety wash over her. 'Do you think he's sleeping with her?'

'Who? Adam? I should think so, darling, you know what he's like.'

'No. I mean...'

'Oh. James.'

'Yes.'

'Sleeping with his ex?'

'Yes.'

'No.'

'Really?'

'Definitely not. The man is absolutely and entirely in love with you.'

Felicity felt her cheeks grow hot. 'It's not been long, let's not get carried away.'

'I'm telling you. He's a smitten kitten, pardon the pun.'

'I don't know if I can. That was dreadful.'

'Ha. God it really was, wasn't it? I can only apologise.'

'But you should have seen her though. She's like a statue. Honestly. Like someone's carved her from a block of marble.'

'And just as cold, by all accounts.'

'Well, yes, that too. To be honest I think this whole Erika thing might be the last straw. Sometimes the universe just isn't on your side, is it? Star crossed lovers and all that? They've got history. All that time on the plane to realise how perfect they are for each other.'

'You don't really think he'd do that?'

'I hope not. They seemed awfully close. I mean, they've definitely been in touch since they broke up. This is not out of the blue or anything. I'm sure of it.'

Sophie turned awkwardly in the booth to face her friend. 'You've been in touch with Adam.'

'That's different.'

'Is it?' Sophie patted her hand. 'The thing with love is–'

'Here we go. Is this where you tell me to stop being such a cynical old witch?' Felicity grinned.

'No, I'm serious. This is where I tell you that you can't love someone without trusting them. The two go together, I'm afraid. Like salt and pepper.'

'Or Soph and Marcus.'

'Hmm, not the best example I can think of but okay. Yes. Like us.'

'I know you're right. But it's so scary.'

'That, my darling, is the point.'

# CHAPTER FORTY-SIX

AND THEN, at last, it was time for James to come home.

She had received a somewhat curt text, outlining his plans for his journey home, one solitary 'X' at the end. But he had asked to see her so that was potentially encouraging. Or terrifying.

On the upside, he had offered to bring a takeaway.

On the downside, he hadn't asked her what she wanted.

So, when he arrived at 7pm sharp with her very favourite pizza and beer combo, Felicity let her shoulders drop an inch or two. She was so relieved to see his face that she had to swallow down the tears that sprang to her eyes.

'Hello. Or should I say, *Konnichi wa*? I looked that up earlier. Are you impressed?'

James looked tired, his blond hair even more mussed up than usual. He gave a wry smile and trundled into the hallway holding the pizza boxes aloft like he was a silver service waiter. He lowered them onto the side with a flourish and turned towards her.

'You know more Japanese than me, and I've been to the flipping country.'

Tentatively, she moved into his arms and his lips brushed her hair. *And breathe.*

'How was it?' she murmured into his chest. His lovely, comforting Disney chest.

'It was rough. Let's eat, then I'll tell you all about it.'

And so they did, huddled together on the sofa watching *Britain's Got Talent,* munching on stringy cheese and soft Italian dough in virtual silence except for the occasional snigger at the dreadful auditions. But, thought Felicity, as they watched an elderly gentleman balancing five plates on his nose while playing the harmonica, it felt like a good silence. An I'm-tired-and-I'm-appreciating-my-pizza silence. Not an I'm-about-to-break-up-with-you silence. Not an I've-just-had-two-weeks-of-amazing-sex-with-my-beautiful-Japanese-ex-girlfriend silence.

*Not that.*

*Please God, not that.*

When they were finally full, and each of them had polished off a bottle of beer to boot, James started to speak.

He told her about the funeral – 'tough, there were lots of tears, but it was nicely done' – he told her about the beauty of the landscape of Japan, or what he had seen, at least – 'I'd love to see it in cherry blossom season' – and he told her about the incredible sight that was Mount Fuji – 'like it's been painted on the sky'.

They sat side by side for a few moments, and then Felicity cracked.

'And how was Erika?' She tried to keep her voice light. 'I mean, I assume she was there...' *Please God say she wasn't there.*

'Ah. Yes, of course she was there,' said James, running a hand through his hair.

'And?'

'And what?'

'Well... I mean, she's lost her dad, so I guess I'm asking, how was she?'

'That's not what you meant.'

'No. You're right. It's not. But then I felt like an absolute cow because she must be really going through it—'

'She wants us to get back together.' James was staring at the floor.

*Andrea was right.*

Felicity bit her lip to stop herself saying 'I bloody knew it' as she realised that being right wasn't the most important thing right now. It was also to stop herself from crying although that felt horribly inevitable suddenly.

'And what do you want?'

'I don't know,' said James, and there was a moment or two of silence as the world spun off its axis.

# CHAPTER FORTY-SEVEN

SAY SOMETHING, *Felicity.*

*Anything.*

*Just say some words.*

'You... don't... know?' she managed eventually. Whispered, really.

James looked up at her with his big blue eyes filled with tears.

'Of course I know, you bloody idiot. How could you doubt it?'

He grinned at her then, even as tears were on his cheeks, and Felicity gave a squeal and fell forward into his arms, giddy with relief. He held her tightly for a few seconds, and then she broke the hold so she could punch him hard on the arm.

'You total git,' she said, laughing through her own tears.

'Sorry, that was really mean. But you deserved it. You don't trust me!'

'Of course I trust you,' said Felicity but it came out a little bit squeaky.

*Do I?* she thought.

'Okay, tell me honestly. Brutal truth. Did you or did you not wonder if I'd slept with my ex-girlfriend while I was in Japan?'

Felicity bit her lip. 'I did.'

'There you are then.' James waved a hand as if to conclude the discussion.

'But... to be fair, you did just bugger off and leave me.'

'Hold on a moment, I didn't have a choice, I had to go–'

'I know you had to, but it was pretty sudden. And you didn't even think of taking me with you.'

'I assumed you needed to help Andrea. I didn't think she'd let you go away again for at least a million more years.'

'And also... I don't trust anyone,' she said suddenly, as if it had just occurred to her. Which, in a way, it had.

James looked up at her with wide eyes and put his hand on her knee. 'Go on,' he said, and his voice was so tender that the tears started to roll.

*It's time.*

Felicity sniffed and wiped her hand across her face like a small child. James smiled and handed her a tissue from the box on the table.

'You're right. I don't trust you. I'm so sorry. I don't think I've ever trusted anyone,' she said, taking it and balling it up in her hand. 'And with good reason. I seem to be surrounded by people who can't be trusted. As you can see.'

A large sob came out of nowhere and it took a few moments to regain the ability to speak.

'My dad walked out when we were tiny. You know that. And I don't know if you remember but I always thought he was the cheater. You know, because men.'

James winced, and then nodded.

'But when I went to Guernsey... I met this couple. This lovely old couple who knew my family, told me all about it. In fact, the man... well, he knew my mother *really* well, as it happens.'

James raised an eyebrow.

'Yup,' said Felicity. 'You got it. My mum, it turns out, was cheating on my dad. When he walked out, I guess he was just at the end of his tether. I feel so bad that I blamed him all these years, thinking he'd just been heartless, basically, when it was really both their faults. There was this picture of my mum at a party and she's staring at the camera and ignoring my dad. I couldn't work out why until I realised she was staring at the photographer.'

'No!'

'Yes. The photographer was having an affair with her. That was the guy I met. He's really old now, but he clearly remembers her. Still loves her, I guess. His poor wife. She was so kind to me and all I've done is open up some really nasty old wounds...'

Felicity drew in a long breath.

'I don't think he was the only one,' she said quietly. 'When I look back now, I can remember lots of other men who I guess I've blocked from my memory. She was an absolute minx, I reckon.'

James looked impressed for a moment, until Felicity gave him a mock slap on the leg and he changed his expression back to one of polite listening.

'After Dad left, things got way worse. I think I told you some of it. Mum let us down constantly. My brother couldn't wait to get out of there. He went to live with my dad and left us all alone. She was never there for me when I needed her, so I had to learn to cope, to deal with stuff on my own. But it was bad. I mean, really bad. I had to get myself to school. I had to deal with puberty. Often I was dealing with basic things like, I don't know, finding food. Sometimes mopping my own mother up off the floor.'

James gave her knee a squeeze.

'It wasn't just the men. She drank. A whole lot. Especially at Christmas. It started at Christmas but then it was more like every day.'

'I'm so sorry,' murmured James, his face pale.

'When she died...' Felicity said slowly, feeling a physical pain in her jaw from clenching. She tried again. 'When she died, it was sort of a relief, which I know is a dreadful thing to say out loud but there, I said it. The irony is, I spent so many years worried I would turn out like my dad, never realising I should be even more worried about turning out like my mum.'

'You are nothing like either of them,' said James emphatically.

'It's kind of you to say. And let's be honest, it's a pretty low bar.' Felicity gave a forced laugh that came out like a snort and covered her mouth in horror. She grinned at James and tried to relax, tried to get the rest out. It felt good to say it out loud.

'God knows where Dad is now. I never heard from him again. I mean, you don't get much of a lower bar than that, parenting-wise, do you?'

James' eyebrows flew up so high it looked as though they might touch his hairline. But a soft, 'Wow,' was all he said.

'Yeah. Wow. That's about the size of it. As you can imagine, I brought all those issues with me into my adult life, of course I did. My crap childhood, my crap parents, my tragic life, poor me, etc., etc. The upshot is, in case you hadn't noticed, I'm still totally useless at having grown-up relationships. And apparently all the important people in my life cheat. All of them. My best friend. My childhood sweetheart. My parents. All a bunch of big fat cheaters.'

James looked as if he was about to say something and then clearly thought better of it.

'So... I've been having therapy to try and get it sorted.'

A warm smile spread across James' face. 'That's great.'

'I'm trying, I really am... So no, I don't trust you but if it helps, you are not alone. How am I ever supposed to trust anyone?'

Felicity finished this little outburst and put her face in her hands, letting out giant heaving sobs and not even trying to hide them. James didn't say a word, he just shuffled along the sofa and wrapped her in his arms. They stayed like that for a long time.

# CHAPTER FORTY-EIGHT

'Please say something,' said Felicity, eventually, into James' lovely comforting chest. 'Unless you're going to say you think I'm an overly dramatic wreck. In which case, please don't say anything.'

James pulled her back and held her by her shoulders. He looked deeply and intently into her (very swollen) eyes.

'I think you are an incredible person, Felicity Brooks.'

Felicity made a motion to dismiss him, to pull away, and he immediately dropped his hands. She covered them with her own.

'Sorry, sorry. I'm not good in these situations. Go on.' She tried to look him in the eye, but it was so intense it was almost overwhelming. Normally she would crack a joke, try to break the tension but she knew she had to attempt to stay in the moment. Just once.

*Right here, right now, this is happening.*

She focused on their hands, hers on his, hanging on for dear life.

James spoke quietly. 'Don't you ever apologise. You have nothing to be sorry for. And you're right, that was a bit full-on, but I'm glad you told me. It's my turn to say some things now, okay? I'll go gently. You don't have to look at me if you don't want to.'

She nodded and clasped his hands more tightly.

'Firstly, I'm so proud of you for getting therapy. That's so brave. Just amazing.'

Felicity's eyes filled with tears. Again.

'And I know I will have to prove this to you, I don't expect you to just believe me or anything. But you can trust me. I promise you can trust me. I have such a strong sense of obligation to anyone in authority that I have never so much as cheated on an exam. Or nicked a chocolate bar. Honest. Never. Not in my whole life. I just... can't.

'The thing is, I have never met anyone like you before, Felicity. You are an incredible person, you are brave, and strong, and funny,' he said, very slowly and very carefully. 'The things you've been through, I just can't imagine how hard that must have been, and for you to come out the way you have, so kind and loving and wonderful, it's a miracle quite frankly.'

A single tear rolled down Felicity's cheek and James wiped it away with his thumb.

'Now listen... I do have a problem, though.'

Felicity thought she might throw up all over him. 'What kind of problem?' Her voice sounded pathetically thin and reedy.

'My problem is that I'm afraid you are completely and utterly stuck with me because there is no way in hell that I'm ever letting you go. Do you understand me? So, you are just going to have to not-trust me in your own special way until you do trust me. I don't care how long it takes. Okay?'

Felicity nodded, her heart thumping in triple time like it might leap right out of her rib cage.

'I'm not done yet.'

*Oh God.*

'I'm not done yet because, Felicity Brooks, I need to tell you that I love you.'

Felicity gave a huge shuddering sob.

'I'm going to kiss you now,' said James, and she nodded through the tears.

He flashed her an enormous smile as he bent to kiss her, and his blue eyes crinkled right into her heart.

*I'm home at last.*

The next day Felicity floated to work.

She floated through the door into the corridor, and she floated into the office to put down her bag. She floated to the coffee machine and made herself a latte without spilling a drop, then she floated across the room to change her shoes. Effortlessly, of course.

Andrea watched these proceedings with amusement. 'Morning, Felicity.'

'Oh, good morning, Andrea,' said the new and improved Felicity, who was loved – really loved – by an amazing man and had spent the entire night being naked with him and his broad Disney chest and his handsome face and his blue, blue eyes and his kisses like lightning.

'Your face will get stuck like that, if you're not careful,' said Andrea, and went back to pretending to work on her computer.

Felicity ignored her. She floated through to the cat nursery to check on the cats who all mewled with excitement at her arrival and scrambled up their various cages to try to get to her first. She felt like a Disney princess. All elegance and grace with hundreds of small animals falling at her feet. The feeling even lasted while she cleaned out their litter trays. Which was a first.

After break she floated back to the nursery to play with the cats and do some training (cuddling). This time Andrea followed her and told her that someone was coming after lunch to see if they'd like to rehome Holly and Gennie.

'Wait, what?' Felicity felt her feet hit solid earth for the first time that morning.

'You heard me. There's this lovely family who live down the street who'd like to take on a couple of cats. They were really excited when I told them about those two,' she explained, nodding towards Holly who was snuggled in Felicity's hands, and Gennie who was perched on her shoulders.

Felicity smiled fixedly but didn't reply.

'You are okay with this, right?'

She felt strangely emotional. She put Holly back in her cage and wrestled Gennie down from the back of her neck, quite against her will.

'Yeah, I'm fine, of course. It's great news.'

'I know this always feels the toughest part,' said Andrea, putting her head on one side as she watched the three of them. 'But it's the happy ending bit. That's what we want, right?'

'I know. It's just, with these two, I felt... a connection.'

'But you can't take every cat home, you know.'

'I've been very restrained so far! Not a single cat or dog taken home yet. Personally, I think there should be some kind of award for that. "And tonight, the award for Best Will Power goes to..."'

Andrea laughed. 'Well, if you're serious then you know the answer to that, now don't you?'

'Sounds like it's too late.'

'Not necessarily... there are other possibilities...'

'You mean Itchy and Scratchy?'

Andrea made a face. 'We'll have to change those names but, yes, them. They will be turned around pretty soon, won't they?

They're both healthy and strong. I suppose I could ask if they would wait for them instead. You know, if you want? You did save these two, after all. Not that I'm trying to encourage you, you understand.' Andrea put her hands on her hips and gave her a hard stare.

Felicity chewed her lip.

She walked along the corridor and back.

She chewed her lip a bit more.

She made a phone call.

# CHAPTER FORTY-NINE

## NINE MONTHS LATER

A YEAR to the day since they first met over a freezing cold kitten.

Christmas Eve, no less, and this year it found them both standing on the doorstep of a very smart Victorian house near the town centre, bags of brightly wrapped presents at their feet. James rang the doorbell again.

'I may never forgive you for this,' hissed Felicity, flapping one (dry) penguin wing at him.

James put his own winged arm up to her face and stroked it gently. 'You look so cute as a giant penguin,' he said.

She raised an eyebrow.

'Hot, you look hot as a giant penguin, that's what I meant to say.'

She giggled. 'Not as hot as you.'

James did a sort of awkward penguin bow and nearly lost a flipper.

'Not tonight, of course, tonight you look like something out of *Mary Poppins*.'

'Oh, thanks a lot.'

'No, I just mean, it's so *clean*. Last time, you were all filthy and wet and I fancied the penguin suit right off you. Which is weird, given that you were a total stranger, and I was a bit worried you might be a murderer. And, you know, the whole dying kitten thing.'

'It *is* weird,' said James. 'A bit erotic, but definitely weird.'

At that moment, the door finally opened revealing a tall girl of about eight or nine, dressed as an Easter bunny. She had long dark hair tied in plaits on either side of her pretty round face, and enormous green eyes. *Like a young Wednesday from* The Addams Family, thought Felicity. *But a lot less creepy.*

A cloud of warmth and noise came wafting out of the door, wrapping its tendrils around them. Enticing them in.

'Hi, Uncle James! Hi, er, Penguin Lady,' she said cheerfully, eyeing Felicity up and down.

*So, this was the niece.*

'Thank God, it is fancy dress. I was convinced we'd dressed as giant penguins for nothing,' said James, pretending to mop his brow in relief.

The girl giggled.

'Next year it's going to be fancy dress too. We know how much you like it.' She said this with a cheeky grin. 'The question is, are you going to dress as a penguin again?'

'Hey, that's a low blow,' said James.

'What are you saying? Don't you like the penguin look?' said Felicity, doing an awkward flippered-foot twirl.

The little girl/Easter bunny laughed out loud and before Felicity knew what had happened, she was giving Felicity's foam-padded belly a big hug. The bunny ears tickled her nose.

'Wow, okay, er, this is Felicity, Harper,' said James. 'And Felicity, say hi to my very special – and only – niece, Harper.'

'Hi, there,' said Felicity, hugging her as best she could manage with wings for arms. 'Happy birthday, Harper.'

Harper extricated herself and gave her a huge beaming

smile, and Felicity inwardly congratulated herself on her swift work winning over this particular relative. *Only the rest of James' family to go.* 'Why not just meet them all in one night?' he had said. 'Get it over with?' *Oh, sure. That was a great plan.*

'Um, Harper?' said James. 'Please tell me I didn't get Easter and Christmas confused again?'

'What?'

'Your outfit?'

'Oh, that.' She pulled one bunny ear and giggled again, an infectious, tinkling sound. 'I was bored of being an elf. I'm a Christmas Rabbit of Good Cheer.'

'Fair play,' said James. 'Can we come in?'

Harper stepped back from the door, then abruptly turned and ran down the hall into the house, letting James and Felicity find their own way in.

In the distance they could hear her telling someone excitedly that Uncle James had brought a *girl*. As they approached the end of the corridor, where they could hear what sounded like roughly a million children having a rave in the living room, Felicity smiled up at her penguin man.

'Okay, Harper is super cute but I'm still not going to forgive you for this.'

James looked down at her, his blue-grey eyes sparkling, and slipped his arm around her waist, which was rather unfair as Felicity had already been working hard at keeping her face free from he's with me smugness. His arm was warm and even in these circumstances she felt a thrill of excitement at his presence.

'You'll love it when you get going. You'll see.'

And she did.

The next day – Christmas Day, in fact – it was just them.

Rug on the floor? Check. M&S snacks? Check. Percy Pigs? Check. James and Felicity had decided to start their own Christmas traditions. Later there would be *Die Hard*, of course. James had even cracked out the John McClane outfit again for her edification. It was a good look. And there would be chess, played on a very fancy new chess set because although they had agreed no presents, they had both broken their own rule.

And tomorrow there would be dinner with Sophie and Bex, Andrea and Javier (newly divorced, surprisingly twinkly and handsome). Even Tristan and his boyfriend ('Pete, enjoys dogs and baking but not both at the same time') had promised to make an appearance, although she wasn't holding her breath. They had all, in spite of themselves, agreed to attend a Christmas do hosted by Felicity, providing she promised not to swear too much or complain about the Christmas telly. Maybe it was just because of the copious amounts of Prosecco on offer.

Bex was not going to be bringing Adam, for obvious reasons, although she was still insisting on going ahead with the wedding. An event which loomed in all their futures like a giant question mark.

For now, there was James and Felicity consuming much beer, and the finest cheese and onion pasties money could buy. Eaten on a pile of Felicity's beloved cushions, leaning against the comfiest sofa in the world, in their now shared house in Chelsea Gardens. Surrounded by three cats, of course. Yes, that was three. Because you can bet your life that Bobby Charlton was not about to be left behind.

Felicity had grudgingly given up her anti-Christmas playlist although she had insisted on curating the day's music herself. Bublé, Carey, Richards, they were all banned. She would just about tolerate Wham!. Mainly it was Elvis' 'Blue Christmas' on repeat until James pleaded with her to put on something more cheerful. Finally, they agreed on the Jackson 5 and anything by Crosby or Sinatra. The room filled with the comforting sound of smooth-voiced crooners, interspersed every so often by Michael Jackson's high-pitched vigour.

*Perfect*, thought Felicity.

*We'll work on it*, thought James.

They had even put up a tree, of sorts. It was more like a large branch, which James had spray painted white. It was wrapped in a solitary string of tinsel and some twinkly lights. It rather spoiled the minimalist look of the room but for some reason, however pathetic it looked, it brought Felicity joy in a way she couldn't quite explain. She resolved from now on that she would do everything she could to disrupt the minimalist look whenever she could manage.

The tree was also proving fairly cat proof so far, despite the fact that Bobby and Holly had taken to launching themselves at it from the end of the sofa with increasing gusto while Gennie looked on with... what? Envy? Scorn? It was hard to tell with Gennie.

And dinner? Dinner was in the freezer. Two frozen pizzas and two tubs of Ben and Jerry's ice cream.

*Perfect*, thought James.

*We'll work on it*, thought Felicity.

James stroked a finger down Felicity's neck, and a thrill crackled down her spine at his touch.

'So, Crazy Cat Lady,' he said, pulling her close until she was pressed up against him. 'How do you feel about the C word now then?'

'Dirty bastard,' said Felicity, jabbing him with her elbow.

'Not that kind of C word, you numpty.' James laughed.

'Actually...' said Felicity, holding her beer aloft. 'Actually, I think this might just be the best C word I've ever had.'

And as she said it, she realised she meant it. Genuinely,

genuinely meant it. For the first time ever she felt completely safe, completely secure, completely happy.

*So, this is what it feels like.*

'Even better than last year?' said James, looking down at her with lowered lids in that way he had that made her toes curl with delight.

'I guess I now have two good Christmases in the bank,' she said, looking up into his eyes. 'What about you?'

'I think this is the single best day of my life full stop,' said James softly. 'Christmas or otherwise. But if you're asking me whether I still hate Christmas...?'

Felicity nodded encouragingly.

'Then I'd have to say I'm coming round to it.'

And he bent and kissed her lightly on the lips.

'Maybe everyone who hates Christmas is really just waiting for the perfect one?' replied Felicity, wondering if she might drown in his blue-grey eyes.

He nodded and kissed her again, harder this time. One slightly left-field thought flickered through her mind – *I wonder what our children will look like (part ginger ninja, part blond titan)?* – before she abandoned herself completely to his embrace.

Her secret news could wait just one more day.


THE END

# ACKNOWLEDGEMENTS

*The Night Before Christmas* is my debut novel. At every turn on my journey over the last three years, often while I've been in a state of total bewilderment, authors and professionals in the industry have offered me their time, their advice and their encouragement and I will forever be grateful. Very special thanks must go to Stephanie Butland, Jo Thomas, Sue McDonagh, Jenn Ashworth, P A Staff, Jenni Keer, Joanna Cannon, Jane Walters, Kathryn Mannix, Heidi Swain, Catherine Cho and Laura Shepperson for all their cheerleading and guidance, and to the wonderful Sara Cox of the Cheshire Novel Prize whose sage advice has been absolutely priceless.

Huge thanks to my agent, Katie Fulford, who believed in Felicity and her story from the very beginning. To my editor, Abbie Rutherford, for gentle correction and brilliant insights, and to Betsy Reavley and the entire Bloodhound Books team for making my first novel experience so incredibly smooth and angst-free. Special mention to Tara Lyons for her patience, kind words and the beautiful snowflakes!

To my horde of beta readers, many of whom didn't even know that's what they were doing until it was all over – you are truly amazing. Thank you. Love you, Diane, Gemma, Nicky, Jo, Claire and of course my dear Auntie Gill, cat expert extraordinaire.

Thanks to my friends Imogen and Charlie for inspiring me with their penguin-based meet-cute. To my wonderful family and friends for their endless support and listening to me waffle on about the extraordinary and sometimes baffling world of publishing, and my incredible work colleagues including Lynn, Debbie, Rachel, Jude, Jennie, Leanne, Georgia, Charlotte, Helen, Katie, Rachael, Andie, Lydia and Steph for asking all the right questions and never letting me give up.

And to you, dear reader. I hope we meet again. But for now, thank you for making it this far. Treasures in heaven will be yours.

# ABOUT THE AUTHOR

Nicola Knight is a former journalist and chartered public relations professional, who works in communications at an animal welfare charity.

Writing has always been her obsession and she has recently been placed runner up in the Daily Mail First Novel competition and for Comedy Women in Print flash fiction and longlisted in the Mslexia Novel Prize. In 2023 Nicola published a chapter which formed part of a collection of stories around mental health called 'Will You Read This Please?', edited by Dr Joanna Cannon and co-authored with renowned writer Jenn Ashworth.

*The Night Before Christmas* is her first novel.

Nicola lives in South Norfolk with her husband, young daughter and three* chaotic cats.

(*number correct at time of going to press ).

# A NOTE FROM THE PUBLISHER

**Thank you for reading this book**. If you enjoyed it please do consider leaving a review on Amazon to help others find it too.

**We hate typos.** All of our books have been rigorously edited and proofread, but sometimes mistakes do slip through. If you have spotted a typo, please do let us know and we can get it amended within hours.

**info@bloodhoundbooks.com**

Milton Keynes UK
Ingram Content Group UK Ltd.
UKHW032124310824
447708UK00004B/69